# HART & SOUL

By

Sarah Kaye

Copyright @ 2023 by Sarah Kaye All rights reserved.

No portion of this book may be reproduced in any form without written permission from the publisher or author, except as permitted by U.S. copyright law.

This is a work of fiction. Names, characters, places and incidents are the product of the author's imagination on use fictitiously. Any resemblance to actual events, locales, or persons, living or dead, is entirely coincidental.

"In the heartfelt dedication of this book, I extend my deepest gratitude to the people, places, and things that have shaped my journey as a writer.

To my beloved Andrew, you are the love of my life and the driving force behind these words.

In loving memory of my mother-in-law, whose spirit guides my pen from beyond.

To my cherished family, you are the pillars of my strength and creativity. My author friend, whose brilliance shines through even a white sheet, I thank you for your invaluable guidance.

In remembrance of my dear Aunt, your wisdom remains an everlasting presence.

To the places that have inspired me, from Fudgy's Ice Cream to the distant landscapes of Taiwan, and the cherished things, like watermelon gummies and family jewelry, you are the tapestry that weaves this narrative together."

# About The Author

Sarah Kaye, a first-time Author, is a mother of three sons and a grandmother of four. Her journey has been marked by resilience and determination since her diagnosis of Lupus in 1994.

In the face of adversity, Sarah found solace in writing, allowing her to explore her creativity. Her debut novel, "Hart & Soul," is a passionate romance tinged with erotica.

Sarah's personal journey as a Lupus survivor, mother, and grandmother adds a unique depth to her storytelling. Her book is a testament to her strength and the power of pursuing one's dreams, even in the face of life's challenges.

Author Contact Information.
Sarahkaye1st@gmail.com
Sarahkaye@Facebook
Sarahkaye1st@Instagram

# Table of Content

*DEDICATION* . . . . . . . . . . . . . III
*ABOUT THE AUTHOR* . . . . . . . . . . . . IV

*Chapter 01* . . . . . . . . . . . . . . . 1
*Chapter 02* . . . . . . . . . . . . . . . 10
*Chapter 03* . . . . . . . . . . . . . . . 19
*Chapter 04* . . . . . . . . . . . . . . . 28
*Chapter 05* . . . . . . . . . . . . . . . 34
*Chapter 06* . . . . . . . . . . . . . . . 47
*Chapter 07* . . . . . . . . . . . . . . . 58
*Chapter 08* . . . . . . . . . . . . . . . 63
*Chapter 09* . . . . . . . . . . . . . . . 68
*Chapter 10* . . . . . . . . . . . . . . . 73
*Chapter 11* . . . . . . . . . . . . . . . 92
*Chapter 12* . . . . . . . . . . . . . . . 98

| | |
|---|---|
| *Chapter 13* | *108* |
| *Chapter 14* | *112* |
| *Chapter 15* | *116* |
| *Chapter 16* | *127* |
| *Chapter 17* | *135* |
| *Chapter 18* | *140* |
| *Chapter 19* | *150* |
| *Chapter 20* | *163* |
| *Chapter 21* | *168* |
| *Chapter 22* | *174* |
| *Chapter 23* | *187* |
| *Chapter 24* | *194* |
| *Chapter 25* | *197* |
| *Chapter 26* | *205* |
| *Chapter 27* | *216* |
| *Chapter 28* | *220* |
| *Chapter 29* | *225* |
| *Chapter 30* | *230* |
| *Chapter 31* | *235* |
| *Chapter 32* | *245* |
| *Chapter 33* | *250* |
| *Chapter 34* | *256* |
| *Chapter 35* | *261* |
| *Chapter 36* | *266* |
| *Chapter 37* | *271* |

| | |
|---|---|
| *Chapter 38* . . . . . . . . . . . . . . . | *277* |
| *Chapter 39* . . . . . . . . . . . . . . . | *283* |
| *Chapter 40* . . . . . . . . . . . . . . . | *288* |
| *Chapter 41* . . . . . . . . . . . . . . . | *293* |

# Chapter 01

May 25, my fifty-sixth birthday. By this age, most people think of a relaxing retirement with their grandkids around and probably lovely scenery in front of their house to stare at every day. And, most importantly, every year, you would count down. All your kids and grandkids and your spouse would stand right by your side, cheering you on for passing another year. However, I... I just found myself. My freedom, my worth, my esteem, and myself entirely. And I was celebrating my birthday -- not for another year down, but for finding myself. I smiled at the choices I made and having the years ahead with them.

"You look happy?" one of the customers who had just received her ice cream noted and remarked. I guessed that when you smile genuinely, it shows. And it showed. "It's my birthday," I told the happy customer.

"Oh, Happy Birthday," she wished me and went her way out of the parlor.

I was waiting in line at Fudgy's, my favorite ice-cream parlor. I was tenth in line, but I knew it was worth it. Amenia was a small town and I knew almost everyone ahead of me. I looked up to allow my face to soak up the sun. I closed my eyes for a second and immediately I saw his face. Drew. I wondered if he accepted my friend request. I opened my eyes when I heard someone ask for a banana split and thought about what I was going to have. A hot fudge sundae, or maybe my favorite chocolate cone. Then I thought about why I was standing in this long line. 'It must be special, today's my day.'

"Savannah Rowe," someone called out to me.

I turned around and waved to Sue. We used to work together years ago. We had a typical small talk, asked each other how we were and she left the parlor wiping her hands on a napkin.

It was my turn to order, I got a cone with sprinkles to make the celebration official. The woman handed me my colorful cone and said, "A dollar-ninety, please."

I handed her two dollars and dropped another one in the tip jar. When she gave me my change, at first, I was going to drop the dime in the jar, but something strange came over me. I felt a wave of emotion. It was an odd, yet beautiful feeling. I reached up and grabbed two napkins, wrapped the coin in one, and put it in my pocket for safekeeping.

I sat on the stone wall at the end of the building and ate my ice cream reflecting on the past thirty years of my life. I was still in high school when I met my husband. In fact, a month after I graduated, we got married. Over the years, he would cheat on me and that devastated me. Together, we raised three sons, my handsome sons. I stayed with my husband until my youngest son left home for the Navy. As soon as he was out of the home, I told my husband I was leaving. I planned my departure not only from my beautiful home but also from a marriage that I once relished and celebrated but that he breached and broke. I saved up enough money to get myself a small apartment a few towns over. I took a second job, securing my independence; I was determined to stand on my own.

I rented a U-Haul truck and moved all my belongings to my new apartment. It was small but cute; a one-bedroom offering a small porch and the best neighbors I could ask for. They made me feel safe. The man who lived above me was a teacher. In another unit, an elderly couple promised to look out for me, telling me if I needed anything at all to call them.

Believe it or not, being on my own felt wonderful. Fixing my apartment up to mirror the home I had left behind gave me a feeling of comfort and familiarity. Still, I was lonely – I guess I had been lonely for a long time – so I created a profile on Match.com. I had no problem finding men interested in dating me. I did, however, discover the dating pool was not for me. It just didn't feel right. I had tried dating but I couldn't connect with any of the men. Maybe, because I had gone from high school to my husband, I was ignorant of the world of love and relationships.

I finished my ice cream, thinking about the party I was throwing myself. My family and my new neighbors were coming over for dinner. My eldest son, James, and his wife Kelly were coming with their children, Lynn and Andy. Michael and his wife Summer didn't have any children, yet. But my youngest son Samuel and Jessica also had two children, Eli and Nessa. They were my heart. My sons were the reason I stayed, kept going, and probably felt a little bit of happiness after marriage. Now, I live for my sons and my grandchildren.

As I got back in my car, I heard my cell phone ding, I rummaged through my purse to find my phone. 'It was just a promotional message. Dang it.' I somewhere thought I was overreacting, but none of it was intentional. Despite keeping myself occupied, I couldn't seem to forget about him. *'Drew, I'm waiting for your response.'* I pulled out of the parking lot, making a mental note to log onto Facebook to see if Drew accepted or sent me a message. I had goosebumps just thinking about him.

'Maybe, he's the one?'

I had so much to prepare for: cook, set the dining table, set the extra LED light I bought; a lot on my to-do list, and yet Drew was on my mind. It was as if I already knew him. He was a beautiful man, self-employed. As far as I could tell, he had great friends. I had to wonder if he looked at my profile. Perhaps he asked anyone about me. 'Did he even notice today is my birthday? I mean come on, we have over forty mutual friends.' I liked the idea that he did not live in my old small town, in fact, he lives in Connecticut.

It was my day, my children, grandchildren, and newfound friends were all coming to my home, and I wanted to spend time with him, but a stranger, a damn man I found on Facebook of all places was on my mind.

I rested my hand on my leg, and when I did it brushed up against my pocket and again a chill went down my spine. I stopped at the traffic light and took out the dime, unwrapped it, and almost cried. A warm feeling rushed through me. The elderly woman in the car behind me blew her horn for me to drive.

I drove the rest of the way home with the dime in my hand.

After a good few minutes of reminiscing and dreaming about my new fantasy man, I raced into my apartment to get ready for my dinner party. I set the dime on the counter and went in search of a jar to put it in. I was just about to open the upper cabinet when I heard a knock at my door. The local grocery store had delivered my groceries. I tipped the person two dollars and carried my bags to the kitchen.

'Is he a gentleman? Or just some rude dude? You can tell a lot from how they treat other people. Am I into rude dudes? Definitely not. I had one jerk and I am not having another one.'

As soon as I put the cold stuff in the refrigerator I opened my computer. My heart raced, and my hands trembled as my fingers kept typing the wrong letters. Finally, I entered the right password. I had no idea what was going on inside me. I had never felt like this before. I shook my head thinking, how strange it was to feel this way over a picture and a friend request.

"Yes!" I squealed with delight. Drew accepted my friend request. He even wrote on my wall. "Happy Birthday, Savannah. I hope you have a good one." I read it aloud. I was back in high school; it felt like he was my high school crush and just couldn't get over him.

I glanced up at the clock, I had twenty minutes before I start preparing dinner. *'In five minutes, let the stalking begin.'* I hit the about section and read: fifty-two, self- employed, Hart Electric in Sharon Connecticut. He's at least a half-hour away from where I live. I didn't care. As far as I was concerned, there were no boundaries between us. *'Goodness, I was really into him.'* I sometimes even surprised myself. I looked at his photos, uploads, and at his albums, but nothing. *'Is it all private or no uploads at all? Of course, I wanted to see more of his handsome face.'*

I wanted to search more, but I had guests arriving in less than two hours. I wanted to show my family how independent I was and that started by arranging the dinner party all by myself. It was important to me for my sons to know that I was going to be fine living on my own. I turned the music on and started preparing the eggplant parmesan. Then I began to make the baked ziti. I set the table, lit a few candles, and tossed the LED lights aside, 'No time for these,' I thought and waited.

I glanced at the clock again, there were still ten minutes till my guests arrive. I looked around, gave everything one last look, and felt proud of myself. I did well. I thought I needed help, but I managed. It was one of those few moments when I felt like I have achieved something and I did it all on my own. Of course, not without my children's support. It was for these little moments, these times that I would choose over and over again to be with myself than with someone who never knew your worth. But somewhere,

I wanted the one who knew my worth, who could truly cherish me.

'*Maybe he is the one?*'

I couldn't get this thought out of my head. It felt like a certainty. Immersed in my contemplation, I heard the doorbell.

'Ahh, finally.' I opened the door and hugged my son Michael. He was my middle child – the one who always made me laugh. He was also the one who told me to leave my husband. He had said, "Mom, if you're not happy, you need to leave." He made me think hard about myself and my own future. I was scared. Unsure about whether I could financially make it on my own. Prices were high, everything was expensive, food, gas, and especially rent. But after that conversation, I really started thinking and seriously planned my departure.

"Happy Birthday," Summer said to me as she handed me my card and gift. "Something smells delicious," Michael said as he turned around.

"I made your favorite," I told him. "Eggplant parmesan."

He hugged me from behind and kissed the top of my head. "It's your birthday and you made my favorite for dinner. Mom, you always put everyone else's needs ahead of yourself."

"Yes," Summer said adding, "You're an independent woman now. Start doing something wonderful for yourself."

I inhaled knowing I raised three amazing sons. I was glad they understood why I had to leave. I didn't want them to think marriage, loving someone else, and relationships were supposed to be like their father's and mine. I wanted them to know what true love felt like, so I spoke of happier times. I asked an old friend once, "How does it feel to be turning fifty?" I smiled at his answer, "I have another whole half of this life to live."

It was a good way to think about the rest of my own life. The doorbell rang and this time it was my upstairs neighbor, Hank. Hank was a teacher. He taught special education. He was a middle-aged single man, who seemed lonely at times. A bit shy if you ask me. I thanked him for the bottle of wine and introduced him to my son and daughter-in-law.

The men shook hands and I wanted to say, 'Hey, Hank. Do you know you snore? The walls between his apartment and mine are very thin.' In fact, I could hear Hank do a lot of things but I just kept it to myself. I laughed thinking about how I started mirroring my daily routine to Hank's. As soon as I smelled his coffee, I made mine. When Hank vacuumed, I did the same. I also found the aromas coming from his apartment every evening to prove he was a good cook.

I turned around when I heard my eldest son call out my name. James, his wife Kelly, and my grandchildren, Lynn now twelve, and Andy who just turned five were all holding gifts. Being their grandmother was the greatest gift and feeling a woman needed. I loved all of my grandchildren, but being her grandmother was special. After all, she was my first.

"Grandma, I love your department," Andy said, and we all laughed. "Apartment," his sister corrected him. Grandma, can we go outside?"

My apartment complex had a nice playground and an area safe for the children to run around and play in. I watched as they climbed up on the swing set. My heart hurt remembering the day I had to explain why grandma and grandpa would not be living together anymore. Maybe, having the coolest play area around helped.

"Aww," I said aloud. "My other neighbors aren't feeling good. They can't make it." I set my cell phone down adding, "I'll have the kids take them up a plate, later."

I was in the kitchen taking the eggplant out of the oven when I heard someone at the front door. My youngest son was home on leave. First, I hugged Samuel, then Jessica before bending down to hug Nessa and Eli.

"I have a playground in the backyard." I pointed toward the door. "Lynn and Andy are outside if you want to play with them. You have twenty minutes before we eat."

As soon as Eli jumped up and down, I knew they were going outside to check out Grandma's new backyard.

"I'm so proud of you," Samuel said to me. "I know this was a big decision for you and moving out here alone wasn't easy. But I'm glad you did it. You deserve to be happy."

I offered everyone something to drink. Of course, the men chose beer and the women wine. I set the salad on the table next to the two waiting hot plates. I called out to the children and told them it was time to come and wash their hands. Then I set the eggplant and baked ziti on the table. On the side table was the apple pie I had picked up from Paley's Farm Market in Sharon.

After dinner, the kids went next door to deliver dinner and dessert to my neighbors.

"You're such a good person," my daughter-in-law said to me. "Always thinking of the other person. Umm, I noticed you made everyone's favorite. You realize today is your birthday, right?"

Four hours later, after laughing so loud I was sure the neighborhood heard us, I smiled knowing everyone had a great time and, it was our first memory in my new apartment.

I was in the kitchen when it dawned on me. The dime. I put it on the counter and now it was gone. I looked at the empty jar, down at the floor, even in the sink. It was nowhere to be found.

"What's the matter?" Jessica asked me. "You look like you saw a ghost." "I'm just being silly. I put a dime right here and now it's not there." Andy held up his hand. "Grandma, is this your dime?"

My heart settled in my chest. "Where did you get it?" I asked, holding out my hand.

"Right here," he said resting his hand on the counter exactly where I had put

I explained that the dime was very special to me. "I'll trade you one dollar for that dime."

"That's not necessary," my son said. "Andy, give grandma her money back. You know better."

I bent down and hugged him before taking back my dime. Then I set it in the jar and closed the lid. We talked a little more and as the night deepened, they all decided it was time to return to their homes. Somewhere I missed them all very much, however, I knew they were proud of me and it was time that I did something for myself. Only for myself. My kids were right, I needed to start my own wonderful life.

After everyone went home, I ran back inside and logged onto my computer. 'Huh, no message other than my birthday wish. Should I send him a private message?' I laughed aloud at the thought, 'Oh, by the way, you are all I can think about.'

I typed and retyped several messages, any way to talk to him without sounding like someone who was waiting for his reply. I realized, sending any message this soon would be a message in itself that I was desperate for his message.

*'Desperate?'* I didn't like that word to be associated with me, I was a woman of esteem. I decided to abort the idea of messaging him and prepared for the night.

I went to bed thinking about Drew, and the feeling that came over me when I held that dime in my hand. Every time I picked it up, a chilling sensation rushed through me. I dreamt I messaged him, but he never got back to me.

And in reality, as days went by, there wasn't a single message or any notification with his name. I felt dejected like my heart felt lost.

*Sarah Kaye*

## Chapter 02

It was another morning. A usual morning when the coffee smell wafted in my room, filled my sense and rose me up. How much I wished that the coffee smell was from my kitchen and not upstairs. I stretched my arms out, thanked Hank for brewing coffee every morning, and headed for a shower. I needed to stop thinking about Drew. After all, we were both adults. If he wanted to get to know me, he would have reached out to me on my birthday with more than a single sentence. I hated the fact that I had to be in this damn new-age dating world.

My friend told me, "It's the twenty-first century. Things are different. Savannah, you're no longer a childhood bride. You're a grown woman. If you want to keep him coming back, you need to prepare yourself for sex by the third date." I laughed at the thought of having sex by the third date.

I made a pot of coffee, grabbed two slices of toast, and sat out on the back porch listening to traffic going by. "Sex?" I hadn't even met the man and I was already thinking about having intercourse with the man. Once again, I laughed hoping no one heard me say the word out loud. I went back inside, set my plate in the sink, and poured myself another cup of coffee.

For at least five minutes, I stared at my laptop before logging onto Facebook. I was looking out the window when I heard a ding. 'Oh, my goodness.' The little lightning icon had a red number one on it. I had a message. I was too excited to click on it. I wanted to think it was Drew, but something inside of me thought otherwise. I was sure it was one of my sons.

'Oh, hell.' I clicked on it.

"How was your birthday? Did you do anything special?"

My heart started beating so fast, I spilled coffee all over myself when I jumped out of my chair. I tried to contain myself. Ran to the kitchen, grabbed a dish towel, and cleaned up my mess. I took a deep breath and sat back down. I needed to respond to him, but what do I say? I couldn't tell him about my dream. He would think I was obsessed with him and thought about him all the time. I decided to tell him about my dinner party.

"Hi Drew, thanks for the birthday wishes. That was very kind of you. I had a small dinner party at my new apartment for my family and a few of my neighbors."

"Great. Sounds like you enjoyed yourself. Can I take you out for ice cream to celebrate with me?"

I laughed before typing, "Sure. When would you like to go?" I typed out the message, not believing that he asked me out. Or was he not asking me out? My mind raced, trying to make sense of this.

"How about tonight at six-thirty? I'll meet you at Fudgy's in Amenia."

I almost typed, 'It's a date. See you then.' But quickly backspaced and wrote, "Sounds wonderful."

"Okay, I'll be driving a white Jeep."

My heart smiled. Seriously, I could feel it in my chest. I jumped up and started dancing. "I have a date." Then I quickly sat back down. Am I really going on a blind date? I looked at his Facebook page again and told myself to relax. "We have more than forty mutual friends." If the date goes fowl, we could just talk about all the people we know in common. I looked at his picture one more time and felt something inside of me as if I knew him or at the least, the feeling of how much I wanted to know this man.

For once in my life, I felt good inside. I was happy. I smiled when I saw all the wrapping paper on the dining room table. I started cleaning the apartment but stopped when I thought about what I would wear on my ice cream date. I had hoped no one would mention the fact that I visit that place often.

I stood in front of my closet trying to decide on something casual or nice. I checked the weather and it was supposed to be a little breezy later on. I decided on a pair of jeans and a short sleeve blouse. I grabbed my blue sweater just in case it got cold. I glanced in the mirror.

"I'm going on a date with a dreamy man." Did I just say that?

I wondered if he was feeling the same way. Is he as nervous as I am right now? I hoped he wasn't a player. He was sexy and handsome and there was something else, I just couldn't put my finger on it yet. What I did know was he made me feel good and I hadn't even kissed him. I was hoping all my questions and concerns about him got answered tonight. Like why I was so attracted to him?

I made my bed, set my clothes on top, and took my shower. By the time, I finished cleaning the apartment it was almost five. I got dressed and left the apartment a half-hour later. I wanted to be early.

Before I got into my car one of my neighbors hollered out to me, "You look gorgeous. Are you going out on a date?"

"Thank you. Yes," I replied and got in my car.

I sat at the picnic table trying to calm myself, hoping I didn't make a fool of myself. Do I hug him? I don't shake his hand, right? I should have thought to ask my neighbor. I focused on the drive out here. We live in the country, and it can be very beautiful. Driving down De Lavergne Hill and seeing the many farmlands out in the distance is worth the drive alone. They say you can see three states from the top of that hill. I saw a vehicle pull in and my insides tumbled again.

I tried thinking about what ice cream I should order. A cone? Oh, hell no. No licking on the first date. I rolled my eyes at the thought of him watching me.

Six-thirty on the nose, a white Jeep pulled in. No top. He has one foot dangling, and he looks just like his picture. He was dressed in shorts, a blue shirt, and sneakers. I was mesmerized by him. He was cool and casual and he made my heartbeat again. A lot faster.

I stood up and met him halfway. We both said hello and hugged. I followed him to the order window. At first, I felt awkward standing next to a man I didn't know. He turned to me and asked, "What would you like?"

"I'll have whatever you're having," I replied. I was thinking he looked like he just stepped out of the movie set for Hawaii Five-O. Jet-black hair, porcelain complexion, and eyes that made me want him more than ever.

I had a twenty-dollar bill in my hand. I was prepared to pay for my own. Until he touched my hand and motioned for me to put it away. When he paid for our ice cream, I knew he was a gentleman. We sat at the picnic table, talking about our mutual friends, living in a small town, and friends we both shared other than those on Facebook. Then, I spilled my chocolate sundae. Knocked it over. The spoon went flying and I had chocolate on my sweater.

*What must he think of me?*

Drew got up and picked up my cup and ran to the window to get napkins so I could clean myself up. I was so embarrassed. But he made me feel better when he said, "And here I thought I would be the one so nervous I would spill ice cream all over myself." Then he bent down and picked up the spoon.

"Look at this. It was under your spoon." He handed me a dime and I put it in the pocket of my jeans.

I wanted to say, no way, but instead, I asked him if I could have it. "I'll save it as a reminder of our," I stopped myself from saying the words.

Drew smiled at me. "I'd like to continue our first date a little longer if that's okay with you?"

I wanted to tell him that I didn't want to leave, I wanted to stay there, for hours.

Or maybe not leave at all. But I just resorted to a humble 'sure.'

Three hours went by, and as we talked, shared our backstories. The sun set all around us as people came and left. I didn't want to leave. I told him about my children, and my separation and I shared my desire to do more with my life.

He moved a hair from my face, and I felt flutters in my stomach and my mind did a cartwheel twice. I was head over heels, I knew I was. Why, that I was unaware and uncertain of.

"Do you ski?"

"No, but I'd like to try it one day," I replied, briefly looking at him. Drew smiled. "Good. How about scuba diving, snowmobiling?"

I gave him a wry grin and shook my head. "Nope." He laughed softly. "Camping?"

I looked into his eyes knowingly, willingly. "Can you teach me?" I was still looking at him when I added, "I heard camping can be fun. Campfires, sleeping outside amongst nature."

The old Savannah would have felt out of place. She would have thought we had nothing in common, but sitting with him, feeling the way I did, I wanted to explore everything new with him by my side. He was adventurous, an explorer and I was going to have all the adventures I never thought I would have. As soon as the thought appeared so did the feeling of being out of my league. I was a mom; he had no children. I had a husband; Drew was never married. Worst yet, I lived a sheltered life. Suddenly, I had no idea how I was supposed to adjust to this new lifestyle, his way of living.

I knew the smile vanished and he noticed it. He took my hand and said, "Well, Savannah. I think it's time we changed all of that." He smiled. His perfect, white teeth stare at me, waiting for me to respond.

*'He was interested in me.'*

I could feel myself catching my breath, I didn't want him to know. I returned the smile and slightly nodded.

"Drew, can I ask you something?"

He nodded. "Anything, I'm an open book."

"How is it that you're still single?" I finally found the courage to ask this question.

"I never found the right person, and no I don't have any children anywhere either." We both laughed.

"Okay," I said. "But?"

He took hold of my hand for a second. "I have been taking care of my mother for the past few years."

My heart melted. "You take care of your mother? That's very compassionate of you. I like that about you."

"You do? My mom would have been glad to hear that. Thank you by the way."

I laughed, "I'm sure she knows her son is a great man."

"I just told her that I had given up on finding the right woman." His eyes sparkled. "She said, 'It will happen when you least expect it.' She told me to be patient."

"How long have you been caring for her?"

"My father left when I was a teenager and that left me to watch over her. I have two sisters, but my mother and I always had a special bond."

"Do they live nearby?"

"No. My older sister Karen and her son live in another state. Tanya has two children. I'm closer to my nieces and nephews than I am to my sisters." He mentioned his neighbors, Stacy and Greg. "They made me godfather to their son, Kevin. He's a great kid. We get along well."

"How about your father?" As soon as the words left my mouth, I wished I hadn't asked, but he seemed comfortable with his answer.

"My father was in the Air Force. He was in Taiwan when he met my mother. That's where we were all born. My sisters and I were born in military hospitals. When I was a year old, we moved to the States. My mother didn't speak any English. Everything was foreign to her."

He told me about the cultural shock his mother faced and how she coped with raising three children alone. "She had a mighty spirit. She wanted to give us a better life and wanted us to be better people."

"I'm sure she is proud."

"I would like to think that."

I could feel his voice fissure as if he was holding up. He paused and stared outside. It was getting dark out. As I looked around, I noticed the owner had taken in the Open Sign. It was also getting chilly out.

"Hey, would you like to go for a ride?" He managed a smile. "In my Jeep." "Let's go!" I said, without giving it a second thought and probably a little louder than I should have.

He followed me over to the passenger side, lifted me, and handed me a blanket from the backseat. I thanked him when he put it across my legs. I watched him climb in. It was such a cool vehicle. No top, just a cool breeze in our faces. Before he started the engine I declared, "I've never driven topless before."

He nearly snapped his neck looking at me. Then he flashed me a smile. "You're referring to the Jeep, right?"

I could feel my face turning red as he backed out of the parking lot. "Yes, Drew."

Apparently, there was a Jeep wave in place, because every time one went by, Drew raised his hand. As we drove around the town of Amenia, I thought it really was a great place to raise my sons in.

Main Street had a lot of old architectural buildings, the bank on the corner of Main and Route 22 dated back to the eighteen-hundreds. The town always hosted my grandchildren's favorite drive-in located at Four Brothers Pizza Inn. At night, when they turned the lights on, it took on the appearance of a carnival. Retro lights, flashing signs, and old-time music streaming from loudspeakers. Everyone loved their pizzas, but I couldn't get enough of their Greek Salads. I must have been looking at the place intently.

Drew looked over at me and asked, "Hey, would you like to go to dinner there tomorrow night?"

"I would love to go to dinner with you."

"Great. I have a few things to do in the afternoon and then I'm free. How about we meet in the parking lot at six-thirty?"

"You got a date, Mr. Hart."

Drew drove back to where my car was parked and I didn't know why, but I did not want to get out of the Jeep. He came around to my side and helped me down. Then he opened my car door.

*'Was I dreaming?'* No man had ever done that before. For the first time in my life, I felt like a real lady. I looked into his eyes, hoping he would kiss me so I could feel his lips on mine all night long, but instead, he tapped me on my nose.

I drove home thinking that was a big brownie point. I got home in half the time. Daydreaming about him and all there was to come. When I pulled into the parking lot my neighbors were sitting outside.

"Hi Savannah, thank you for sending over the food and pie. It was so sweet of you. Your grandchildren are adorable," she said.

"The food was delicious," her husband called out to me. "I heard you went on a date?"

"Yes, to an ice cream parlor. I met him on Facebook." I looked at his wife. "You would like him. He's a fine gentleman."

She winked at me. "You get some rest now." And then she motioned for him to get up and follow her inside.

"Good night," I shouted. "I have work tomorrow."

"Oh, Savannah. Wait, tomorrow night I'm making your favorite Hungarian dish, chicken paprikash. I'll send you over some in your baking pan."

I waved to them. "Thank you so much," I replied and opened my door.

My jammies were on and I was in my bed, reading before I tried to fall asleep.

I loved reading, especially, love stories.

*"Dear God, please make my wish of finding my one true love come true."* I turned the light out, put the book on my nightstand, and added, "Thank you for Drew."

I knew I was going to sleep better than most nights. I couldn't wait to dream about him, about us.

# Chapter 03

'Ahh, coffee. Good morning, world. And Hank.'
I stretched my arms out trying to touch the rays coming in through my bedroom window. When I sat up, I looked at myself in the mirror remembering I had the most beautiful dream. I smiled broadly at the thought of it, feeling so real, and boy, was it a good one. I was looking forward to our second date, wishing it was six-thirty already. I jumped up when I realized I had to go to work today. It was Wednesday. *'How will I work with him on my mind?'* Work seemed to be a struggle now. I wondered what errands he had to run.

'Oh, maybe it has something to do with our date.'

First, I checked my phone for any messages, then Facebook. Nothing. I took my coffee outside thinking about my dream and how it felt so real to me. I was so excited that the day dragged on at work.

"No."

We left the parking lot without exchanging phone numbers. *'I'm such a klutz.'* First, I spilled my ice cream, now I was going on a second date with a man I had no idea how to get a hold of. Thank goodness for Facebook. 'Wait, I hope he doesn't message me to cancel because of whatever he had to do today.' I had gotten so used to being disappointed. I never got my hopes up.

*'But Drew is different. Right?'* What exactly was different? Weren't people supposed to disappoint? Living up to hopes, perhaps, is a burden that most won't willingly bear. I wouldn't go with expectations; I was going on a date to just have some good moments with the man of my dreams. And we would see from there. After all, I had nothing to lose.

I kept telling myself, keeping my emotions at bay – I knew I couldn't endure another disappointment.

I raced home after work, suppressed the teenager in me, and started to get ready for our date. I looked in the mirror and smiled at myself. For the first time in a long time, my heart was filled with joy. My soul felt comfortable with the presence surrounding me. I was in a new place – a spiritual bubble. Someone, somewhere out there was watching over me, guiding me on this new path in life and love.

I picked out a cute dress I had bought a few weeks ago when I thought I would try dating. All of them still had the tags on them. I laughed when I looked at my selection. A red, white, and blue tank dress. *'Perfect. Very memorable.'* I slipped on my red shoes, grabbed my purse, and touched up my makeup.

I paused and looked at myself from head to toe; I liked myself tonight. I generally liked myself, but tonight I wore happiness proudly. Selfish happiness some may say, but happiness like I had never felt before.

*'I am going to have a good time.'* I grabbed my key and paced outside the door.

The drive to Amenia made me feel anxious. *'In thirty minutes, I will see him again.'* Of course, I was early, I couldn't wait. I parked my car and felt my heart fluttering in my chest. I turned the radio on and listened to some eighties songs. Tears filled my eyes when "Somewhere Over the Rainbow" played. It was one of my favorites.

I sang along, "And the dreams that you dare to dream, really do come true."

I closed my eyes and pictured myself with Drew. I dared to dream a blissful life with the man of my dreams. I would dream of it again, every day.

'And I won't give up on it.' I confessed to myself that I liked him, liked him more than he knew, more than I thought I would like anyone. The steadied tears breached the barriers and flowed down.

'I dare to dream of us,' I said to myself, repeating it like a mantra. 'I dare to dream

…' my repetition was interrupted by a familiar horn, and I quickly grabbed the tissue and dried my face.

'Here he comes.' He pulled up next to me in a silver BMW convertible. I couldn't help staring at him, he was my knight in shining armor. He got out, came over to my car, and opened my door. I looked at him in awe, such gentleness was new to me.

Drew smiled at me and asked, "How are you tonight?"

I was speechless, but somehow, I said, "I'm so happy to see you." I accepted his hand and stepped out of my car.

"You look very festive." He raised his eyebrows adding, "Gorgeous."

"Thank you." I seriously had to get used to his compliments and the way they make me feel.

He took my hand as we entered the restaurant. We sat in a booth, across from one another. I kept looking at him. His flawless milky skin, his perfectly arched eyebrows, his not too pointy or not too blunt nose, the forehead that was starting to welcome a receding hairline, that small almost undetectable black mole right above the lip, and that dimple. I scanned him and thought to stop but I couldn't help myself. I was so attracted to him. My last crush on a man was in high school. I cracked a smile. Maybe middle school.

Our eyes met, and he paused and smiled back at me. I broke the stare, took a sip of my water, and said, "I didn't get anything done today and it's your fault. I spent my day thinking about you and our date. How did your day go? Were you able to get everything that you wanted to get done?"

His face turned red as if he wanted to tease. His lips parted to reveal his sparkling teeth and a smile to show off his adorable dimple. For the first time, he seemed bashful. He was so different than all the other men I knew, he was sensitive and sensible, handsome and humble, and cautious and caring. I was surprised at myself for observing him in so little time.

"I was able to do everything," he said just as our server arrived at our table.

After I told him they make the best Margaritas, we both ordered one. Knowing it was only our second date, I allowed myself one drink. 'Am I old-fashioned? Hell, yeah, but I think Drew is too.' Drew ordered the chicken parmesan, and I got the veal cutlet special.

I was nervous, calm, and needed to say something. I wanted to tell him I was glad he accomplished everything on his list. But I chose silence, I thought my silent observations said enough.

He looked at me and put his head down before looking into my eyes. "My mother passed away two days ago."

*On my birthday?* I was taken aback. I was ready to progress our relationship with him, but was I ready for him to be vulnerable to me? I reached out and touched his hand. "I'm so sorry for your loss."

"I had to make her arrangements today." He took a sip of his water. "She died from complications due to COVID." He shook his head. "She was in a nursing home." I had lost my own mother many years ago, so I knew exactly how he was feeling. I was grateful I still had my Aunt Dolly, she was like a mother to me. She meant everything to me. I was not sure how I would handle her passing. Ninety-six years old and she was still as vibrant as a woman half her age.

The server brought our cocktails over to the table. Drew held his up and tapped mine to his. No words, just the clanging of our glasses. I sipped mine and asked him to tell me about his mom.

"Savannah, I will, but not tonight." He put his drink down adding, "I'm on a date with a beautiful woman. Right now, I'd like to enjoy every minute."

"I completely understand. I'm sorry." I felt so bad for him, yet I understood.

He was hurting and yet he wanted to lend me a good time. I wanted to console him, hug him and make his pain go away. I had hoped he knew he could talk to me about anything.

"Tell me about you," he said.

"I love being outdoors. Taking long walks, riding my bicycle on the rail trail, and I like riding in your Jeep." That made him smile.

"I'm afraid I'm not very exciting. Married out of high school, mother, and domestic engineer."

"If you stick with me, I will make sure you see, and do everything you have dreamed about."

*'Well, I have dreamed a lot about us together.'*

I knew my cheeks were turning crimson, but before they revealed my true emotions I responded to his remark, "I hope so. Can't wait for our adventures."

"Can't wait," he paused, smiled, stared, and at that moment I felt the world around me vanish as if there were only the two of us. Just us – no one else, nothing else.

Somehow, I knew he was sincere. Somewhere, I believed he was the one.

After we finished our dinner, Drew asked me, "Would you like to go to the drive-in and see a movie with me?"

*Oh, he speaks my mind and my heart.* I thought to myself. I wanted to end my night with a good movie, but never had the idea of watching it in a drive-in cinema. I guess, I had been pretty conventional all my life.

I didn't care what was playing. I was excited he wanted to spend more time with me, so I replied, "I would love to."

While I used the restroom, I decided to refresh my makeup. With a little pat of compact, I reapplied the lipstick; it seemed to fade away. Then, I ran my fingers through my hair. I stood there for a minute, probably preening myself in the mirror. 'I look nice.' Not many times, but it was the one time I praised myself. 'It's not makeup, it's called happiness.'

"I paid for dinner. We can leave." He lightly placed his hand on my back and we left the restaurant together. We got in his car and drove across the parking lot. The movie was Batman versus Superman, starring Ben Affleck. Drew parked in a perfect spot. The screen was right in front of us. To my surprise, he got out, opened the trunk, and handed me a blanket and a sweatshirt. Then he set a basket filled with crackers, cheese, and other snacks inside. It was like falling in love with him over and over again, especially when he did things like this.

As soon as he started talking about Marvel and DC Comics, I knew he was a big fan of science fiction movies.

"Star Trek is probably my first love," he said.

I looked at him, hoping I was his second. Then he offered to get me some hot cocoa from the snack stand. All I could do was hope I didn't spill the cocoa in his car. *Please Savannah, don't be a klutz tonight.*

When the movie was over, I told Drew, "This is my first time seeing a movie in a convertible."

"We're going to have so many firsts together," he replied. The dimple appeared again, "I hope so, and only if you want to."

"Of course, I do." I nodded my head, and we shifted back in the car. We drove over to where my car was parked. He got in my car and started it for me, and then he handed me his cell phone. "Can I get your phone number?"

I put my number in and handed it back to him. He immediately sent me a text message so I would have his number.

"Don't read it until you get home," he said jokingly.

"Thank you for dinner and the movie. I had a great time." Then I tried to be funny and told him I put my friend's name and number in his phone. When he didn't say anything, I quickly told him it was a joke.

He laughed. "I'm glad you have a funny side. You're good for me, Savannah." Right there, I wanted to kiss him. To make him feel better. To myself feel better, or the best I had ever felt before. I spent most of my days crying, and I knew it wasn't good for me. It was the last thing I would want him to experience. A little laugh is what we both needed.

I drove home, hoping Drew would open up about his mother. I wanted to know everything about her. I was curious to know her even though she was gone. I felt a connection to her; she was his mom. No one knew him better than his own mother. I had hoped his family was there for him, helping him get through his loss.

At eleven-thirty, I pulled into the parking lot, tired and not wanting to go to work. As tired as I was, I could not fall asleep. Yet, I knew I had to be at work at seven. A part of me was awake, remembering his tenderness. Sometimes I thought about his mother, and mostly my imagination ran wild thinking about us. What could we be? How far would we go with this relationship?

'Relationship? Were we exclusive? Are we together-together? It felt like we were. We would be, right?'

And the night passed with a hundred questions that I could and couldn't answer.

The next morning, I was dragging at work. Everyone was talking at their desks when I arrived. They asked me what I did for my birthday.

"Oh, it was memorable," I said. I decided to tell them about Drew. "Turning fifty-six has proved to be the best year of my life. I met someone very special. We went on two dates and we exchanged numbers."

They were happy for me. For a while, I enjoyed telling the married women about my crazy dating experiences, living by myself, decorating my apartment, and eating whatever I wanted, whenever I felt like it, but even I knew I was ready for a real man – a gentleman in my life. I think my work and family lived vicariously through me. I was glad they were protective of me, asking me every detail, and ensuring my safety. I appreciated them.

It was three o'clock and I was glad the day at work ended. I hollered, "I'll see you all tomorrow."

I walked out to the front parking lot and my car was nowhere in sight. I was so tired, I parked in the back lot. I got in and the damn radio was playing "Somewhere Over The Rainbow" I yelled at the top of my lungs, "Yes." It was a sign. My dream was coming true. As soon as the song ended, I turned the radio off. I wanted it to linger in my head. I wanted this song to stay with me for the rest of the day.

I was almost home when I tried figuring out what I was going to have for dinner. I had a few dishes left from Blue Apron that I could choose from. Chicken and fish were my go-to meals. I was so tired I didn't have the strength to heat anything. Maybe I could call Drew and we could cook something wonderful together.

And then I saw my neighbor, sitting on her porch holding a dish filled with her delicious Hungarian food. I got out of the car and yelled over to her, "Thank you."

I ate in front of the television. I was so tired I couldn't tell what was on. I wanted to rest or do something much more relaxing than resting.

'Oh, how easily I drift toward Drew.'

## Chapter 04

I Had been an over thinker my whole life. Maybe, he was busy with funeral arrangements. I checked my phone again, but there was no message, nothing even on Facebook. I certainly could understand if he needed to be alone for a while. I was cleaning the kitchen when I heard my cell phone ding. I dropped the dish in the sink and ran for my phone. I laughed aloud when I read, "Hello, Jenny. How are you doing tonight?" I liked the fact that he had a sense of humor. Last night, when he asked me to put my name and number in his phone, I typed Jenny. It was an old trick I used when a guy asked me for my number, and I didn't want to hear from him again, I would pull my Jenny card out.

"Hey, can I call you, I would like to talk to you?"

I blinked a thousand times. "Umm, yes!" I typed, "Of course, you can." "Hello, handsome," I said after the first ring.

First, he asked about me and how my night was going, and then I listened intently to his Jeep excursion stories. "We're going for a ride this Saturday," he said. "I would love it if you would come along."

"Yes, sure, thanks for asking."

When he said he would see me then, I felt deflated. I wanted to see him again. I wouldn't mind seeing him every day, waiting to see him made me impatient. I didn't want to wait three days. I went back out to the kitchen and finished the dishes, cleaned the bathroom, and then spent the rest of the night on Google. I wanted to be Jeep ready. I ordered a hat from Amazon that read: 'Jeep Hair and I Don't Care.' I closed my laptop thinking, 'Wait, what time?' Where? Should I call him back?'

I logged onto Facebook, read his posts, and saw he was in a group called Jeeple People. "Wow, there's a lot of people in this group." I kept scrolling. "Found it!" Come join us this weekend as we ride through Mount Riga in Salisbury, Connecticut. "Oh, nice. Lunch will be at When Pigs Fly in Sharon. I love barbecue." I started to get excited about my new adventure and try a new restaurant for the first time. I trusted Drew to call me with the game plan before Saturday.

During our ride, I would ask him if he would like to come to my place for a nice dinner. I have a fantastic dish to prepare from Blue Apron. After dinner, we could go for a walk on the Walk over the Hudson on the bridge from Poughkeepsie to Highland. Hopefully, it will make for a fun date. Besides, it will be good exercise, a great way for us to hold hands, talk and get to know one another. My heart was happy just thinking about spending time with him. I had planned our entire days and nights.

It all, however, came with a realization of how lackluster my life had been. In fact, my life had been a chronicle of selflessness, where I mistakenly assumed selflessness as 'not wanting, not wishing, and not doing anything for myself.' All my life, I ensured that what I wanted tallied with what my husband wanted. And then, fulfilling my children's wants, wishes and desires became my sole ambition. However, I was proud of my children and proud of myself for being there and being what it meant to be a mom.

I spent the next few days daydreaming about Drew. I was at work, sitting at my desk when Fred tossed a wad of paper at my head. "You're thinking about him again," he said and laughed. Fred was like a father to me. When my dad died of a stroke back in nineteen-ninety-nine, I was shattered, and hopeless. I missed his wisdom, hugs, and sweet kisses on my forehead every time he saw me. Fred was not only my co-worker, he was my ninety-four-year-old sidekick. Never married, no children, but oh how he loved life. Still working full-time, packing the best lunches of all of us. We were his family. Everyone at work watched out for him. I could not wait to introduce him to Drew. Daily, I would talk to Fred about Drew and how I felt about him. A whole new chapter was about to get started and I was more than ready to make Drew a part of it.

I was especially excited to introduce him to my Aunt Dolly. I knew the first thing Aunt Dolly would ask me was, "Is he a Christian?" Honestly, I didn't know. Drew told me his mother practiced Buddhism, but he never said anything about his own faith. If the second half of my life meant I was about to become a Buddhist, then so be it. I closed my eyes remembering my friend, Brenda. She was a Buddhist and if she didn't pass away as tragically as she did, I would call her right now for my first lesson, and how enthusiastic she would have been about teaching me Buddhism.

I pulled the covers back, asked Alexia to play "Somewhere Over the Rainbow" and fell asleep dreaming about my man. The next morning, I woke up rested and ready for work early. I laughed out loud, rehearsing all the conversations in my head. I beat my neighbor to the coffee pot. I checked on my order and noticed my new hat was supposed to be delivered this afternoon. I clapped my hands and grabbed my cup, lunch, and pocketbook before heading out the door. The air was so hot, I turned around and headed back inside to change my clothes. I ripped my pants and shirt off and threw on a sundress.

We were so busy at work; I never had a second to do anything but get my job done. At three o'clock one of my co-workers asked me if I wanted to go out for chicken wings. "Come on, it's Friday night," she said. I agreed to go. I liked Andrea, she had always been kind to me and gave me great advice every time. I told her about my husband. We agreed to meet at the Public House in Pleasant Valley. Andrea believed she would find Mr. Right someday. Her bitter divorce was three years ago, and just listening to her scared the crap out of me. I hated the "D" word. I honestly thought marriage was forever. Little did I know, marriage without care, appreciation, and love may last years but it actually is nothing more than a relationship on a piece of paper.

I arrived first, sat at a table, and ordered my go-to beer. "I'll have a Bud Light Orange, please." I didn't drink beer until one of the other ladies I worked with introduced me to the flavor.

As soon as Andrea walked in, I knew she went home and changed. She even had on a little more make-up. I smiled at her. She sat down and ordered a drink before telling me that she was ready to find her prince charming.

"I cannot wait to know about your prince charming, and can you help me find my prince charming? I am serious about this. I know it all happens when you least expect it, but I am expecting my prince charming to find me. I mean it's time. High time!"

"And you seem quite patient about it. So, yeah, is time to reap the fruit of your patience."

We shared a laugh and I told her how I found Drew on Facebook. "It was magical. I can't explain it. There's something about the timing of it all and how he makes me feel."

"I would love to feel that way," Andrea replied.

Then my cell phone chimed. I put my glass down and read Drew's text message aloud, "Savannah, I need your address, so I can pick you up tomorrow." I texted him my address and smiled at Andrea. "Yikes, nine o'clock sharp."

"Girl, you better drink up, go home, and get yourself ready."

I was grateful for our friendship. "I'm going to the lady's room, and we are going to order dinner," I said. "This is our time."

She smiled at me. "Okay. As you say. But I told you so."

By the time I got back to the table, our wings and another round of drinks were there. As much as I wanted to give her my full attention, I could not wait to go home and get ready for my date. I told her about my cousin Randy, told her what he did, and how I found him to be.

"He is a great guy, single, honest, and a very generous man. He's a little older than you. Divorced eight years ago, and never found anyone. I think the two of you would make a great couple."

"Age doesn't bother me," she said and continued to eat her chicken. "Is he nice?" Before taking another bite.

I smiled at her. "Extremely."

Andrea nodded. She seemed almost excited and curious about Randy. We were almost done with our wings when she offered to pay for dinner and drinks. We agreed to split the tab.

Before leaving, I quickly ran through my Facebook and typed my cousin's name, Randy Miller.

"Aha, he's on Facebook. Look." I handed my phone to Andrea for her to look. "Not bad, actually," Andrea seemed a little impressed.

"Check him out and let me know on Monday," I told her.

We both walked to our cars by the light of the moon. I sat in my car for a second. I was glad to see the stars were out. I wanted nice weather for Saturday. I started the car, put it in drive, and noticed a dime on the passenger seat. I looked outside trying to find a streetlamp or headlight, but Andrea was gone and I was alone. I picked up the shiny coin and held it in my hand until I got home. I raced up to the front door and was happy my package was there. I set it on the counter for a second before putting the dime in the jar with the other two. I hurriedly opened the envelope and tried the new hat on.

"Perfect."

I went on with my night routine, did dinner, wash dishes, and prepare for a good night's sleep. I was just ready to fall asleep when my cell phone chimed. My heart started racing. "Oh, no. He's canceling our adventure. Crap!" I pushed the thought away and picked up my phone. I read the message aloud, "Please fix me up with your cousin Randy." I laughed when I read, "I've spent the past hour stalking his page. He's perfectly my type."

I texted her back. "He will be blown away by this. Sweet dreams. You just found your prince charming!"

I set my phone down and rolled over before turning back. "Hey, I hope you like baseball. If not, do your homework. He's a die-hard Yankees fan."

"On to the basketball trivia," She texted and I responded with laughing emoji's and set my phone aside.

I recalled the moment when Drew wished me goodnight and closed my eyes.

## Chapter 05

I Slept like a newborn last night. Maybe, it was the two beers. Perhaps it was the thought of spending the day with Drew. I reached over and slapped the alarm so hard it fell to the floor. I had two hours to get ready. While my coffee brewed, I logged onto Facebook to see how many other Jeeps would be in attendance. "Nineteen!" I said aloud. "That's a lot of people to meet for the first time."

I poured my coffee, took a few sips, and headed for the shower. I stood under the overhead sprayer petrified. "Stop," I told myself. "You can do this. You're not a shy person." I washed my hair laughing, knowing it was about to be wrapped up in a hat all day.

After I got dressed, I put on some foundation that included sunscreen, mascara, and lipstick. I pressed my lips together hoping for my first big kiss today. "Wait, will he think I'm a good kisser? Huh, is he?"

I quickly checked if everything was in order; I would be leaving my house for two days, and I didn't want to return to a house that was messed up. I checked the gas, the switches, and the taps. Satisfied with them all, I grabbed my hat and headed out.

I closed the door behind myself, sat on the front porch, and waited. "Where are you going today?"

My neighbor asked as she walked to her car.

I smiled graciously. "I'm going on a date with Drew again," I replied. "Nice, where you are going so early?"

"We're going trail riding in his Jeep and then out to lunch in Connecticut." "Well don't be nervous, you look great."

"Thank you," I replied and waved goodbye just as Drew whipped into the parking lot.

He got out, opened the passenger door, and kissed me on the cheek before telling me I looked amazing. "Are you ready?" He asked as I stepped up.

"I am," I said and took hold of my seatbelt.

"Ha, ha ha," he laughed, adding, "Nice hat. I'm glad you're prepared to be topless all day."

I don't think he saw my wide-eyed expression until he got in the Jeep. He pointed to the sky.

"Topless." Then he winked. "Ready?"

"Oh, yeah!" I inhaled, rested my elbow on the armrest, and felt his bare skin next to mine. When he touched my pinky finger with his own, we laced fingers for the next several miles. My heart settled and once more I took a deep satisfying breath.

Drew broke the silence and told me, "You look great."

"Thank you, that makes me feel good. I wish I wasn't so nervous."

First, he kissed the back of my hand and then he turned on the radio. "Eighties?

I love the eighties."

I looked over at him. He's either been doing a lot of research about me or he has a damn crystal ball. Suddenly, I felt calm, and apparently, my nerves had settled down enough to allow me to sing the rest of the way to the state line. When the weather report came on I looked over at Drew and thought, this was the way I wanted to spend an entire afternoon. I was in the coolest vehicle I have ever ridden in, my favorite music was on the radio, and I was with him – the most gorgeous man and he was with me.

Drew turned the radio down and told me he liked the way I sing. "I could listen to you all day."

I didn't know what to say. I just smiled at him. "Thank you."

"You're going to love the others. They're all good people. Friendly, considerate and we have a lot of fun together." Then he looked down at my sneakers. "I'll order you a pair of hiking boots for our next trip. You're in luck, your sneakers are fine for today."

"Sorry."

*How can I forget about the shoes on a hiking trip?'* I guess, I should have asked him what I needed to take care of before doing my research.

His voice was deep, kind of edgy when he said, "Don't ever be sorry. I like taking care of you."

I nodded my head; never met a man who cared even about how I think about myself. I knew it wasn't just his gorgeous looks or his gentleness, it was also about how he had confidence in me.

"We're here. Two-hundred and seventy-six acres of peaceful hiking trails and scenic views that will take your breath away."

My stomach started to flutter as he drove through the entrance. I glanced at the clock, it was almost ten-thirty. I noticed a few Jeeps parked in the upper lot. Drew must have sensed I was nervous.

He reached over and took my hand in his. "You have nothing to be nervous about, you're with me. They are going to love you. They're good people, most have children. I was the only single guy in the group, until today."

He was smiling so hard that his dimple was showing. "You have the sweetest dimple. I bet a lot of people have mentioned your dimple, but I think it is adorable."

"Actually, only my sisters tease me about them. I can't wait to introduce you to them." He parked the Jeep and waved to a few couples. One by one, he introduced me to his friends.

I watched as they pulled in, smiling, waving, and eager for a good time. The Jeeps came in an array of colors. I found every one of them to be more fascinating than the previous one. Our Jeep had something special about it, it had Drew. I stood on my tippy-toes and kissed him on his cheek.

"You smell so good," I told him.

Drew was correct, everyone was super nice. He made me feel so special. I didn't want to get back in the Jeep, I wanted to hang out with everybody. We got in our Jeep and got on with this ride. I was used to smooth drives on roads, and I never thanked whoever laid those roads for us, but as soon as we were on that trail, I paid my gratitude to those people.

With every bump, Drew asked me if I was okay. "I think my butt just took a leap of faith."

As we drove through the park, Drew played the role of tour guide. When he pointed to the left, I sat up and saw a beautiful waterfall. On the right, a gorgeous, panoramic view of the mountains.

"This is so fantastic; I would love to hike it one day." I looked at him waiting for a reply. Then I saw what he was looking at. A dime.

"Is that your lucky coin?" he asked as he parked the Jeep next to the others. "No," I replied and picked it up. Drew's Jeep was the cleanest, neatest of all the others. Not one crumb, coin, cup, or item, except that dime.

We got out and followed the others to the edge of the parking lot. The view filled me with awe. I could see for miles. I imagined how the sun must dip behind the mountains, and a tapestry of colors must take over the sky. And somewhere there would be a serene lake, mirroring the sky-high mountains.

Drew told me about the secret swimming pool. "Not a lot of people know about

Did he want to take me there? He knew I didn't have a suit with me. I glanced over at him.

'Maybe, if you kiss me first then I'll go skinny dipping with you.' I felt shy at that thought.

As we pulled into the barbeque place, I started to get that embarrassing feeling like I was about to have a Tide Eraser moment in front of everyone. Of course, the chicken was my favorite. I started thinking I should order something that required a fork.

We stood in the middle of the line. The couple in front of us asked me how I met Drew. I wanted to say fate, but instead, I told her, "Facebook. We have a lot of mutual friends." There's that dimple again. Everyone agreed that we made a great couple, and they were pleased to see Drew happy for a change.

"Hey, I'm always happy," Drew said laughingly.

"Not like today," his friend told him and then he told me.

"Well, I can't argue that," Drew responded.

"Savannah, we hope to see more of you." His friend patted Drew's shoulder, received his order, and moved to make space for us.

It was our turn to order. Drew turned to me and asked, "What would you like?"

I ordered chicken breast. I laughed when he ordered the triple BBQ – baby back ribs, chicken, and pulled pork on a slider Brioche roll. I ate mine using a fork and knife. We all sat outside at the picnic tables laughing and talking about our next adventure. When Drew got up to take our plates to the garbage can, I caught the scent of his cologne.

We all chatted a little more, let the night deepen, and allowed ourselves a few more carefree moments. Each of us told some things about ourselves, letting everyone know us better, I told them about my children and grandchildren. They all adored them just by listening to a few of their stories. Soon, we called the night, and each of us bid farewell.

While saying our goodbyes, I asked him, "What are you wearing? It smells so good on you."

He smiled broadly. "CK by Calvin Klein."

I inhaled and when I did my inside exploded. If he only knew how he made me feel. "Well, it smells so good on you."

"Thank you, Savannah. May I put my arm around you?" I smiled at him. "I would love that."

Drew was such a gentleman. Often shy. I did not want the date to end. I wanted to go back to his house and stay with him until he made love to me.

"Savannah, would you like to go back to my house and walk on the rail trail?" "Okay," I replied. Maybe, I could ask him about his mom, her passing, and if there was anything I could do for him.

Drew parked the Jeep, and we walked hand in hand up the eighteen-mile trail toward Copake, New York. If he only knew how much I loved walking, hiking, and riding my bike. Or doing anything with him beside me.

I asked him, "Drew do you have a bicycle?"

"I have a trail bike," he replied.

"Perfect," I said and told him, "Maybe, we can ride our bikes one day. This trail is spectacular."

Drew stopped walking in front of a park bench, took my face into his hands, and kissed me. The sun was starting to go down. I was not sure if it was the warmth of the rays or my body. I was hot from my toes to my forehead. I was sure my face was glowing. I closed my eyes and returned his kiss before telling him, "Thank you for a wonderful day and evening."

*Sarah Kaye*

With quivering lips, he kissed me again. A little longer, lingering, and tender; truly, it was a kiss I would remember for the rest of my life.

'Oh, how I hoped and hoped for the rest of my life to be filled with such kisses.'

We pulled apart and our eyes met and I smiled. My first kiss from Drew. "I will never forget today," I said.

He took my hand, kissed it gently, and said, "I won't either."

Hand in hand, we walked back toward the Jeep. Drew cautiously scanned the area as if looking for something or looking out for something. He saw me noticing him and told me,

"There's been a few bear sightings on the trail lately." He squeezed my hand. "Don't worry, I'll protect you."

Then he laughed. "Actually, I'm afraid of bears and it's getting dark." I squeezed his hand. "Your secret is safe with me."

We arrived back at his Jeep and before he started the engine I asked him, "Drew, would you tell me about your mother?"

When he looked at me, I thought perhaps it was too soon to ask.

"You care about me. Thank you for that. You're a very caring person. Most women want to use me and take advantage of my generosity. You're different."

I reached over and held his hand on my own. "I deeply care about you."

"My mom was a great lady. Her name was Lu-Anne. My dad left her for his secretary. My mother took it very hard. She was faced with many obstacles, living in

America, a language barrier, no real friends to guide her, and she had to work in a world she knew nothing about. My sisters were gone, living their own lives. They had families to take care of. I was all she had. As the years went by, her health declined in a variety of ways. It got harder for me to take care of her. Eventually, I had to put her in an adult daycare facility while I was at work. She deserved to be taken care of with dignity. I worked even harder to pay for her care."

When he looked over at me, I wiped my eyes listening to this beautiful man talk about his mother and the care he provided for her.

Drew placed his hand on my cheek and stroked it lightly. "My evenings and weekends were spent caring for her. I loved her so much. It was my turn to take care of her. I tried to include her in everything I did. One day, I told her I didn't think I would ever find anyone to share my life with. She looked at me and replied, 'Son, you will find someone special. She will come to you when you least expect it. I promise you.' I thanked her and told her I was okay being alone." He tapped me on my nose. "I wish you had met her. I truly wished she would have met you and wished us a happy life together.

"She passed away due to COVID on your birthday. At first, she thought it was just a minor allergy. And I thought that too. But it got severe with time, so we took the COVID test and it came back positive. She was given every help and care that was needed. But maybe this time, she needed a peaceful rest, like my Mom used to say. I miss her so much. So much."

I felt blessed to have Drew in my life. The way he spoke about his mom. I knew it took a special man to do what he did for his mother.

We were still sitting in his Jeep when he turned to me and said, "She liked to be called Lu."

I looked up at the sky and whispered, "Thank you, Lu." I promised her I would take good care of her son.

Drew smiled warmly at me as if he knew. "Because it was during the pandemic, I had to stand on the other side of the glass to say goodbye to her. Rest in peace, Mom."

I held his hand in mine. "I'm sure she's watching over you right now. I hope she likes me."

"She loved you before me. In fact, she knew you before me,"

he replied, and there was his usual smile with a dimple.

At that moment, I felt more feelings for Drew than ever before. More respect, more care and I honored him more. His mother raised a son loved and respected by all. I reached in my pocket for a tissue and of course, I felt the dime.

"Now you know what I had to take care of before our first date. I had to meet with the funeral director and pick out her urn. I chose an eagle wrapped all the way around it. She would have liked the 3D image. For now, I'll keep her with me in the house. Someday, I would like to take her home to Taiwan." He looked up to the sky and whispered, "I promise, Mom."

"Drew, take all the time you need. If you need to mourn, cry, or be alone, I'll be right here by your side." I squeezed his hand a little and he returned the gesture.

"I know you are. I know you'll be. Thank you, Savannah." He dried his tears with the tissue, inhaled a few long breaths, and turned to me with a smile. "As much as I hate this moment, but it's getting late. We should go home but let's get together again on Wednesday. I don't want to wait until the weekend to see you again."

My heart melted; it melt a million times over. "I feel the same way. How about you come to my place and I'll make you dinner. I have a great new recipe I'd like to try."

Drew answered me right away. "I would like that very much."

And before I knew it, we were back at my apartment building. I was upset; upset at the idea of both of us sleeping separately; upset that I didn't want to part so soon; upset that I wanted to tell him how much I loved him and I hadn't yet; upset that I found him later in life. I realized I felt gloomy when he wasn't around like a part of me was craving for him. Always.

I wanted him to come inside, hold me, and just keep me there. I wanted to hold him, make the pain in his heart go away but I totally understood why he was taking his time. He held out his hand as I climbed down, walked me to my door, and kissed me harder than before.

"Thank you for a wonderful day, and evening and for trusting me with your mother's story."

He kissed me again and said, "You are a gift from God."

"You dropped your keys," he said, bending down like me to pick them up. I laughed as we banged heads. Then Drew handed me my keys and the dime sitting next to them on the floor.

"This is getting strange," I said.

"Very," Drew replied and handed me my keys and the dime.

I laughed aloud. "Remind me to look up finding dimes everywhere I go."

"I'll see you in a couple of days, sweetheart." He turned to leave before I had a chance to tell him I thought they were a good sign.

I put both dimes in the jar, took a long hot shower, and climbed into my bed. I felt blessed knowing he wanted to spend time with me so quickly after his mother's death. I almost felt guilty for feeling so good, and happy.

I spent Sunday catching up on my soaps. It was a habit I had started when I moved into my new apartment. I would tape them during the day while I was at work and watch them every night. I was still wearing my pajamas when my cell phone chimed. I thought it might be Drew. I had hoped he missed me and wanted to get together, but it was my friend telling me about her chat with my cousin.

I popped some popcorn and settled back down in front of the television. At seven o'clock, I finished watching all the episodes. I went back to the kitchen to plan my lunches for the week. I picked my clothes out too. Monday and Tuesday flew by at work, maybe because I never stopped talking about my excursions with Drew on Saturday. Everyone said the same thing about me; I seemed happier. They teased me about being smitten and for being brave enough to cook for him.

Wednesday arrived just in time. I was almost tempted to change our plans and take him out for dinner, but at three o'clock sharp I finished work, and got a text from Drew, checking to see if our dinner plans were still on. His message was sweet. "I can come early and help if you'd like. We'll have fun in the kitchen together, me chopping and you swinging to the music while preparing our food."

I texted him back. 'Yes, come early, I'll chill a bottle of wine for us. Five if that's good for you.'

It seemed like weeks since we had seen each other. I was looking forward to our dinner date. I felt like a teenager getting ready for a prom night. What should I wear? Do I curl my hair? How much make-up is too much for a Wednesday dinner date? Should I dress casually? Sexy? My friend told me people have sex on the third date. 'Oh, my. This will be ours.' When I turned the shower water on, I caught sight of my reflection and noticed I was blushing just thinking about him making love to me. I stepped in and thought, 'Nah, we barely know each other.'

I stepped out of the shower knowing I was falling for him. Hard. I decided to put on a pair of comfortable jeans and my Marilyn Monroe tee shirt along with my best push-up bra and matching lace panties. 'Just in case. I mean, I am in the second half of my best life. Right?'

Even if he didn't make any signs of wanting sex with me, I was hoping tonight brought our hearts closer to each other. The other night, he told me a funny story about calling his sister, Tanya. When he told her he had a date with a woman named Savannah Rowe, she told him she works with my son, Michael. I laughed so hard when he told me she thought I was an old lady. I said, "Why? Because I have a son old enough to work?" So, I had my boys when I was young. I liked people thinking they were my brothers.

At five, Drew was at my front door. I opened the door and

smiled. He was holding a bouquet of tulips and a six-pack of Bud Light Orange. I kissed his cheek and told him he was a great listener. "You remembered."

"Yep, and I assume you like these?" He handed me the flowers.

"Come in, I'll put them in a vase and grab two glasses." He followed me into the kitchen. "I'm not used to men being so thoughtful." I thought my ex barely remembered Valentine's Day. As I filled the vase with water. I set the flowers on the table.

"You look great. I love your shirt. Very hot."

'Too soon?' I thought. "Thank you." Drew had on a nice pair of boots, black jeans, and a black button-down shirt. "Now roll up those sleeves. We're making pesto chicken pasta with zucchini and tomatoes." We prepared everything without a hitch while sipping our beer. We set the table together and enjoyed our first meal in my home. I confessed to Drew that I never thought to make dessert.

"Let's clean up and relax in the living room. Maybe, something good is on Netflix." "Do you like comedy, drama, or action films?" I asked as I picked up our dishes. "Wait, love stories?" I laughed out loud. "Anything, as long as I am watching it with you."

I smiled. Once again, he made me feel so good. We cozied up on the couch and watched three episodes of Mad Men. It was one of my favorites. Drew on the other hand had never seen the series. I knew Drew was a respectable man the moment he spoke about his mother. I was not used to this much respect.

We knew it was getting late and we both had to work the next day. "Savannah, would you like to go camping this weekend?" He knew I had never been and always wanted to go.

'Is he for real? My every wish.'

"Do you have a camper?"

He laughed. "No, but I have a tent."

"Count me in. Just tell me what I need to bring."

"Okay, I'll call you on Friday and let you know when I

figure out all the details." He sat up.

"Thank you for a lovely evening. Dinner was great."

"You're welcome." We both stood up and moved toward the front door. He kissed me long and hard before saying, "Good night, beautiful."

I stood in the doorway as he walked to his BMW. I yelled, "Thank you for the tulips." Wait, did I just agree to spend the weekend with him? I closed the door. "Yes, yes, yes."

## Chapter 06

"I miss you, too. A lot, in fact."

I couldn't help but smile at the last conversation I had with Drew. It was Friday night, Drew called me to say he missed me and was excited about our camping trip.

I was so excited to have this camping weekend with Drew. Honestly, I didn't think twice about my answer to camp with him. Should I have said no? Was it too early to do something so serious together? All I know is that the word yes just flowed right out of my mouth when he asked.

I wondered if he was going to give me a call tonight when he got home from work. I need to know what to expect.

Finally, my phone rang; it was Drew. He said, "Are you packing for our camping trip?" I told him that I had no idea what to bring. "Where are we going? Should I bring my pillow and some extra blankets?"

*Should I bring some condoms? Oh god, am I going to have to buy some? This might be a little embarrassing for me. The last time I bought something like that was for my sons. They were teenagers with raging hormones. Am I a teenager again? I could feel myself* blushing just thinking about that purchase.

As I started putting a duffle bag together, my mind was wandering all over the place. I needed to be ready by eleven in the morning, he was picking me up. He told me to bring some comfy clothes for two nights and two days.

*Where are we going to camp? There are not very many campgrounds around. Maybe we will take a road trip.* The curiosity was driving me crazy, along with the thought that we were going to spend the night together.

*Would I have gotten myself into it? I am just going to let nature take its course. Besides, we were going to be out in the woods, sleeping under the stars. It's going to be so fun. I think I packed everything I might need. I should go to bed early tonight so I can be rested for the weekend. I set my alarm for eight thirty. That should give me plenty of time to double check my bag.*

I woke up to Hank's famous coffee aroma. Oh, it smelled so good. It was heavenly. I jumped out of bed and started my coffee. Sitting at the table trying to visualize our weekend. Drew seemed to me to be quite romantic. I bet he is planning something so special; I just have the feeling.

Already ready to go. Now just sit and wait. Sit and wonder about the new adventure we are about to go on this weekend. It's eight-fifteen, and I hear that masculine sound coming around the corner.

He pulls up and sees me standing by the door with my bag in my hand. Felt like I was going away to camp. He was dressed as though he was camping. Khaki shorts and a buttoned-up olive-green shirt. He looked so handsome; the shirt was the same color as his eyes. Oh, and that dimple.

"Are you ready for our adventure, Savannah?"

"Oh yes, I am. Can't wait."

Drew said we have to go to the store to get a few more groceries and we have to buy a new grill. Apparently, his grill rusted out over the winter and wasn't working.

"Have you ever been to COSTCO?"

We spent a few hours shopping. He took me to COSTCO's. I have never been there before. It was the most interesting store I have ever seen. You can buy anything from household items to underwear. They even had a liquor store attached to the main store. Drew wanted to know if I wanted something from the liquor store for the weekend. I actually saw a really nice Margarita mix that looked really yummy. We bought two bottles and a bottle of tequila. Now we are ready for the weekend.

Off we went to Drew's house in Connecticut.

He pulled over before he got to his driveway. "Savannah, I want you to put this handkerchief around your head. I want you to cover those beautiful hazel eyes of yours for one minute. Don't get weirded out."

I agreed so eagerly.

We pulled into the driveway, I thought. Then I could tell by the way the Jeep was turning that he pulled around a corner. He reached over to the passenger side and removed the blindfold

There it was, there was our weekend getaway all setup. There was a two-man tent set up with two Adirondack chairs sitting next to the fire pit all ready to go. He pulled his Jeep around to the side of the tent and parked it as if we were at a campground.

It was so cool. I really felt as though I was all set up for an s'mores, sleeping bag, snuggly kind of weekend. He had everything all set up. He even had music playing on his Bluetooth speaker. My whole body began to relax as if I was on a retreat.

He transformed his backyard into a beautiful scene. Something right out of a movie. Speaking of movies, I saw a 24-inch screen television set up on a table by the tent.

I asked him, "Are we watching movies, too?"

"Of course, we are Savannah. It's all for you, girl. You told me you liked camping and here we are. Now let's enjoy ourselves."

I took a picture of this scene and posted it on Facebook. Within an hour, all my friends were posting, where are you Savannah, who are you with Savannah, what campground are you at?

I replied to all, 'I'm just in a peaceful backyard made to look like a camping weekend and oh yes, he succeeded.'

"There is only one rule. House is off limits this weekend. That will be another time when I show you around my home."

"How am I going to use the bathroom all weekend?"

Drew explained that he had a garage for the business next to the house, and there was an upstairs with everything you'll need.

I was very happy to hear that. I pictured myself squatting down in the woods behind us, using some random leaf to wipe. But you know what? I didn't even care, I would do that if it meant that I was with Drew. I felt so comfortable with him there. He made me feel so special and loved. He said he wanted to make this special and he succeeded so far. I can't wait to see what he has planned for us tonight and tomorrow. Music, campfire, s'mores, margaritas and movies, that's what I can see so far. It feels like a movie in the making. *Could my life feel so right? All I know is that I am going to enjoy every minute of this, whatever happens here.*

It was around four in the afternoon, and I was getting kind of hungry. I wondered what he had planned for dinner. Maybe, I should have thought of bringing some snacks. I looked inside the tent and noticed one mattress, a blanket, and two pillows. When I first saw the bed, I immediately jumped on it. "You do realize, I have never slept on an air mattress before."

"Huh?" he replied and then added, "another first."

As I put my bag down in the corner of the tent, I realized that I was spending the whole weekend with this dreamy guy. Someone right out of a fairytale novel.

He came into the tent and noticed that I was off in la-la land, staring at the whole scene. I was in awe that Drew would go out of his way to make my camping experience so cool.

"Are you hungry?" "Starving."

"I'll start the grill. We are having shrimp and chicken shish-kebab, baked potato, and some homemade coleslaw. I hope you like it."

I smiled warmly at him. "When it comes to food, I have an appetite of a man."

He laughed. "Okay, but you are all woman to me."

I smiled back at him. Glad he approved of my five-foot-two, one-hundred-and- thirty-pound frame because keeping the pounds away wasn't easy. Thankfully, I was very active. I chose to stay active, I had the choice of not moving around much. I was hoping Drew would take an interest in my passion for bike riding and long walks. He said that he did enough at work, but I knew it was well to keep up the cardio and eat healthy foods. He looked more Hawaiian than Asian, but that didn't matter to me.

Drew had picked up an array of flowers from Paley's Garden Center and placed them on the table next to the tent. When dinner was prepared, he pulled out the chair for me. "Sit down, I'll serve you." I wanted to say, 'I haven't been served by a man except for waiters,' and I knew it was a first for me but I held my word. He made me a plate that looked like it came out of a fancy restaurant. I suddenly felt more in love with this man. He ran inside and got two margarita glasses and made both of us a salted on-the-rocks drink. I loved drinks made with tequila.

He sat across from me, held his glass up, and said, "Cheers." I tapped mine to his. "Cheers, to us."

I took one bite of my shrimp and felt an explosion in my mouth. 'He is an exceptional cook.' I was certain, at that moment that I would love this man more.

After we finished our delightful meal. Drew said, "Now, it's time to relax in front of a nice warm fire." I obliged.

I sat down in one of the two Adirondack chairs. I thought I was on vacation. Drew put on an eighties station, and of course, I started singing. "Dream On" by Aero Smith. The Beatles sang another favorite of mine.

I had no idea how many cocktails we had. Music was playing in the background, as we laughed, talked, and joked about our own lives. He spoke about his sisters and I told him about my children and their families. We decided that we needed to host a barbecue. "Maybe at Lake Taconic in New York," I suggested and he agreed.

"That would be a nice venue for a family picnic. It just seems like the next thing to do. Family means a lot to me," he said.

We decided to revisit the idea in a month. "Maybe on the 4th of July. I will ask my family if they are available and you could ask your sisters. Hopefully, we can make it happen."

"Hey, we haven't watched anything yet. Do you want to watch an episode of Mad Men?"

I knew right where we left off. Season one, episode four. "Oh, yes," I replied.

It was like he knew me so well. He really paid attention to me. Yes, he had a television set outdoors.

Drew turned on the episode and I jumped on his lap. We were both sitting on his chair, snuggled under a blanket. He put his arm around me and hugged me – the hug that made me feel so close to him. The blanket was an oriental thick colorful throw. He said his mom brought it back from her home country, Taiwan, many years ago. It was a bright pink with big bold flowers printed on it. It was almost as though his mom was hugging us too. A real connection.

By the time the show ended, I knew he was falling for me, as much as I was for him. I could feel it.

Drew made sure the fire was out and we decided that it was

a good time to turn it for the night.

'Oh no, I am starting to get a little nervous.' I brought my Adidas sweat suit and big heavy socks to wear to bed. Not very romantic. I grabbed my bag and quickly walked up to the bathroom to change, brush my teeth, and freshen up. It was very dark out. Why I insisted on going alone, I had no idea. All I kept thinking about was that I hoped the bears didn't get me.

I returned to the tent entrance and announced, "I'm ready for bed if you are." "Do you think we need any more blankets? Do you want something to drink or eat?"

"No, thank you. I'm good."

Drew excused himself and went back to the house to get ready for bed. Suddenly, I thought about my looks in the morning, my breath, my hair. 'What is he going to think? Hopefully, he doesn't look at me and run.' I might need to brush my hair before he opened his eyes.

I still couldn't believe we were sharing the same bed tonight. I was waiting for him near the tent when I saw him standing on the deck. He yelled to me, "Savannah come here for a minute, please."

I grabbed my small blanket and wrapped it around my shoulders and ran to the deck. There stood Drew with a lighter and a sealed plastic bag. He opened the bag, there were these odd-looking flattened paper decorations.

He said, "These are Chinese lanterns, have you ever seen these before?" "No, never."

Drew explained, "I really like doing things that are your firsts. But this is my first, too." He gave my hand a quick squeeze and continued, **"By lighting these lanterns you are wishing for happiness and luck in your relationship."** Both of us lit them and sent them off into the sky. We looked up as a dozen red lanterns filled the sky above us. Drew was the best weekend planner ever!

I leaned in and kissed him. "This was the most romantic experience I have ever had."

After we watched the lanterns fly into the sky, we were finally ready for bed.

Drew unzipped the tent for me. It was so cozy and warm in there. As we both climbed in the bed, my senses were heightened, by the smell of trees and all the flowers planted in the yard. I closed my eyes, feeling unusual and genuine happiness. My heart was beating as though it was my first time in bed with a man. Well, it was, with the man of my dreams. 'Is he feeling the same?'

Drew reached over to get his phone and when he did his fingers brushed up against my breasts.

He immediately started apologizing for mistakenly touching my chest. "I'm sorry, I didn't mean to do that."

I told him it was fine. "It was nothing," I replied.

He took hold of his cell phone. "I thought I'd play some relaxing music for us to fall asleep."

Then he unzipped the ceiling part of the tent. We laid on our backs, listened to the music, and gazed up at the stars. He started telling me about the constellations and how much he wanted to see the stars closely when he was young. However, he was quite disappointed to learn that stars die, too.

"You see if we arrange the stars like this," he drew in the air with his index finger, "We get a Hyades cluster."

"Uh-huh," I said, managing to hold my yawn.

"You're sleepy. I'm sorry for boring you with my starry talk." He gently stroked my hair, held my chin, and landed a brief peck on my forehead. "Good night, my sleeping beauty."

"Good night, my prince charming." I snuggled myself in his arms tightly and closed my eyes.

He held me there until we both fell asleep.

I woke up a few hours later and Drew's arms were wrapped

around me like he was holding on for his life. When I opened my eyes, he was staring at me with an alarm in his eyes. He was a little embarrassed to say that he heard some noises in the woods and thought it was a bear. He was afraid of bears, which I didn't blame him for. There were a lot of sightings around Sharon recently, in garbage cans and knocking down bird feeders. "I heard rustling noises very close to the tent," he said and we squeezed each other tight until we fell back to sleep again.

I woke up at eight. Before I opened my eyes, I giggled to myself. 'And I was worried about condoms.'

I smelled coffee brewing. Drew had an electric percolator. It smelled so delicious. I grabbed my brush and quickly ran it through my hair, hoping he didn't take a good look at me while I was sleeping.

I unzipped the opening of the tent and said, "Good Morning, Drew." "Good morning, sunshine. How did you sleep?"

I told him I slept like a baby. "The fresh air was delightful."

I didn't think he remembered the whole bear thing. I wasn't going to say a word about it. It was kind of cute in my opinion. He must have gotten up early. He was all showered and ready for the day. He had the table set for breakfast, scrambled eggs, bacon, and wheat toast. Of course, orange juice and champagne.

"Would you care for a Mimosa?" "Yes, please."

"How about a little music this morning? Or would you like to watch the news, or something else?"

"I would like some tunes."

He turned on iTunes and played 80s music just for me. The first song played was "Waiting For a Girl Like You" by Foreigner. He started singing it to me.

"I've been waiting for a girl like you, Savannah."

Drew made me feel exceptional, almost one in a million. Made me wonder what happened in his past relationships. He mentioned that he was tired of being used by women and he was going to give up on looking for one. It made my heart melt to hear that out of his mouth.

His stories made me sad. How some women can be so mean and selfish? Maybe that's the reason he was so guarded with his relationships. He will not have to worry about me using him. Maybe that was the reason he and I connected well; we both had been used in our relationship and would rather stay alone and single for the rest of our lives rather than be used again.

*'I feel you should treat people the way you want to be treated. If you wouldn't want it done to you, then don't do it to others. It's easy to do. Why is it hard for some people to get that?'*

Drew stood up from the breakfast table and said, "Let's keep this nature weekend going."

"I'd like to take a shower." "Great, I'll clean up."

"Do you want me to help you first?" "I got this. Go get ready."

I grabbed my bag and set off to the office bathroom. I dressed in my comfortable clothes, not really knowing what we would be doing. "I'm ready for my next adventure, Captain."

Drew drove the Jeep around the front of the house. 'Your chariot awaits, my Anna,' Drew said. No one had ever called me that before. He asked if I minded if he could call me Anna. I told him, "Not at all." I actually liked it, I was starting a new life and apparently with a new name. *'And with the man of my dreams, how magical is this?'*

Besides, Anna and Drew, that sounds so perfect.

He held his hand out to me as I jumped in. "I hope you will like the next part of our day," he said. He drove north about twenty miles. It was a nice drive through the mountains. I could see the rail trail through the trees most of the way as we drove. I could see lots of bicycles and people walking, enjoying their beautiful Sunday in June. I know we weren't going biking because there were no bikes on the back of the Jeep. 'Where could we be going?'

We ended up at Copake Lake in New York. It was so exciting seeing all the boats on the lake. Some were fishing, some just hanging out in a cove with other boats, and some were just riding around the lake pulling people on their inner tubes. That looked fun. I have never done that before. *'Of course, I haven't. Little Miss Sheltered.'*

Drew parked the Jeep, got out, and went toward the back. He opened the back door and pulled out two boxes and an air pump. I still had no idea what we were about to do. Then Drew opened the box and suddenly I got it. It was an inflatable kayak, two of them.

"Are we going?" "Yes, Anna we are."

"Oh my, I have never kayaked before."

As usual, Drew was all prepared. He handed me one of the life preservers. While he blew up the kayaks, I put my life jacket on. I felt safe. *'But was it safe? I have seen one too many videos of kayak capsizing and kayakers having a good deep dive in the water. I wasn't the deep-diving type. And drowning was my worst fear.'*

"I'm a great swimmer," he said. Now, I felt actually safe.

★★★

## Chapter 07

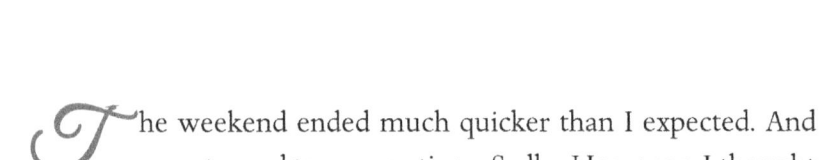

The weekend ended much quicker than I expected. And we returned to our routines. Sadly. However, I thought returning to our routines kind of kept the anticipation of meeting each other. And somehow, it made me grow fonder of him, and I guessed he grew fonder of me, too.

Never thought I would enjoy the mundaneness of my routine.

"Andrea, hey, I can't wait to tell you about the weekend with Drew. Oh, my goodness!"

"Slow down Savannah, I can't understand you. Take a deep breath and calm down."

I pulled over to the side of the road, took a deep breath, and told her, "It was the most fun I have ever had. I'm talking for a long time. Drew is such an amazing man. He had the whole weekend planned out. I felt like I was living in a different world. Being with him was incredible. The chemistry is exploding between us. It's so natural and magical all at the same time. We are so compatible. It is almost like he is exactly what I was looking for and apparently, I am what he was searching for all this time." I said it all in a breath. He was becoming my happiness – my whole happiness. "Maybe his mother had a vision about you when she told him someone will come to you when you least expect it. Oh, Savannah, I am so happy for you." "Do you think he believes I am the one for him?"

"Not to sound cliché or anything but, it sounds like a match made in heaven." "Andrea, I think I am falling madly in love with this beautiful, dimpled man named Drew Hart."

"Wow. I can feel your excitement through the phone. I'm so happy for you." "Okay, I need to get home. I will tell you more at work tomorrow."

"Hey, wait. I have been stalking your cousin's page. He sounds amazing, could you please put a bug in his ear about me? I sent him a friend request, but he hasn't responded."

"Give him a couple more days. He might be checking you out as well. I will give him a call during the week."

Half an hour later, I pulled into the apartment complex, I thought there was a murder or something really big going on there. There were around twenty black Mercedes vans lined up on the lower part of the lot. *'I left for one weekend and came home to this. What the heck is going on?'* I quickly got my phone out and texted Hank.

"Hank, I am in the parking lot, and I am afraid to get out of my car. I see all these strange-looking vans out here. Do you know what's going on?"

"Hi, Savannah. Yes, I'll come down and meet you at your door and explain. It's kind of cool."

"Okay, see you in a minute." I felt better. I hurried out of the car with my duffle bag and purse and headed toward my door. I couldn't wait to hear the news.

"Hank, tell me."

"You need to hear this. There is going to be an HBO movie filmed here at our very own complex. They rented two apartments to film in. They are renovating them to look like the eighties. It's going to be a six-part series and guess who the main star is?"

"Who?"

"Mark Ruffalo."

"Wait, what? You mean he's going to be here filming for months?"

"Yes, the movie is called, I Know This Much is True. Check it out online, you can read the story for yourself. It's a dark drama involving twin brothers. And Mark is going to play both parts."

"I can't believe this is all happening right here in our little town of Pleasant Valley. I wondered if I would get to meet him. He's one of my favorite stars."

*'I must call Drew.'* I thought.

I quickly called Drew and told him what was going on here, he was glad things were ok and was super excited the Hulk was going to be hanging around.

"You do love your Marvel stars. I hope we get to meet him and get our picture taken with him."

I emptied my duffle bag, put my clothes in the laundry, looked for anything to eat, and then rehearsed my first-ever meeting with Mark Ruffalo.

*"'Hi, sir. Nice to meet you. Big fan."* Wait, do I call him Sir or just Mark? *"Hi, Mark, I am your biggest fan."* God, I sounded like a teenager. Meeting Drew brought that chirpy, bubbly, and happy teenager right out of me. Well, I wasn't sure if it suited me at this age or not. I just knew it made me happy. And I liked being happy. *'I'll figure out what to say to him whenever I meet Mark Ruffalo. I have met people before.'* I gave my rehearsing a rest and prepped myself for the night.

After years, I decided to follow a strict nighttime skincare routine. I brought a few products and opened the saved YouTube video on 'Quick 10-minute Nighttime Routine for Glowing Skin.' I peeled the seal off the first product and gently rubbed it in circles on my face (as was told in the video).

The routine made me sleepy too. And I dozed off after checking my cellphone for fifteen minutes. I whispered and wished myself good night, already feeling my skin fresher than before.

The next morning, I woke up and noticed my skin looked a tad bit better, or so I thought. It was the power of believing in whatever you did. I readied myself for the office and dragged myself out for the mundaneness of the day. *Why do I feel that way? I was okay a few days before. Maybe I just want to be with Drew more often, that's why.*

'It's a bright new day and I am going to make the most of it.' I said my affirmation out loud, felt a little better, and headed out.

I had a letter taped to my door. I opened it in my car. HBO was going to compensate all of the tenants with one hundred dollars a month for our inconvenience. The paper needed me to acknowledge and accept. I signed it. Who wouldn't want one hundred dollars a month? I couldn't wait to follow this whole production right from the window of my own place.

Of course, with me working full time and my weekend getaways with Drew, I probably wouldn't be seeing too much of it. I stopped at Panera's on the way to work to get a dozen bagels for the office. Those bagels are the best. *'That was one way of adding some flavor to my day.'* Everyone at the office had their own special bagel that they liked, and I knew who liked what. It was easy for me to pick out twelve. My favorite was the cranberry walnut one.

I got back in the car with the bag of bagels and turned on the radio, the song that was playing was "Rainy Days and Mondays Always Gets Me Down" I shouted, "Not this girl, not anymore."

Got to the office right on time, I was struggling with all the bags I was carrying. My hands and arms were full. I usually brought all my lunches for the week, and I brought my sneakers to wear during my lunch breaks. It looked as though I was moving in for the week.

Mr. Fred always made the Monday morning coffee. Same as every other first day back to work, everyone gathered around the break area to share a breakfast snack. I started to choke up the moment I realized I had something special to share. I decided to keep everything about me and Drew quiet for the time being. I was excited about us, I wanted to tell the whole world about us and have all of them join us to celebrate us. But I didn't want to jinx it. I would just tell Andrea when we walked at lunchtime.

"Guess who is going to star in an HBO movie?" "What? You? Drew?" Andrea squealed.

"Shush. No. Neither of us. My apartment complex is." "I didn't get it."

"They are using the apartment complex for a movie with Mark Ruffalo. Can you imagine? It's super exciting."

I told this to all my coworkers, all of them said it was pretty exciting. "Do you realize how popular he is? Mark has been in around 150 movies so far."

"And he is the Hulk," Mr. Fred said.

Half an hour later, everyone was back at their desks and things were settling down for the day. Of course, my mind was wandering the whole day. Reliving the whole weekend. Rewinding all the conversations Drew and I had the entire time. I felt like I was floating through the day. I realized I didn't tell everyone that I was going to be a grandma again. I was so excited about all the other things I wanted to share. Especially, for my new Wednesday date nights.

## Chapter 08

Tuesday night, I didn't hear from Drew since I called him with my news of Mark Ruffalo. I watched a few episodes of Mad Men, read six chapters, cleaned my bathroom, and checked my cell phone a hundred times.

Finally, my cell phone was going off. 'What the hell?' I couldn't find it. I heard it but had no idea where I left it. I usually put it on my kitchen counter or my bedside table. But it wasn't there. I searched my lounge, tossed all the cushion off the couches, looked under the tables and bed, it was nowhere.

I could hear the faint ringing of it. *'I was in the bathroom the last time.'* I rushed to the bathroom and there it was, right next to my shampoo bottle. I grabbed it but couldn't receive the call as it went to voicemail.

"Hello."

"How are you, Anna? How work has been so far this week? How is the Hulk?"

"Things are going well at work. I haven't seen Mark yet. I am going through Drew withdrawals."

He laughed at that. "I'd like to take you to dinner tomorrow night at a place in Connecticut. Would you mind driving to my house so we can go from here?"

"Not a problem. I would drive anywhere just to be with you."

"Anna, I have to admit something to you. I have been missing you, too. I've never had that feeling before. You are really getting to me, girl."

"What if I say feelings are mutual? I dreamt about you last night," I said, wishing we were together so I could see his facial expression.

"Oh yeah? What was it about?"

"We were horseback riding at the beach. It was such a peaceful feeling riding side by side. It seemed so real. I swear I could smell the ocean and feel the sun as we rode along the coast. Then, I woke up. I wanted so badly to go back to sleep to finish the dream, but I had to get up for work."

"Darn, I wish I knew what happened next. Anna, I promise to make all your dreams, a reality."

"If you were here, I would kiss you. Can you give me a hint as to where we are going tomorrow night?"

"No, you will have to wait. Just dress fancy."

Wednesday at three o'clock, I was on my way home feeling excited about my dinner date. I picked out a cute summer yellow dress. It was V-necked exposing just enough cleavage. The minute I slipped it on, I felt like Cinderella. *Wow, it's short.* I smiled at my reflection. *I'm coming for you, Drew Hart.*

He was waiting for me in his little convertible car. He had the top down. There goes my hairdo. He told me, how sexy I looked and handed me a hat. Not fashionable, but it would do the job. I took the hat and put it on as he opened the door for me to get in.

"You know I have been feeling breathless around you. Careful, girl." I kissed the back of his hand.

"I hope you like the restaurant. It's in New Preston, Connecticut called The White Horse. It's a country restaurant with a fireplace and a great menu. You can Google the place and check out the menu on our ride. Maybe we will sit outside on the patio, it's nice out tonight."

He wasn't kidding, this place was very well-known. "Hey, they stencil a little horse on all the food."

"Wait. Didn't you have a dream about horses?"

"Ah," I agreed, fascinated about the details he remembered.

We arrived at the White Horse right on time for our reservations. The place was packed on a Wednesday. Apparently, this was the date night for a lot of couples. It was our night, Drew and Anna's night. We sat outside on the patio. There was a beautiful roaring brook close to where we were sitting.

"How relaxing is this, Drew? I am so happy you brought me here tonight. The menu looks great."

"What are you going to have? Is there anything you would recommend?"

"Their French onion soup is the best. You should try it."

"I'll have the French onion soup, pear and blue cheese salad, and a chicken pot pie. I read on their website it's their specialty."

Drew said he was having the seafood pot pie. We ordered and sat with our glass of water.

"Anna, speaking of pot pies, what are your thoughts on pot? You know marijuana? It's legal in Connecticut. We have a dispensary in the area. Have you ever tried any edibles?"

"I have tried gummy bears. I enjoyed them. It took a couple of hours to take effect, but I liked the way they made me feel. Can I tell you something personal?"

"Anna, you can tell me anything."

"I think they work as an aphrodisiac for me. They make me horny." "Oh, my Anna, that was unexpected."

"I'm sorry, I was just being honest with you."

He choked on his water. "I guess we will have to make a date night to the closest dispensary."

"Oh yea, we will," I replied, teasingly.

"Oh good, here comes the food," he said and then added, "I can feel my face getting red. Anna!"

"The French onion soup, it looks delicious."

Drew was quiet for the next few minutes. We both finished our soup at the same time. When they delivered our pot pies; I took a picture of the horse cutout on the top and posted it on Facebook. My Facebook friends were quite interested about my whereabouts.

"Would you like dessert?"

"Oh, do they serve kunafah made by Chef Drew?" He laughed and said, "You're overselling it."

"Well, maybe." We shared a laugh and I continued, "No I am so full. I couldn't eat anything else."

Drew ordered a coffee and a piece of pie. When the pie arrived, it looked so good, I asked for a bite. He made a good spoonful of pie and said, "Open wide." I did and had the bite.

"I am not a kid." I said protesting against the act.

"I know. I won't be doing it." He accepted the protest. "That was easy." I said to him.

"I am an easy-going kinda guy. Well, how do you like the food here?" "Everything was delicious. Thank you so much."

We got in the car and Drew raised the top. I would have frozen with the top down.

"Anna, I probably won't see you until Saturday. I have a big job I am working on and I have to get it done if I want to go and play on the weekends."

"I understand. It's your business." I smiled warmly. "I'll try to survive two days without you." However, I knew I wouldn't survive well without him.

He was looking at me with a catlike grin on his face.

"Let me know if you finish that dream," he said and kissed me goodnight. "If I get Drew withdrawals, can we Facetime?"

"Every night," he said and waved me goodbye.

I texted Drew to let him know I made it home and thanked him again for the lovely evening. I wanted to sit outside and breathe in the night air. Hell, I wanted to get back in my car, strip down naked, climb in bed with him, and never leave.

'Two more days, Savannah,' I sighed at the thought.

## Chapter 09

I spent most of Thursday and Friday having lots of talks with Andrea. Her desk was right next to mine so we could easily talk back and forth all day without anyone knowing. She really wanted me to fix her up with Randy. I could tell she was very serious about meeting him. Andrea was involved with a married man before and I was trying to steer her away from that. She deserved better than being someone's mistress. She was so sweet and beautiful and looked like the actress January Jones from Mad Men. I wanted her to feel the same way about Randy, as I did about Drew.

"Did you brush up on your Yankee trivia?"

She smiled. "Quiz me. I am a hundred percent certain I won't disappoint you.

Or him." She grinned.

"I have three questions for you. Who was the most famous Yankee player of all time? What do Yankee fans call themselves? What is the motto of the New York Yankees?"

She answered all three perfectly.

"As soon as I get home tonight, I am going to call my cousin and tell him that you will be calling him. I will let you know tomorrow if he agrees." Andrea was smiling from ear to ear.

When the shift ended, and before I stepped out of the office, I stopped by Andrea. "Do you know what you are going to have by next week?"

She picked up her lunchbox from her desk, tossed it in her humongous tote bag, and looked at me confused. "What? Are we getting our paychecks early?"

"No. Something much better." I kept her guessing.

"Oh come on, don't play with my little heart. Be a dear and tell me," She insisted.

"You're going to get a man of your dreams," I responded with my eyebrows and did our little dance.

"Oh, my God! I am turning red. I can't now. Savannah, will he really like me?" She asked curiously.

"No. He will love you." I gave her a warm hug and we said our goodbyes.

As soon as I got home, I called Randy. He didn't answer, so I left him a message. "Randy, it's me Savannah, I have someone I want you to meet, please call me back as soon as possible."

Twenty minutes later, Randy called me. He was excited I had some news for him. He was always after me to fix him up with someone. He would always ask me to find him someone sweet and petite. It was a running joke between the two of us. "I found someone I think fits your order. A very nice woman from my office, Andrea. She is in her early fifties and very cute. Can I give you her number?"

"Sure."

"I met a very nice man. I have been seeing him for a couple of weeks now. We met on Facebook. Turns out we had over forty mutual friends. We have a lot in common, too. Hopefully, you will get to meet him soon. I was thinking maybe we could double date with you and Andrea, then you both can meet Drew."

Randy and I had been close cousins for a long time. We always felt comfortable sharing our problems and being there for each other, even if it meant just a few words of encouragement.

"That sounds great, Savannah."

"Oh, and he calls me Anna. It's a nickname he gave me. I think it's cute."

"I think it's great that you found someone. You deserve to be happy. I am so proud of you. The way that you stuck to your guns, moved out, and living on your own, with no help from anyone. I can't wait to meet him and Andrea. She sounds like my type."

It was the start of another weekend – an adventure with Drew. I went online and ordered a matching luggage set. If I was going away every weekend, I wasgoing to do it in style. I ordered a black and white polka dot set. I packed my bags for our trip to Mystic. I checked my cell phone to see what the weather forecast was calling for.

"Perfect." I didn't even put the phone down and was having a call from him. "Hello."

"Happy Friday, Anna." "Happy weekend, Drew."

"Anna, could you please come here to my place tomorrow by nine in the morning?"

My heart deflated. I was hoping we were leaving tonight. "Sure, no problem," I replied, "I am so excited to spend another weekend with you. You fill my heart with purpose. I just feel happy with you."

"I feel the same way about you. A real connection as though someone was pushing us together. Can't wait for tomorrow, I will see you in the morning, bright and early and ready to go."

"See you then," I said and set the phone down. I made my weekly calls to the children.

My granddaughter, Lynn was trying out for her school play

Mama Mia. Andy was getting ready to go to a birthday party. Everyone was healthy and happy. They look forward to my check in calls. I was hoping to start the weekly dinner tradition that we had in Amenia. Every week, if they had nothing on their calendars, they would gather at the house.

I knew I probably should go grocery shopping for the week. I enjoyed bringing my lunch to work every day. Most of my coworkers got takeout. I was on a budget, for the first time in my life and that was fine by me. I enjoyed my new life of independence and happiness.

Off to ACME for my shopping. I made a list from the sale flyer and my lunch menu to go along with it. As I checked out, watching the cash register adding everything up.

Watching very close to the amount I set aside for food. I could only spend seventy-five dollars a week in groceries.

Cashier says, "That will be seventy-four-dollars and ninety-cents."

Fidgeting through my purse to find my envelope that was labeled groceries, I handed the money to her. "Here you go."

She printed my receipt and I put out my hand out as she placed the receipt in my palm along with my change. The feeling, the spiritual feeling of something hovering over me.

The cashier asked me, "Are you ok, Miss?"

I nodded, gathered my groceries and headed to my car. Why am I getting all these feelings? What's going on with these dimes? I headed back to the apartment to put away my groceries. I made a couple trips back and forth to the door. My last trip, my neighbors shouted to me from their porch.

"Savannah, come over after you get your groceries put away, I have something for you."

"I'll be right over." I put my dime in the jar, knowing it was going to be one of my favorite Hungarian dishes.

"Sit down Savannah and enjoy. Then you are going to tell us more about this man of yours."

"I would love to tell you Mr. and Mrs. Farkas." "Savannah, please call us Orshi and Bela."

"This looks delicious. Thank you so much for being my friend, for making me feel comfortable and safe in my new home." That sounded so weird to me, it was the very first time I lived alone.

I decided to have a cup of tea and do some reading before going to sleep. I needed something to take my mind off Drew. I had so many kinds of teas to choose from in my tea basket. *'I think I will have Chamomile.'* I stood on my tippy toes to grab my favorite cup the one with a big S on it. My friend got it for me one Christmas. I started to fill the cup up with water and I saw a shiny dime on the bottom of the porcelain cup resting on the bottom shelf. *'What is it with these dimes? Why am I finding them all over the place? Weird.'*

I grabbed the jar and added it to the bunch that I had collected already. I believed someone was trying to tell me something. Maybe I was supposed to save up for something special.

I grabbed a cookie, my tea, book, and headed for the bedroom. My cell phone chimed in with a text message, so I set everything down on the nightstand and read it aloud, "Anna, what flavor do you like better; watermelon, lemon-lime, or mango?"

I texted him back. "Watermelon. It's my favorite."

He texted me back. "That was easy. See you in the morning."

*'What is he up to now? The flavor of what?'*

I set my alarm for seven. I was so excited about going away. I had never been to Mystic, Connecticut, or the aquarium.

## Chapter 10

My bags were packed, so all I had to do was take my shower and head over to Drew's. This time, I packed my hat because we would definitely be going topless. "Of the Jeep," I whispered and chuckled to myself. This is such a beautiful feeling, to be with someone so deeply. I loved it.

This was a whole new world to me. I was unhappy for so long in my marriage and I didn't realize what relationships were supposed to feel like. I guess, I started to think that relationships demand such grave compromises and discounted feelings for the other person. I, somehow, thought that I was being a bigger person by compromising on what I felt, what I wanted to do, and what I expected from the relationship. I never experienced that people in relationships are supposed to go an extra mile for each other, they take care of their feelings and make each other feel special, even if it meant opening the car door for the other person. I suspect that Drew was very inexperienced in many ways and at the same time, I myself was very naive about many things. Well, we can both learn together about life and love. It feels like I never had a past of disappointment in my life, it was all moving forward with all good things. I loved my new life, this newness of being in love.

Showered and ready to go, I grabbed my new weekender bag, and off I went. I closed my door behind me and of course, my neighbors were sitting on their porch having their morning coffee.

They were such a cute couple. They called me over to the side of the porch. "So, Savannah, how's it going with your guy?"

"Oh, it's going great. When I get back on Sunday evening, I will stop over and have tea with you and tell you all about what's been going on with us. It's wonderful stuff. By the way, we are going on an overnight trip to Mystic, Connecticut."

"Have a great weekend, Savannah." "Can't wait to hear about it." "Thanks."

"We noticed how pleased you look Savannah. It's like you are walking around in a bubble filled with hearts, we can feel it."

I didn't realize how much it showed, but I guess feelings don't lie. My high spirits were showing to everyone. I threw my bag in the back seat and headed to Connecticut. Of course, I had to turn my favorite radio station on. It seemed to make the ride easier, singing all the way there. Singing was something I never did when I was getting ready to go anywhere in my past life.

Going away with my husband in the past was not a grand time. You see, he was a chronic complainer, every word out of his mouth was criticism about everything. And he hated to spend money, especially on me and the kids. Now when I don't live with him, I do believe that living with him was a daunting task. He never liked what I did, never appreciated what big or small I did for him. I would prepare three-course meals for him, but he never uttered a word of praise. I would doll up for him, but he wouldn't say more than a few complaints about 'wasting' money on 'makeup.' I would educate my children, and tell them how to behave with their father, but he needed one moment and he would thrash my parenting as if I failed as a mother. Come to think of it, I sought his validation, his praise, and just one little pat on my back to tell me I was doing a fine job. I never received one, but a blatant betrayal in return.

I remember, how I felt when Drew mentioned he doesn't date married women. I had to assure him of my separation and how long I had been gone before meeting him. Okay, technically, I was married. I never thought to call a divorce attorney, until now

'Why am I spoiling my mood thinking about all this?' I shook my head as if shaking off the negative thoughts. I put the volume up and focused on the song. After two sing-alongs, I took the turn for the street where Drew's house was located.

I pulled into his driveway, got out, and kissed him. "Good, morning." He grabbed my bag and put it in the back of the Jeep.

I wanted to say thank you, Drew. Thank you for everything. For just being you. I appreciate you so much, but something didn't feel right. Drew was quiet. More than normal.

He quietly checked the stuff in the Jeep, checked the tires, and seated himself in the driver's seat. With one hand on the steering wheel and one hand holding my hand, he asked me to put the radio on and I obliged.

*'This isn't like Drew. At all.'* I thought to myself. He didn't say a word, not even complimented me. *'Something must have upset him so much.'* His silence only grew my anxiety, I wanted to know what was wrong.

In fact, if not for the radio and an occasional kiss on the back of my hand, he didn't say or do anything the entire way. Two and a half hours later, we arrived at the hotel. The Inn at Mystic.

Drew opened the door for me. "This is our room for the night."

The room was spectacular. It had a fireplace, a Jacuzzi tub, and the most breathtaking views of Mystic Harbor. My heart started racing. I was so glad he waited. I wanted tonight to be the night we shared intimacy. *'If he wants to,'* I quickly reminded myself that

Drew seemed lost and somewhat troubled. I couldn't, with all my sanity, expect him to make love to me while being upset with something.

When we drove through the town, I fell in love with the cute little boutiques, the houses with so much character and so many restaurants. Awe, the New England charm was lovely.

"First, we are going to lunch. There is a great place here called Mystic Pizza. It's very well known, a movie was filmed in the place years ago. After lunch, we are going on a wine tour. It's a Connecticut Winery Farms where we can collect stamps from all the Connecticut-based wineries we visit. If we collect enough stamps, then we can enter to win a grand prize and other prize packages. Here, look at the pamphlet about it." Drew explained the first destination on his itinerary.

"Wow, it says we are going to visit Saltwater Farm Vineyard and Stonington Vineyard. I guess, we have to find the other vineyards on our own. Not sure if I am up to going to all of them. We don't need a hangover tomorrow and certainly do not need to be driving after all those tastings. We are not that young anymore, or are we?" Drew then told me he had made reservations to eat dinner at the Inn at Mystic Restaurant where we were staying. That was nice because we could have a few cocktails and just walk back to the room.

Our day and night were planned. In between wine tasting and dinner, we walked the charming streets of the town. We walked hand and hand through the quaint sidewalks. The landscaping throughout the town was amazing. We took a few pictures and selfies in all the right places. One couple stopped us and asked if they could take our picture for us. They told us we made such an adorable couple and looked so in love. They even asked us if we were on our honeymoon.

I was so embarrassed for Drew. He got really red and told the couple, no, we were on a weekend getaway. The thought of us being on our honeymoon was such a dream to me.

I posted pictures of us on Facebook. They did tell a story, the happiness on our faces and the love in our eyes were apparent. Immediately we got all kinds of likes and comments.

'Great picture guys, so happy for the two of you, you both deserve to be a happy, perfect couple.' You could tell that our friends were very grateful that Drew and I found each other. That made me feel so good that everyone was seeing what I was feeling. In fact, I have never posted my pictures so frequently on Facebook. And posting them regularly, with someone I love, and our getaways, only I knew how much confident I was now.

We made our way back to the Inn and got ready for our dinner. I thought of wearing a pretty dress with heels. It was a fancy place, I looked it up online and was quite pleasantly surprised that Drew had booked such an amazing place for us. So I had to dress accordingly. Drew was always dressed up. He always looks like he is going to a wedding or some special event and that was so sexy to me.

"Mr. Hart, we have your table ready, follow me."

"I hope you like this place, Anna. Do you want seafood tonight?"

We followed the hostess over to a table next to the fireplace. Before I sat down, I noticed the reservation card: Hart's Table. *'Oh my heart! This couldn't get any better. It was the most romantic spot in the entire restaurant.'* Drew held my chair out for me and I knew I was dining out with the most exotic, charming man in the whole place. I stared into the fire and romanticized our night.

*'What if no one was here? Not a single soul, only me and him. In this blazing fire, our hearts would have blazed in the fire of our love. This whole restaurant would be our dance floor, our slow dance with this ever-ticking away night. No one to see, nothing to watch for, our eyes locked with each other, every second, as we fall deeper and harder in love with each other. And a finale, the finality of the*

night. Embraced in each other's a...'

"Your order, ma'am."

The waitress came over to the table with our orders. I didn't realize how long I have been dreaming with my eyes open. She poured water, and asked what we wanted to drink.

"I'll have a Margarita," I said.

Drew ordered an Old Fashion.

"That's a strong drink," I said smiling, hoping it put him in the mood.

"I am only having one this evening. I have something else for us tonight. A surprise."

"Hmm," I replied. I was intrigued. Wondering what else he had up his sleeve. Drew lifted his cocktail. "To us. To, tonight."

My inside surged. I clicked my glass with his glass and repeated, "To us."

*'Us, it sounded like a fantasy to me. A beautiful fairytale.'*

I ordered the pistachio-crusted salmon and Drew asked for the veal parmesan.

"What surprise do you have for me, if I may ask?" I asked again, just to make him talk.

"It's a surprise. It won't be a surprise if I told you what it is." Drew replied, sipping on his drink.

"Can I take a guess?" I persisted.

"Sure. Go for it, But only three guesses," Drew smiled and looked at me intently. My heart did a little dance whenever he looked at me that way – with a smile that make me forget that there is a whole wide world around me.

"Alright," I managed a response, stealing my sight away from him. "I think it is a gift, a very beautiful piece of jewelry." My silly heart wanted him to give me a ring.

"Nopes. Far from it. Next guess." I did feel a little disappointed but I knew I was expecting a little too much, too early.

"Okay. If not jewelry then I think you've bought tickets for our next getaway. I think you're planning our next weekend out of the city." My head kept telling me to say, 'one intimate night' but I resisted the urge to say it out loud.

"No. but I take that as a suggestion and I'll work on it. Thank you for this idea. Your final guess. You aren't going to guess it, let me tell you that," he said, assured I wouldn't have an idea.

"What is it? I am out of guesses now. Well, it is my last guess, I think it is a secret celebration somewhere for us that you've planned."

"Again no, and again a good idea. Thank you for giving me ideas. We should play more of these guessing games." He laughed heartily, I missed his laugh so much throughout the day.

"Now, you'll have to wait until I reveal the surprise at the right time." He gave my clasped hands a little squeeze and winked at me.

'God, I wanted him.'

The servers came with our orders and placed our dishes in front of us. "Enjoy your meal," the waitress said in a chirpy tone and walked away. Their aromas filled the air around us, and we inhaled it for a moment.

"Dig in," Drew said as he held up his knife and fork. You could have cut his veal with a feather. I couldn't resist when he offered me a bite. His eyes sparkled as he slowly took the fork out of my mouth.

After dinner, Drew asked me if I wanted to order anything else. I assured him I was full, satisfied, and ready for the rest of our evening. 'So ready,' I thought.

"Would you like to go to the bar for a nightcap before we head back to our room?"

"Absolutely," I am hoping the cocktail would calm my nerves.

We sat down and ordered two Baileys on the rocks. "Why do they have to taste so good?" I said holding up my empty glass, hoping my remark would get some response from Drew.

A woman in her early seventies came in and sat down next to us. We introduced ourselves to her.

"I'm Mildred from Norwich, Connecticut." As soon as she told us where she was from, I immediately asked her if she knew my father's family.

"My father and all his relatives were from Norwich. When I was a little girl, we used to go visit my aunt and uncle. They owned a candy shop."

She looked at me and told me, "I know exactly what candy shop it is. I used to go there after school every day." She knew my whole family. She was traveling all around the States with her camper. Her husband had passed away and she wanted to tour the country, they were supposed to do it together.

I was glad we took the time to talk to her. It seemed she wanted a companion then. Once again, I was grateful to have Drew in my life.

We left the bar hand and hand. I thanked him for a great dinner. He looked at me and smiled. I took a deep calming breath. That dimple got me every time. Every single time. We walked to our room and I couldn't contain myself for his surprise.

"Anna, stay here for a moment. I need to do one thing before you go inside."

*Finally.* My heart did that little dance again. I knew it was time. The right time.

A few minutes went by before I saw Drew waving to me to come in. I suddenly had butterflies in my stomach. He held the door open and gestured for me to step inside.

"Anna."

"Drew." I stepped inside and was in awe of what my sight beheld.

Hidden away from the hustle and bustle, lies this room set to ignite the flames of love. The soft glow of flickering candles greeted us, casting warm shadows on the walls. The air carried a delicate fragrance of lavender and vanilla, all for relaxation and intimacy.

On one corner of the room rested a lavish Jacuzzi, its inviting waters shimmering with the reflections of more candles scattered around its edges. The Jacuzzi was adorned with rose petals, their velvety touch enhancing the allure of the space. The soft melody of 'Take My Breath Away' by Berlin was playing in the background, a soothing atmosphere to let you focus solely on each other.

*'It is an unforgettable romantic escape.'* I thought to myself.

"Oh, my. Is that a new Angora throw blanket?" He had it perfectly placed on the bed.

I started to cry when the singer said, "My love, take my breath away."

*'This is beyond perfection.'*

Drew took me by my hand and brought me over to the bed. We sat down and started kissing, passionately. One kiss on the lips followed by my neck, and bare shoulders, and when he French kissed me, I became moist. Everywhere.

He whispered, "Anna, close your eyes and open your hand." He placed something in it. "Open your eyes, sweetheart."

I looked down and there it was, a watermelon marijuana gummy – my favorite. "It's up to you if you want to take it." He held my face in his hands. "I would never force you to do anything you would not want to do."

I popped it in my mouth. We both knew how the aphrodisiac made me feel.

Drew smiled widely. "How about we put our suits on and take a nice relaxing bath in the Jacuzzi?"

I inhaled. "Sounds great. Can we have a glass of wine?"

He tapped me on my nose. "You can have whatever your heart desires. Tonight is your night."

I went into the bathroom, put my suit on, and was the first person to enter the water. He handed me my glass of wine before he came in. I sat closer to him. I wanted to feel his skin next to mine. I kissed him several times before taking my first sip. I laughed when Drew emptied his glass.

When he turned around to grab the bottle, I lifted my empty glass for more. I rested my head on his shoulder, as he gently massaged my scalp. I would have returned the favor except the water started getting cold and that bed looked so inviting.

This time, when I took my suit off, I stood in front of him. Drew took his towel and dried my face, arms, and body and when he knelt in front of me to wipe my legs, I thought I was going to scream right there in the moment.

Then he held back the covers and asked me, "Would you like a massage?"

"You're killing me. Please."

"Turn over, I'll do your back first." The oil was so arousing. "Siri, play relaxation music for a great message."

"Am I dreaming?"

He kissed the nape of my neck. "Nope." Then I felt him pour warm oil on the back of my legs, my butt, and my shoulder area. The warm sensation felt so good on my skin.

It was not my first time, but boy, it sure felt like it. Then I thought, it was my first time. I have never felt this way about intimacy before. First, he massaged my legs, then my buttocks before straddling my torso and giving me the best back rub I had ever received. When he reached my neck and shoulders, I knew I would have to roll over next. I was nervous for him to see my breasts. Don't ask me why, but when he asked me to roll over, I closed my eyes.

"Anna? Are you okay?"

I looked up at him and almost cried. He was the most beautiful man I had ever seen. "I'm shy about my stomach area."

His body was perfect. He had no hair on his body. He was like a porcelain man. "You are beautiful. You have a gorgeous body. Don't be ashamed of giving birth to your children." He bent down and kissed me before taking my hand and touching his stomach, chest, and face. Then he kissed the palm of my hand.

He slowly released one drop on my right breast, left, and then my stomach. When he stopped at my belly button, I grabbed his hand and moved it down to my pubic area. I could see he was very aroused by me. His cock was hard. I wanted him as much as he desired me.

The watermelon gummy took effect precisely when I reached my first orgasm. I thought I had known how it felt to be aroused before, but oh my goodness, I was in a whole new level of sexual satisfaction.

When Drew rolled off me, I told him, "I am going to rock your world." I grabbed the oil off the bed stand, ran over to the sink, and turned the hot water on. When it was warm enough, I told him, "I am going to massage you in places you never knew you had." First, I squeezed the oil in my hands and rubbed them together vigorously, then I sat on his torso and started massaging his shoulders, neck, and chest.

I had to catch my breath. "You are simply luscious, and you are all mine." The gummy was making me hallucinate. But I loved it. I wanted hot sex. I wanted him to make passionate love to me. The gummy had nothing to do with the way I felt for Drew.

He looked at me and said, "Anna, I am falling hard for you."

I tilted my head back, caught my breath, and replied, "I fell for you the moment I looked into your eyes." For the first time in my life, I was experiencing the real thing. I let go of my inhibitions. Then I slowly moved down his hairless body. When I reached his cock, he was erect with desire. He was into me and that made me want him even more. Between his eyes, the gummy, and his erection, I was so horny.

I put my mouth around his manhood licking and sucking it until I could feel his member throb. He started moaning with pleasure. The saliva from my mouth was pouring all over his manhood.

Drew asked me in a soft voice, "Would you like me to enter you now?"

I raised my eyes. "Yes, please." My body was craving him to be inside of me.

First, his mouth made its way to my pussy. It was pooled with moisture, and I was ready for him.

He grabbed my inner thighs and started licking all around my inner lips. His tongue was like nothing I had ever felt before. He was doing all the right things to turn me on. When he slid his finger inside of me, all of my juices started flowing. He stopped for a moment and looked up at me and said, "You taste so good."

"I don't want you to stop." I wanted him more than ever. "Please enter me, I need to feel you inside of me."

He sat up, entered me, and started kissing me passionately. It felt so perfect. We made love for several hours. He was smiling from ear to ear. We were both naked, holding hands and talking.

"So, this was your surprise?" I smiled teasingly.

"Yeah." He said with a bit of shyness. I smiled when he asked me, "How did I do?"

I kissed him before telling him, "You, did great. My hot delicious stud."

I was in another world. Drew actually cared about me and loved me the way I needed to be loved. And how I wanted to be loved.

My heart was smiling knowing he was proud of himself for pleasing me with all that pleasure. Men are usually so conceited about things like this. Not Drew, he was a gentleman.

I kissed his temple. "Would you like to take a shower with me and get ready for bed?"

Drew walked behind me, hands on my hips, telling me how beautiful I was. I turned the water on and stepped in waiting for him to follow me. When he closed the door, I handed him the bottle of shampoo and asked him to wash my hair. I didn't have to ask him to wash my body. I returned the favor and of course, we made love one more time before drying off and climbing back in the bed. We kissed goodnight right before the sun came up.

He whispered in my ear, "I'll see you in a few hours, my love."

Sunday morning, I woke up first, thinking about our night. It was perfect. I wouldn't mind if he had nothing else planned, I could gladly spend another day doing what we did last night. But I knew Drew, I knew he had made plans to make a full day in Mystic and head back later in the evening. I had no idea what he had planned for us, but I was sure it would be great. That was one of the things I loved about him. He was comfortable taking care of me and our day. He understood it was like a whole new world for me and he promised to show me what I missed out on. He was ready to show what I have never seen before and share all he had seen and known before.

Drew woke up smiling. "Are you ready for day two of our trip?"

"Yes," I replied and smiled back at him.

He looked over at the clock. It was nearly eleven o'clock. "I have a full day planned for us. Let's get ready and check out."

"Huh, and I thought I would make love to you."

He jumped out of bed and picked me up. "Easy, woman." Then he handed me our itinerary for the day.

I read it aloud, "The Shipwright's Daughter for breakfast, Mystic Seaport, and a tour through the village for a little shopping. Shopping?" I winked at him. "Oh, and then Bravo an Italian Restaurant for a late lunch."

He set his bag next to the door. "I had the most romantic night with you last night."

I leaned in and kissed him, he held me by my waist and returned my kiss. "Now, my sun has risen," I said with a wide smile on my face.

"I like this side of yours. This rather naughty side."

"I like it, too." We chuckled together, and exchanged a peck.

I set the papers down and picked up my luggage remembering how quiet he was coming here. I wondered if he was nervous about making love to me or if he had something else on his mind. I made a mental note to talk to him on the drive home later.

"We sure did work up an appetite," I said, "That was delicious."

As we stood in line at the Aquarium, I realized I had never been there before. I should have brought my boys. Thanks to Drew, another first for me. Suddenly, I was super excited to go inside and observe the sea creatures.

As if he read my mind, he said, "Sweetheart, you are going to experience a lot of things with me if you stick around."

'If, I stick around?' I reached for his hand. "I'm not going anywhere."

We stepped up to the ticket booth and I immediately felt like a kid on a field trip. "Do you know how happy this makes me?"

He kissed the back of my hand. As soon as we entered the aquarium, we saw the African penguins. We both looked at each other and shook our heads. I had to take a photo. There were two of them having sex. Right there, in front of us.

I never realized how beautiful sea life was. The place was amazing. Watching them, even through the glass was captivating.

Our next stop was the sea lion show. It was very interesting to see how they trained these mammals. We sat in the bleachers, holding hands. I stared at the pool and the three sea lions, watching them perform all kinds of tricks. It was so enjoyable.

"Thank you, for this amazing adventure of the sea." "Are you getting hungry?"

"Honestly, I'm famished."

"Okay, and then I'm taking you shopping."

"Sounds good, I'd like to buy the baby some onesies."

He opened the door for me laughing. "Maybe, you'll get lucky and find one that says, 'my grandma went to Mystic and this is all I got.'"

"Ha ha," I replied. "You know the baby is coming in November?"

It was four-thirty, and I was exhausted and starving from all the shopping. However, Drew couldn't find the right onesie for the baby. We bought shirt-trousers sets, a baby grooming set, and a few washcloths. Drew insisted on buying the toy penguins, we added that to our shopping cart and decided to go for our late lunch which turned into an early dinner. Bravo was simply the cutest little Italian restaurant in the village of Mystic. We sat at a table for two.

"Anything look good to you, Anna?"

"I am going to have the great big antipasto salad," I replied and set my menu

"That sounds good, too. I think I'll have the eggplant parmesan with a side of angel hair."

The waitress came over and took our order. Of course, I had to tell her how famished I was.

"I'll put a rush on the order," she said and picked up the menus.

Drew laughed aloud. "You are hungry. I think it's kind of cute, normally you are so patient."

I smiled back at him. "Just think. With every minute that goes by, we learn something new about each other." I took a sip of my water. "While we are on the subject of getting to know each other, can I talk to you about last night?"

"Of course," he replied but looked away.

"I don't want you to think that I am some sort of hippy druggy from Woodstock."

"Not at all Anna, I think it's really cool that you are so in tune with your sexuality to admit that little secret to me, why do you think I bought them?"

"Ha ha, funny."

"Ok, as long as you aren't judging me."

"No, not at all. As a matter of fact, you just gave me a great idea for our next adventure."

"Oh yeah, where?" I asked as our salads arrived.

"Woodstock, New York, I always wanted to go there and check it out. Let's go next weekend. We'll leave first thing Saturday morning."

"That's a date."

'So he does think I am a hippy but all in a good way.'

"But, don't forget about our standing Wednesday date night though." "Oh yeah, I have that on my calendar for every week."

He picked up the basket of bread and asked me if I wanted a piece before taking one for himself.

I went to take my first bite, but pulled the fork back out and told him, "You know, I have never been to that part of Ulster County before."

'Maybe I should wear my tie-dye tank dress and forget to wear my bra that day.'

We ate our dinner, paid the bill, and left for our journey home.

It was getting late and all I wanted to do was go home and climb into my own bed. We both had to work tomorrow. I didn't say anything to Drew, but I quit my second job. I only worked one weekend a month, but still, I wasn't about to give up one second away from him. The man I just had the most intimate night with. The man of my dreams. I would tell him if he asked. He might not even remember that I told him, it was very early in our relationship.

"Anna, reach in the glove compartment for me, please. There is something in there for you."

I opened it. And found an envelope with my name on it. I showed it to him. "This?"

"Yes, open it."

It was a card with a dragonfly on the front that read, "There are still a few remnants of magic left in this world." I opened the card and read, "Because of you, I believe it's true." I kissed his cheek. "How sweet."

"Did you read what I wrote?"

I had tears in my eyes. "Dearest Anna, being with you, this first month has been so magical to me. I never thought or expected to meet a woman as special as you. I can only look forward to the months ahead for us. With all my love, Drew."

After I read that, I was so choked up, I didn't know what to say, "Thank you for this." I couldn't manage to say anything more. I couldn't believe we found each other. He was the most genuine man I have ever met. He drove for a few miles before I regained my composure and added, "Thank you so much for your thoughtful card. You don't even know how much it means to me. For someone to actually write in the card their own words to me is special. I will keep this forever."

I wanted so badly to say, I love you. Right then and there, but I was afraid to scare him away. I actually felt like I swallowed my sentence down my throat.

*'I love you Drew, I love you with all my heart.'*

He reached over and held my hand. I squeezed it tight and kissed it. "Drew, I was thinking. I'd like to take you out this Wednesday for our date night. Will that be ok with you?"

"Are you sure?" he replied.

I knew he was old-fashioned and enjoyed treating me like a queen, but I wanted to show him my appreciation.

"Yes, I'd like to treat you to a special evening." 'For once, I will be the event planner. This will be fun; I will have to think of someplace really nice.

'A first for him. I know it would be tough to find such a place. He has been traveling and going places. He probably knows more places than I ever will.'

We were about fifty minutes away from his house and I wanted to talk to him about why he was so preoccupied on our drive to Mystic. "Can I ask you what was on your mind Saturday morning?"

"I didn't even realize I was so quiet. I'm sorry, Anna. I don't want you to think it was you. I have a lot on my mind lately. I am having some trouble with my sisters about my mom's death."

"I am so sorry to hear that. Is there anything I can do to help?"

"I asked them to come and help me clear out some of my mother's stuff, but they gave me a lame excuse. I am not sure why; maybe they mourn differently. Or they just don't feel responsible for any of it. Maybe they feel guilty now that she passed. They were not that much help when she was alive. I am not complaining at all, I took care of her because I wanted to. I loved her so much. I was her one and only son. I think my sisters should have helped me more than they did. Guess it bothers me more than it should. *'I was an only child, so I don't know what it's like to share responsibilities with siblings.'*"

"I am sorry it's weighing on your mind. I am here to talk or listen at any time." I rubbed his leg before adding, "I'll help you in any way I can."

"Thank you, Anna."

Drew was once again quiet. I sat there looking out the windshield remembering how I used to tell my sons, you can always tell how a man was going to treat their wife, by the way they treat their mothers. I always tried to instill good qualities in my children because their father had no clue.

I blurted out, "Let's put that aside for a while. Try to think of something else." I turned on the radio. "How about enjoying our ride home? It's not too long anyway." I smiled at him. I wanted to sing the rest of the way home.

"I would like that," he returned my smile.

I glanced over at him. I wanted to say it. Those three little words, and let him know how I felt.

Still, I felt like those words should be said in a special way – may even be celebrated.

# Chapter 11

We were home in no time. *'Such is the charm of singing.'* I thought to myself. He braked the car and we sat in silence for a moment or two, just cherishing the togetherness we shared. Before I got out of the car, I said, "That was the most magnificent adventure, Drew. Thank you."

"You're welcome, I had a great time as well," he said and leaned over for a kiss. "I should get going, I have work tomorrow and I haven't made my lunches or picked out my wardrobe for the week."

"I understand, I just hate to see you go."

"I hate to go," I said with a smile, reassuring him that I, too, hated to go. "I love spending time with you. I can't get enough of you."

"We will see each other on Wednesday, don't forget, you're the date night planner this week?"

"Yes, I know, I hope I can be as creative as you."

"I am sure you will plan something really memorable."

Drew kissed me goodnight and I started my engine and turned my car to head home. I immediately turned my radio on and started to hum along. Halfway home I realized I didn't call the children. I pulled over and quickly sent them all a group text. "Hey guys, hope all is well. I went away for the weekend. I promise to call all of you tomorrow evening. Talk soon. Love, Mom."

*'Can't wait for tomorrow. Andrea will love to hear what I have to tell. Should I tell her all the details?'* I wondered, excited for a new day. *'Oh about that. I hope she has some things to share as well.'*

I realized I needed to catch up with Andrea and see how her romance was going. I couldn't wait to get to work. We'll catch up on each other's weekend on our lunchtime walk.

I sang all the way home; my heart filled with memories from my weekend with Drew. I parked my car, grabbed my bag, and threw it over my shoulder while singing the rest of the song that had been playing in my car.

*I can't believe how happy I am, never in my life did I believe this would happen to me.* I dropped my bag on the bed and headed for the kitchen for a cup of honey-ginger tea and read my mail. I was trying to ease my way back into reality for the week ahead. Honestly, I was living a fantasy – a dream came true. I grabbed my phone and sent a goodnight text to Drew.

He replied with a bunch of hearts and a kiss emoji. "Good night, my princess."

*'I'll be dreaming of you.'* I wanted to send the text but resisted as that would have started a conversation and it was already too late.

'Good night, Savannah,' I whispered to myself, filled with pride for myself – pride in choosing my happiness and living it.

It was light out when I jumped out of my bed and my heavy eyelids peeked at my alarm clock. 'Seven o' clock!' Oh no no no! I overslept.' I had forgotten to set my alarm with Alexa. *Maybe I should call in Love Sick.* "Ha-ha," I said and quickly sent a text to my office manager and told her I was going to be late. That was a first for me, and that was a relief for me, too. I was never late and I hoped I would be excused this one time.

I spent as little time as possible getting ready, grabbed my lunch, and headed straight to the office. Everyone there was concerned, inquiring about my reason for being late. However, those who were close to me were laughing. I put my work bags down and let them have their moment. I knew they were genuinely happy for me.

"What were you doing this weekend? Why Savannah, you overslept."

Another co-worker said, "We might need to talk to this Prince Charming that you have been seeing."

"Ha-ha! Prince Charming has nothing to do with it. I forgot to set my alarm, it won't happen again. I got home late last night."

"Last night? I guess we know they spent the weekend together," another person said and pursed her lips.

"Oh, Savannah, we are all happy for you. If anyone deserves happiness, it's you. We're overjoyed with this newfound love of yours."

Mr. Fred looked at me and gave me a hard wink. "Thanks, everyone, now let's get to work."

Work? I couldn't concentrate for one minute on work. I had to try to build my concentration. Still, wasn't as bothered as I should be, in fact, I felt quite cheerful about it. I supposed I was functioning like a teenager.

"Hey, love bird." Andrea came to my desk, I knew she couldn't wait any longer to know about my weekend.

"Hi, Drea." I used to call her Drea whenever I teased her. "Let's go," she said.

"Yeah, give me two minutes," I told her as I wanted to wrap up this one task before lunch.

She stood there for a minute, eagerly tapping my desk and pacing for a little while.

"God, you can't wait, can you?" I quickly finished the task at hand and headed for lunch.

Andrea and I headed out the door for our daily walk. "I have something to tell," she said excitedly.

"Oh, that's why you were that eager. That was that one time when I was able to concentrate on work since morning."

"Mystic has you mystified, right?" "Yeah," I admitted to her.

"Can't wait to hear all of it."

*No way would she want to hear every minute. It would be a little embarrassing on my part anyway.*

"So, Randy and I have officially talked on the phone three times, and have a date set up."

"I am thrilled for you. Where are you going and when? This is so exciting!"

She smiled. "He asked me to go to dinner and a movie. I am so nervous about it. Please give me some good advice, you seem to have a monopoly on new relationships, lately."

"Well, just be yourself and enjoy each other. Don't worry about anything, or anyone else. He's available and ready for love. I think you hit the jackpot as far as nice guys go. I am not just saying that because he is my cousin. He's the real deal. Just be honest, don't hurt him. I know where you work." We both laughed.

"I won't. He seems like a genuine kind of guy, and I won't ruin it. Now, let's talk about Mystic."

"Oh, Andrea. It was a dream come true. We had the greatest New England experience while we were there. Nice dinner, great shopping, and wonderful erotic sex."

"What? Really? Oh my God. I am so excited for you. Was he good? I want all the details," she said and put her arm around my shoulders.

"No way. I want to keep that sacred in my heart. Maybe, someday I will tell you. Wait, I will tell you my juicy details when you have some of your own to share."

"Deal."

I stopped walking for a second. "Now help me find a good divorce lawyer. Was the lawyer you used any good?"

"Wow, you really like this guy. Yes, she was good but very expensive. You couldn't afford her. Friends of mine used a good lawyer with reasonable rates. You must have had a great weekend if you are talking about the big D. I'll get you the name tonight."

"And would you believe our break is almost over?" I said while looking at my watch.

"No, we just got off."

"We better head back to the office."

As soon as we entered the office, all of my coworkers were smiling from ear to ear.

"What's up with you guys?" I asked. "Look on your desk."

On top of my desk was a vase filled with the most beautiful red roses. My heart overflowed with happiness. "I can't believe Drew sent me these."

My boss teased me by saying, "Wow, you must have had one hell of a weekend, Savannah."

I swallowed the lump in my throat. "We both had a wonderful time," I replied and sat down.

*This was the first time that I received flowers at work. How thoughtful.*

I knew the rest of my day would be wonderful. I finished the day out in la-la- land and headed home. I needed to plan my date night.

In the car, I immediately told Google to call Drew. I had to thank him for the lovely surprise. He just kept making me fall more in love with him every day.

He wasn't home from work yet but I left a message, "Thank you so much. I loved the flowers. Talk soon."

*'Maybe I will let those three words come out of my mouth*

sooner than later, hoping he feels the same way. How would it be to say it out loud? I love you, Drew, I love you so much. You're the reason my heart sings and my days are brighter. Your understanding and kindness make me ...'

The loud horn made me snap out of my reality; wasn't driving at the green light. I rolled my window down and said sorry to the person behind me, hoping he wasn't waiting for too long.

I quickly preened myself in the rearview mirror; my cheeks had turned pink. I was too absorbed in the mental rehearsal of my proposal.

'Get a grip. Get a grip. Mental note, confirm with the kids and Drew about the July Fourth picnic.'

## Chapter 12

$\mathcal{I}$ spent the next two days thinking about the perfect evening for me and Drew. I wanted it to be all about him. Every time I was with him, he surprised me with something I had never done before. I had to come up with something that he had never experienced before. It was Drew's turn to be amazed.

Tuesday night, I made sure I had everything for Wednesday's date night. I went over my list one more time:

Called Aunt Dolly☒. Train schedule ☒

Made sure the special Shoppe was open☒.

Everything was for our adventure. I picked up the phone and called Drew. "Are you ready for your surprise?"

"Surprise?" he said laughingly. "If you planned it Anna, I am sure it's going to be wonderful."

"I hope so. Okay, meet me at my apartment at four-sharp. We have a train to catch."

"What? A train! Where are we going?" "Drew, do you trust me?"

"Of course, I do."

"Oh, wait. I actually have two surprises for you." I heard him inhale before saying, "I can't wait." "See you tomorrow, my love."

As I put the phone down, I realized I had been acting hyped up, especially at work. But I knew they all understand me, and I was glad I found people like them. *'Hopefully, they all find me an equally good person.'*

I made myself a cup of tea and started reading a novel I had gotten from the library in town. It was getting good reviews, and after reading the synopsis, I knew I had to read it. It was called Still Crazy by Judy Marshall Prescott. She was a local author here in Dutchess County. I looked her up and realized I knew her from years ago. After reading the synopsis, I couldn't wait to crack the book's spine.

Wow, I read half the book before I realized how late it was. I could not put the book down. At midnight, I set the book on my nightstand, shut the light, and made myself go to sleep.

I made it through work without any anxiety attacks. Everything was right on schedule. I shouted, "Goodbye," to everyone, and headed home. Tossed my lunchbox on the kitchen counter and went outside. I was sitting on the doorstep waiting for Drew when Hank pulled up to our building.

"Hi Savannah, how are you doing? I haven't seen you in a while. Hope all is well."

I laughed thinking about all the sounds coming from his apartment. *Yeah. Okay,*

*Hank. Let's see. I can hear you snore, make your breakfast, shower, and everything else on a daily basis.* Even with all of his rackety noises, I still adored him. He was there for me whenever I needed anything. "I'm good. How are you these days?" I replied as he approached me.

"Good," he said adding, "Well, I better put these groceries away."

At exactly three pm, I heard a noise coming around the corner, but it wasn't the Jeep. It was some guy on a motorcycle. Maybe, it's the actor living in my building. He took his helmet off and I smiled. *Drew?* "There you are. My handsome dimpled man." *I am falling in love with you more each day.*

"Did you know it was me?" he said as walked up to me.

"No. I thought it was Mark Ruffalo, to tell you the truth. I had no idea you had a motorcycle."

"Stick around and you'll learn a lot more about me. It's a Yamaha YZF-R1."

It was a blue sleek looking ride. "I am not a fan of those things. But you did look hot as hell just now. Pretty sexy, Mr. Knievel. Just so you know we are taking my car."

"That's fine. I'll park it at your spot. I just wanted you to see it."

"Are you ready for the date to start?" I asked and held up my keys.

"Yes, ready as ever," he replied as he hooked his helmet to the motorcycle. "Ok, first we need to catch the five-o'clock train out of Brewster. We are going to get off in Valhalla."

"Sounds like fun."

I handed Drew my keys and let him drive because I was so nervous.

"And we are on time for our train." He parked the car and we hopped out.

The train arrived after a few minutes and we took our seats, and were the first to have the conductor punch our tickets. I snuggled next to him and kissed his cheek. "It's going to be a good evening."

Drew looked at me and said, "You are not going to believe this, but I have never been on a Metro-North train before."

"Really?" I was shocked. "How come? I thought Drew Hart had done everything?"

"It's true, it's a first for me." That made me feel good.

The ride was quick. We chatted the whole way about our July fourth plans. Things were falling into place nicely. I was excited to think that I was going to meet his sisters and he was going to meet two of my three sons and their families soon.

"It feels like it's all meant to be," he said, and I agreed. *'And the urge to say those three beautiful words surged again.'*

I grabbed Drew's hand as soon as we got off the train and led him to this black BMW parked in the lot.

"Hey, sweetheart. Over here." Aunt Dolly had been waiting for us, she held me in her warmest embrace and I relaxed in it, I truly missed her mother-like hugs. In fact, she was my mother after my mother passed away.

"I missed you so much," I said to her under a breath and she quickly landed a peck on my cheek.

"Is this the man you have been telling me about?" She asked as she released me from her embrace.

"Yes, Aunt Dolly, it is. Drew, this is my Aunt Dolly, she is the next best thing to my mother. She's my mother's sister. She fills the empty void of my mom for me. I love her so much."

"It's nice to meet you, you're a doll." Drew complimented her as he shook her hand.

She whispered to me, "He is such a hunk, Savannah."

Can you imagine a 96-year-old lady using the word 'hunk'? Well, she was no average lady, she was what every woman hoped to become when they get that age. She was beautiful, classy, and smart, and a tap dancer. She loved her dancing and all her gal pals who danced with her at her club. Often, she would bring me to watch them all practice for their yearly show. One of her dance partners was Joey Kramer's mom. The drummer of Aerosmith. It was so cool to meet her. They all were classy ladies.

*I wish I had their legs.*

We got in her car and headed to her favorite spot to eat, Pelham Pizza. It was family owned for many years and everyone knew her there. They treated her with such respect when she went in.

"Hi Tony, this is my niece, Savannah, and her boyfriend, Drew. They'll be joining me for dinner. Where should we sit?"

"Dolly, you can sit wherever you'd like," he replied.

Of course, we had their famous pizza. It was delicious. Drew was very impressed with the fresh toppings. Mostly, he loved my aunt. He just couldn't believe her age or her personality. She was a very cool lady.

"Ladies, this was a treat."

"Aunt Dolly was my partner in crime. We did a lot together throughout the years. I became even closer to her after my mother's death."

Drew nodded and then asked, "I have to excuse myself, where is the restroom?"

After he walked away, Aunt Dolly asked me, "Where did you find this wonderful man? Does he have a single father?"

"Actually, he does but he's not for you." "Oh, darn," she said laughing.

Dolly had been widowed for many years and was looking for companionship to enjoy once again. Often, I would be there with her and the owners had to kick us out of our seats because we were there for hours. I looked up at the clock and at Drew, we needed to hurry back to the train for my other surprise.

"Aunt Dolly, could you please take us back to the train?"

"Sure, honey, I am so glad you introduced us. Please come back soon and visit."

Drew hugged her and promised to bring me back another day. She also invited us both to her show in July, and of course, we accepted.

"Aunt Dolly, it was a pleasure meeting you."

We made the train in time. "Where to now?" he asked as we took our seats. "Brewster," I said and inhaled the scent of his cologne.

However, on this ride, we didn't chat too much. We enjoyed the silence between us. Our hearts understood each other even in silence. Our silences said all that was unsaid, and we both heard those unsaid words. Loud and clear. I cherished the moments when we met in the silence behind our words.

*'In the silence of love, you will find the spark of life,'* I recalled the wise words of Rumi and held his arm tighter. *'He is my spark of life.'*

The conductor blew the horn, "Next stop, Brewster." Somewhere I was disappointed that our stop arrived so soon, I wanted to stay inhaling his cologne and rest my head on his broad, muscular shoulders. They were actually quite comfy.

We gathered our things and stood next to the door. I couldn't wait to take Drew to the final part of our date. I closed my eyes and wished for success. *Please come through.*

We found my car and quickly drove to our next destination. Our appointment time was getting close.

"Slow down Anna, where are we going? To a fire?"

"No, but we have an appointment."

I parked the car right on time. We got out and headed towards the store. The ride back was so exciting, there were people on the train coming from work, lots of tourists, and many interesting people. Drew and I both loved to watch people, and that was the place for looking for some eccentric people-watching. Matter of fact, we hit the jackpot tonight. We both looked at certain people and rolled our eyes at each other. The world is made up of so many different kinds. All I knew was I had the one person in my life, that I wanted now and forever. I squeezed his hand. Drew was one of a kind.

"Where are we going?" he asked. "You will see soon enough."

We entered the store, and the bell rang letting the store worker know someone was in the store.

"Hi, I am Savannah Rowe, I have an appointment with Felicia at eight." "I will let her know you are here."

"Thank you," I said, and we both sat down on a small sofa. And I noticed Drew was perplexed. He was looking around and wondering at the weird ornaments and miniatures decorating the store.

Drew looked at me and said, "Quite a place. Synchronicity?" "It's kind of like a magic store."

"What? Are you turning me into a toad or something?" I laughed out loud. "No, you will see in a minute."

"Ms. Rowe, this way."

We both stood up, walked past the portiere, and found Felicia sitting in a small room. I extended my hand to her. "Hi, Felicia. It's nice to meet you. I have heard very good reviews about you."

Drew tugged on my hand.

I stopped walking for a second. "We are going to have a session with a Medium tonight."

"Oh." He replied nodding.

Felicia brought us through this mysterious curtain. It was very calm and peaceful there. "Please take your seats," she said and motioned toward two chairs to her right. "Okay, let's get started."

I closed my eyes and prayed that someone would come through for us. Not sure if Drew was into it but I totally was. I believe Mediums can speak to souls. When someone passes, their souls are still with us. Watching from up above.

"Everyone take a deep breath and close your eyes; concentrate on a person you want to come to me." Then she started chanting and breathing very hard before adding, "I see two women coming through."

"One of them is telling me she is watching over you, she points to me. She sees what a good mother and grandmother you have become. She is very proud of you. She also wants you to know she is surrounded by both husbands and loves every minute."

"I used to tease my mom about having two husbands. She would always say, 'I had two great men in my life.'"

Her first husband passed away from cancer. They had been married twenty-five years and then she met my father. They were married for over forty-five years. My father adored her until the day he passed away. She had two great loves. It made sense she would mention she was with both.

Then Felicia told me, "Your mom wants you to spend more time with your Aunt Dolly. She is very worried that you will have regrets when she passes."

My mom was always a worry wart.

Then she looked at Drew. "I have a female coming through. An Asian woman who has broken English. It's very hard to understand her. I will try my hardest for you Drew." She started clapping her hands gently, almost as if she were trying to cheer her on.

I was disappointed. I wanted his mother to appear tonight. He was pale and he seemed nervous until she raised her hands.

"Your mother is saying, 'She's glad you didn't give up and you were patient.

The right woman came exactly when you needed her the most.'"

My heart started beating in my chest. I hoped she was referring to me. Drew looked happy for the first time since we arrived.

"She also wants you to know that she doesn't want you to have any regrets that you didn't say goodbye. You couldn't get the virus. I am at peace now and I want you and your sisters to know that. I know your sisters are having a hard time with my passing, just be there for them, just like you were there for me during my illness. She says she loves you so much."

I handed Drew the only tissue I had in my pocketbook.

"Wait," Felicia says. "Your mother is holding out her hands as if she is showing me something. She has been sending you signs."

Now, Drew had tears rolling down his face. I reached over and grabbed another tissue from the table next to us. It was a very emotional situation. I wondered if this was a good idea. Maybe, I made a bad decision to do this for Drew. I just thought it would be a good thing for both of us to hear from our moms since their souls passed over. I was happy with my reading, but my mom passed away more than twenty years ago. But Drew's, maybe it was too early to try something like this.

When Felicia finished our reading, I thanked her and paid her by giving her a twenty-dollar tip. We walked to the parking lot in silence. I grabbed Drew's hand and kissed it. "Do you want to stop at Dunkin and get a coffee for the ride home?"

"No, I just want to get back, it's getting late, and you have to work tomorrow," he said as he opened my door.

"Okay," I said and went in.

The ride home was only forty minutes, but it seemed like an hour and forty. Drew didn't say much the whole ride. I hope I didn't ruin everything. I might have just blown the best thing that happened to me in forever.

Drew looked at me and said he was not expecting any of this tonight. "It kind of threw me off track."

"I hope you are not upset with me for having done this."

"No, no, not at all. It's just not my style. I know you are very spiritual, and you have done this before, so you knew what to expect. I was blindsided. Shocked." He brushed my hair from my face. "But I must admit. It sounded real, almost like she was speaking to me through Felicia."

We arrived at my apartment. I parked the car and asked, "Are you upset with me for doing this?"

"Oh, Anna. No."

"I should have asked. I'm sorry. Maybe, I shouldn't plan the dates anymore."

He laughed. "Stop. Hey, it was my first time. A little shocking at first, but I am very glad you took me." He kissed me on the lips, lingering for a minute before adding, "It was an adventure I will never forget."

I smiled a reassuring smile. I never thought, never knew someone's happiness would mean so much to me. So much so that I would trade anything for it.

Maybe I was acting like a teenager. Maybe because I never felt loved – a genuine, only-for-me love.

*'Where have you been all my life, Drew? What would I do with this throbbing heart, this yearning heart?'*

Drew walked me to my door. No goodnight kiss, just "I'll call you tomorrow."

I didn't sleep all night, wanting to hold him and make him feel alright, dreading the moment I decided to take him there, hoping he would love me the same.

*'I hope I didn't ruin everything between us.'* Even the thought of it made me tear up. *'I'm sorry, Drew,'* I repeated the words all night.

## Chapter 13

Thursday, I dragged myself to work, and believe me, it was a chore. I was so tired from the lack of sleep. I wish I stayed home. All I kept thinking about was what if he didn't want to be with me anymore. I knew he had to go to work today as well. I was sure he had a lot on his mind after the reading. I felt bad for him, his mom's death was so fresh. I was looking at the floor feeling sorry for Drew. My heart ached for him and what I had done.

Of course, immediately everyone noticed my silence. Andrea looked at me and rushed over to my desk with a look of concern on her face. "What's wrong, Savannah?"

I held back my tears. "I might have blown everything last night."
"What, how?"

"Long story and I'd rather not discuss it here, maybe on our lunch break." "Okay. Take a deep breath. We'll figure it out. Just don't overthink everything."

I sat at my desk, reliving the whole night in my head, trying to remember what the medium said to make him so spooked. I thought about what Andrea said, but I couldn't help myself. When am I going to learn to stop overthinking everything? It was a bad quality I had. One of my friends used to tell me "Don't put the umbrella up before it rains, Savannah." I always kept that tucked in my mind. It helped me stop going to that place in my head.

It was ten o'clock break time and I left the office and sat on the bench in front of my building. I tried to stop my spinning thoughts of a dreadful outcome. Then, I heard a ding on my phone, it was a text from Drew.

My heart skipped a beat just thinking about what it said. "Good morning, Anna. I hope your day at work is going well. I wanted to thank you for a different kind of date last night. It sure was non-traditional, but I did enjoy it. I'm sorry for the meditative state I was in on the ride home. It was a lot for me to handle. It made my mom's death too real for me. I have been preoccupied with you since the day she passed."

"I am sorry to put you in that position."

"Can you call me? I know you are on your break."

"Sure." My fingers trembled as I tapped his name on my phone. "Drew?" "Hey, you, I want you to know that all the things that I was keeping inside about my mother's death were let out and the guilt was lifted from me. You made that happen for me, I was skeptical at first, but oh boy, she was right on. I believe in the afterlife now and how the body is just bones, and the soul is still around us. I am grateful to you for introducing me to this kind of experience."

"I am so relieved. I'm glad you feel that way. Let's Facetime tonight and talk more about it. I love to see your face when we talk."

"I would love that. And you don't need to think that you didn't do a good job planning the date. You were beyond wonderful."

"You think so?" "Yeah, I know so." "Thank you so much."

"No, thank you, Savannah. Now, go back to work and wait for my call tonight." "I love you, Drew."

"I love you too, Anna."

He sent me kiss emoji's, he really did love me. I wiped a tear, stood up, and looked to the heavens. *'He doesn't hate me.'* I skipped back to my desk. Andrea looked at me and smiled, then she gave me a thumbs up. I winked at her and quietly clapped my hands.

Mr. Fred came over to my desk. "What's wrong Savannah? Is something going on with you?"

"Aww, thank you. I'm okay now. Something happened last night on our date.

I thought I made a mistake, but it seems everything is going to be just fine."

"Yes, I know you were quite nervous about making the plans. Do I have to have a talk with him?" In a stern voice he added, "He better not hurt you or hit you."

*Wow, he really does care about me like a daughter. He is so sweet. I just adore him.* I stood up and gave him a hug. "Thank you. Drew would never hurt me. He's such a gentleman."

I finished the day feeling better about myself, our date, and my future with Drew. As soon as the clock turned three, I headed home. I was excited to Facetime Drew. I remembered him telling me the job was far from his shop. He seemed to have a thriving business. The man didn't even advertise, it was all word-of-mouth. Maybe, someday I could do the books for him. He admitted the paperwork always seemed to build up faster than the checks rolled in.

I didn't feel like cooking, so I stopped at McDonald's. I never got drive-thru food. All I wanted to do was go home, chill, and wait for his call. Before I reached my apartment, I called Andrea. During lunch, we only talked about my weekend, I wanted to check on my matchmaking and see how her weekend went. "Hi, Andrea." "Oh, Savannah. I am so glad you called; I was just about to call you. I want to know more about the medium."

"First, I took Drew to meet my Aunt Dolly in Westchester and then we went for our reading. Have you ever experienced one?"

"No, but I do watch the show Long Island Medium. Where did you see her?" "In Brewster. Felicia was amazing. She told me my mother wanted me to know that she was watching over me and that she was with her two husbands, and she was at peace. She wanted me to know what a good mom and grandma I was. And she told me to spend more time with my aunt, she didn't want me to have regrets. That's the one that got my attention most. I need to think that one through."

"What about Drew? Did he hear from anyone?"

"His reading was very touching. Hey, I want to know about your weekend." "I wish you were here right now. You would see my face blushing. Your cousin is amazing. Hey, I must go, he's calling me right now. We'll talk during lunch, bye." She hung up before I could tell her how delighted I was.

"Wow, who is acting like a lovebird now?" I said it in my speaker, knowing she couldn't hear me.

I pulled up to my apartment and went inside with my fast food. I sat in the living room with my dinner, book, and cell phone ready for my call.

The book I started reading lastly was calling my name. 'Boy, is it good. Maybe, I will finish it tonight.' I looked it up online and found out there was a second book, The Inn in Rhode Island. I called the library and reserved a copy.

I removed the bookmark and started reading where I left it. I was lost in the book, feeling what the characters felt and almost living it with them. Books seemed to be unusually real for me, maybe it is their stories. Or maybe it was the first time I was experiencing emotions so strongly, especially love.

## Chapter 14

*'Eight-thirty.'* Drew was particular about timings, *'He must have been caught up somewhere,'* I told myself. I was starting to worry, but then I remembered his job was farther than his usual electric job. That made me feel better. I put the book down and finished my drink. I checked my phone, read and deleted a few promotional messages, and scrolled my Facebook, constantly looking at the watch ticking time away.

*'Eight-forty.'*

Finally, the Alexa device starts ringing, the one Drew had bought me with a screen on it. He had one as well. Apparently, you can communicate through them by video.

I hit the red button that read, answer and there he was sitting in his black leather recliner. He was still in his work clothes. "Hi, Anna. How's my love? Are you having a good night?"

"I am now. I grabbed McDonald's and finished my book, waiting for your call.

I'm sorry you found our date disturbing."

"Not disturbing at all, it was just very spiritual for me, and it took me a while to process it."

"I didn't think your mom would come through like she did. She is a determined lady, she wanted to get messages to you for sure."

"Anna, did you pick up on when she said she had been sending me messages?" "I did. We better pay closer attention from now on."

"That was a very special evening, and I will never forget it. Thank you." "You are so welcome."

"Anna, I also made some decisions last night on my ride home. I want you to meet my Dad and I want us to take a trip to Taiwan."

"Oh my, wow, but I would have to get my passport. Do you have one?"

"No, I don't. I was born on an Air Force Base in Taiwan, and I don't have my birth certificate."

"Well, I can help you with that, I will do some research on how to apply for it." "That will be great, let's do this Anna!"

"Drew, not to change the subject, but what did you think of Aunt Dolly? She is my best friend and my favorite Aunt. My first son was named after her husband, my Uncle James. He was very special to me, too. When he passed, she was lost, but she is a strong woman and made a great life after his death. He left her with a lot of money, so she didn't have any worries about anything. But then, one of her sons died of brain cancer shortly after my uncle's death. That is what broke her. It took her a long time to come back from that tragedy. No mother wants to bury her child, no matter how old they are."

"How old was he?"

"He was in his sixties, but she was very close to him. That's when our relationship grew to what we have now. I would do anything for her. That's why when Felicia said my mom wanted me to spend more time with her, it scared me when she said no regrets. I know she is ninety-six and won't live forever. I'm just not sure how I will take that bad news."

"Anna, I am here for you always."

Drew's word was gospel. I was so not used to a man meaning what they say. I felt so close to him like we have been together for years. "I wish you were here with me tonight; I need to be held and I want to hold you in my arms."

"Soon, my love. Goodnight."

I blew him a kiss. I started to get ready for my shower and then bed. "Savannah! What's going on over there?"

"What?"

"Well you are undressing in front of me, did you forget we are on video?" "Oh, shit!"

"Well, we could have some fun with this, if you want." "Okay," I said smiling directly into the camera.

"I will just sit and watch you, let the show begin."

I ran over to the radio and put on some dance music. Then I slowly took my bra off. I could see his face get all excited for more. Then I shimmied my pants and underwear off, before running to my bedroom to put on a silk floral robe. It almost made me look like a geisha girl. I put my hair up in a French twist and danced for him with my open robe. He saw everything but didn't. Like it was almost classy dirty fun. He sat back and watched me sing and dance along with all the songs on the radio for about a half-hour.

"Anna, I have to get off here now. This is too much for me. I am getting so horny."

"Me too," I said and waved goodbye.

I was almost a little embarrassed. This kind of stuff was new to me, but I have to say he made me feel good about what I was doing.

After Drew said good night, I decided to take my shower in the morning. I went to bed, reached into my nightstand, and grabbed my sex toy.

I thought about Drew as I pleasured myself. I had a feeling Drew was doing the same.

Just as I climaxed, I heard my text go off, it was Drew. "What a night. That was a first for me, Anna."

"Me, too."

"You were so sexy and seductive the way you danced, are you sure you haven't done this before? I'm joking with you. Tomorrow is Friday, would you like to come to my house and spend the night?"

"Sure, I'll pack my bag in the morning and be over around five. I'll bring dinner and dessert."

"Sounds great, I miss you."

I smiled. "I miss you too, good night, Drew. Wait. I am falling deeply in love with you Drew Hart."

## Chapter 15

I was getting ready for work and realized it was already Friday. I was excited to spend the night at Drew's. I finally got to see the inside of his home. I imagined it to be exotic, full of antiques, and treasures from Taiwan.

All day at work, my mind kept wondering about the evening. What will we do tonight, will we have popcorn and a movie? After the video show that I gave him last night, he might be in the mood for passionate sex, I knew I was. Seriously, how was I supposed to know you had to log off? I thought the video ended when you said goodbye.

'My curiosity will soon be fulfilled. *Ooo, should I pack sexy lingerie?* I'll bring my lace teddy, but also bring comfy pajamas.' I added the nightwear to my overnight bag.

I couldn't wait to spend every waking minute with Drew. I was yearning for him more each day. He was my dream come true. I might have done something right in this world to be blessed like this. Maybe, it was the way I cared for my mother when she was sick, or maybe because I went through such heartache and embarrassment over my failed marriage. Doesn't matter, I was just grateful for this special gift of real honest love, one I prayed wouldn't be broken.

I put my hands together, looked up, and thanked God for Drew. "Wait. Am I staying just Friday night or for the entire weekend?" I tossed in a few extra outfits in case.

Drew shouldn't have to cook tonight; I would bring something from my favorite deli. I would stop on my way there and pick up something hot and a cold dish. I looked up at the clock and realized I should be going soon if I wanted to grab dinner.

I was heading out to my car and saw a ton of people, lights, and cameras and I saw him. Mark Ruffalo. He was definitely just as good-looking as he looked in the movies, but it wasn't the usual handsomeness he had to him. It was a 'dad-next-door' kind of vibe with of course the pronounced masculinity of his features.

They must be going to shoot a night scene tonight. They had everything all set up with black sheets going down the stairs of the apartment. All my neighbors were standing around watching.

"Darn, I am going to miss all the action tonight." I waved my hand at them. My neighbors enthusiastically returned my wave and gestured for me to join them. I declined, as I would be spending the weekend with my own action hero, hopefully, there would be a lot of action. In my eyes, Drew was the biggest movie star in the world.

I got in my car and blared the radio as I sang to myself all the way to the deli. I turned it down a little when I reached the deli. I grabbed my wallet and walked inside, welcomed by the waft of chicken parmesan.

I furtively read the menu board, however, the aroma of chicken parmesan had me convinced about what I was ordering. So I asked, "Can I get two chicken parmesan grinders and the special?" Then I grabbed a couple of bags of snacks and a six-pack of Budweiser Light Orange, went through the checkout and saw these tiny homemade eclairs. "Could I get two of those please?"

*Sarah Kaye*

"Sure, I'll wrap them up for you." "Thanks."

I exited the deli with a big smile on my face, and a woman wearing a tee shirt bearing the deli's logo on it, blurted out, "Have a good weekend." Before tossing her cigarette to the ground.

"Aww, thank you, you too," I replied and put my bags on the floor on the passenger's side. *Oh, I plan on it.* The idea of being intimate with him wasn't leaving my head. *Why was I so convinced?*

I was about five minutes away from Drew's when I started getting butterflies in my belly. *What's wrong with you, you're not a teenager anymore.*

I pulled into Drew's driveway and saw him sitting on his porch waiting for me. "I am so happy to see you, Anna. I've missed you so much."

It had only been two days since we had seen each other. "I feel the same way, only with butterflies."

"Butterflies? Why do you say that?"

"I just realized I might have made a fool out of myself the other night on camera."

"Absolutely not, I enjoyed every minute of that sexy show you gave me." "Really? Okay, I believe you." I handed him my bags and I grabbed the food from the passenger side.

He kissed my lips and said, "Anna, I'm looking forward to another one of your shows tonight." Then he smiled. I silently kept looking at him, as if he knew what I wanted. Or we both wanted the same thing at the moment.

"Why is your face getting red?" "You know why."

"Stop. Before we go into the house, I want to remind you I haven't made any progress cleaning her personal belongings out or done much cleaning."

"It's okay Drew, I understand completely. I'm not here to judge, I'm hoping to make you so happy, you don't worry about anything but what show I am planning on performing."

Drew took my empty hand and led me to the door. I noticed a beautiful Zen Garden to my right. I hadn't noticed it when we were camping. It was filled with bamboo and many Asian statues. I imagined it to be a calming place to sit and reflect. It gave me a feeling of sacredness. Then my eyes went to a white porcelain weathervane in the middle of the garden.

"That was my mom's favorite, she used to sit there and read her Chinese books."

"May I go in for a moment?" He let go of my hand and I handed him the bags. I rubbed my hand along the edges and tried to picture Drew's mom sitting there. Peace came over me. "I wish I could have met your mom, I feel so close to her right now."

Drew put his hand on top of mine and kissed my cheek. We glanced down at the weather vane and saw a dime sitting in the middle all by itself.

We both looked at each other and shook our heads. "Anna, someone is trying to tell you something."

"I have to agree with you. They are definitely showing up whenever we are together."

I grabbed the dime and put it in my pocket, reminding myself to put it in the jar once I am home. Once again, I felt that spiritual magnetism. Somewhere I knew, I was at the right place with the right person, in fact, the right people. I could sense Drew's mom there, watching, praying, and wishing the two of us well.

As soon as we got inside, I immediately noticed this big, almost life-size bronze Buddha statue sitting on the center hall table. It was so fascinating to me, it reminded me of my friend Brenda who passed away. Her home was filled with lots of cultural things.

After we put the food in the kitchen, Drew proudly showed me the rest of his home. "I grew up in this house. I've lived here since I was two years old. I want you to feel welcome. Anna, please feel comfortable here. My home is your home."

I swallowed the lump in my throat. "Thank you, Drew." I was still holding my overnight bag. "Where should I put my things?"

"You can put them in my room or my mom's room, whichever you feel comfortable."

"Oh Drew, we are past sleeping in separate rooms. I'll put my things in your room if you don't mind."

"I was hoping you'd say that." He held me by my shoulder as we walked toward his room.

"Thanks for picking up dinner. How much do I owe you?"

"Nothing. My goodness. You have spent so much on me the past few weeks.

It's my turn."

He laughed aloud. "I don't mind. Are you ready to eat now?" "No, not yet. I am still feeling a little queasy."

"Chill out, you won't have to dance for me tonight." He said.

"Alright. That makes me feel better." "Tomorrow night?" He winked.

"Yay, I'm staying the weekend. Ha-ha, Drew, you're funny."

I put my bag on the floor in his room and ran a quick scan of it. It was minimalistic, his bed being the most outstanding feature of the room followed by the white fur rug on the floor.

"I like your room," I complimented.

"Thanks, Anna. I quite like it, too," he said with a chuckle.

"Come, I have something to show you." He took my head and we walked to the living room. Drew took out some photos of his family.

"You have a lot of photo albums," I said trying to find a picture of him when he was young. It was so interesting looking at his mom's family pictures. "Drew you're right, we do need to go to Taiwan to visit your family."

We sat for about an hour looking through albums, he was so proud of his heritage.

I looked over at him. "Hey, can you cook Asian-style food?"

"Of course, I can. My mom taught me. In fact, I have a lot of family recipes. I will cook something for you someday soon."

"Oh, I would love that, thank you."

I always loved eating Hungarian food when my in-laws used to cook it. It was so good to experience different cultural foods. I was excited about the Asian food coming my way. *'Maybe someday, we can cook together, and build our own recipes.'* I was excited about the new milestone of our relationship.

"I'll be right back." He brought over a beautiful wooden box. "This was my mother's." He opened it and my eyes were blinded by the jewels. It was as if I was looking in a treasure chest. "I haven't looked in here since I was a kid. Shall we look together?"

My eyes were feasting on all the jade in shades of pale and dark green. "Drew, these are so beautiful."

We sat for an hour looking through the box. Drew would pick up a piece and explain the story behind it.

"One year, my mom brought this piece home after visiting her country. Every time she wore it her friends would adore it." There was a twinkle in his eyes every time he talked about his mother; enough for anyone to see how much he loved and missed his mother. Other than his dimple, I adored that twinkle in his eyes. I leaned in and gently kissed his cheek. He returned it with a peck on my forehead.

"Here, look at this one Anna." He picked up a gold bracelet. "My mom gave it to me when I was a little boy. I used to wear it until it got too small for me. She must have taken it and put it in this box." He was putting all his strength not to keep those tears steadied on the eyelid. I took his hands in mine and held them there for a moment. He lowered his head and breathed in deeply.

"It's alright, Drew. I am right here," I said consolingly.

"I know. And I couldn't be luckier." He sniffled a little and looked at me. "Thanks, Anna." He put his forehead against mine, holding me there for a while.

He wiped his eyes and lifted my hand, placing the bracelet on my wrist, it fit perfectly.

"It's yours to keep from me."

"Are you sure? This must be so sentimental to you."

"You are a precious gem to me, and I want you to have it, my mom would want you to have it too, I just feel it."

As he clasps the bracelet around my wrist, I could feel the sensation of approval, it was as if his mom was watching us from up above.

"Anna, go to the jeweler and have them appraise it, I believe it is worth something, so be careful with it."

"Oh Drew, I am never taking it off. Ever. This is the most emotional gift I have ever received. Thank you so much." I looked at the clock and couldn't believe an hour and a half went by, it was so interesting listening to the family stories.

"This is all I have for this treasure chest stories to tell you for tonight," he said touching my hand.

"That's fine, I enjoyed listening. Let's put everything back and close up the box." I could see how emotional he was just reminiscing about the family, it made my heart melt. As we lifted the empty red velvet-lined box to put everything back inside, we both saw a lonely old dime sitting at the bottom.

"Drew, you do see that I am not going crazy here, right?" "Yes Anna, I am starting to understand what's going on." "What do you think?"

"Well, after our visit to the medium. I started going over all the things she told us. I wracked my brain trying to think of what she meant by, 'I am sending you signs.' Then an idea came to me. Of course, I turned to my friend Alexa and asked, what does it mean when you find a single dime in various places? Alexa replied, 'Many people feel that the dimes are a sign of communication from someone that has passed on, letting them know they are not alone. Some other interpretations of dimes are – someone or something is trying to get your attention – guidance or validation that you're on the right path.'"

We both looked at each other with excitement. I picked up the dime. "They must be a sign from *your* mom. Right?"

"She is validating you are on the right path with me."

"Your mom is guiding us together," I replied and had goosebumps. "Yeah, my love. She knew you before I did."

Drew grabbed my face and gave me the biggest kiss.

"I found you when I least expected it. You came into my life when I needed you the most." He looked up and said, "Thanks, Mom, I love you and miss you. By the way, I love the gift of Anna. She is the most beautiful woman I have ever met. And she is very caring, so don't worry, Mom, I am in the right hands."

I laughed before saying, "We are proof of the interpretations. You know people will think we're crazy."

He shook his head. "It makes sense to me. I don't care what that makes us."

"Yeah, it's about us, right?"

"Right. Not to change the subject, but one of the reasons I wanted to bring you over to meet my next-door neighbors. I have been telling them about you since I met you. And they are more than eager to meet you."

That made me teary, Drew made me feel like I belonged to his family and the people he cared about. "I'm touched." I was overwhelmed: the dimes, his mother approving of me, my mom telling me to visit Aunt Dolly before it was too late, and now Drew gifting me and making me a part of his life.

"They are my best friends, they're like family. I've lived next to them since moving to Connecticut. And I want you to meet them, you'll like them."

"I know, I will."

He stood up and held out his hand. "Let's walk over." He grabbed my hand and practically pulled me across the lawn. "I can't wait to introduce you to them. I'm so proud to call you my better half." He knocked on their door with his other hand, grinning from ear to ear.

His friend opened the door. "Greg, this is Anna. Anna, this is my friend, Greg." I noticed how Greg smiled as soon as Drew mentioned my name.

Greg ushered us into the living room, where his wife and son were. Greg has a huge lounge area, or it seemed like one as he might have cleared all the other stuff and I could see his son's remote-control car parked in one corner. Oh, I remember how one of my kids would want to drive their battery-operated car in the living room and kitchen, and wouldn't give up on it. Eventually, I had to move my stuff somewhere else to make room for them.

"Anna, it's a pleasure to meet you in person. Drew hasn't stopped talking about you since the day he met you." Greg introduced me to his wife and son. "Stacy, Kevin this is Drew's girlfriend, Anna."

"Hi everyone, I am so excited to meet you. Drew told me you've been neighbors for years."

"We sure have," Greg replied. "Drew is our son's godfather."

"That is so nice, I bet he is a super one too."

"Oh yes, he has treated my son as if he were his own, but lately he hasn't had any time for him. I am sure you know why," he said, jokingly.

"I am sorry about that. Am I keeping him from you, Kevin? I will make sure he doesn't spend all his time with me, I'll share him."

Kevin waved his hand in the air. "It's okay, I can see how happy he is. I think he will love you, Ms. Anna."

"Kevin!" his mother says in a stern voice.

"Don't feel bad or think you have to share Drew. Kevin is a big boy now and he has a lot of friends," Greg says and I breathe a little easier and don't feel so guilty.

I was looking at Stacy wondering how I knew her. "Stacy, you look so familiar to me, where do you work?"

"I work at the Town Hall."

"That's it, I am constantly going there to get copies of my children's birth certificates," I shook my head. "They lose them all the time. I have a question for you. Do you know anything about getting a birth certificate from Taiwan?"

Drew rubbed the small of my back. "I was born on an Air Force base."

She nodded. "I remember hearing something about that. Of course, Anna. Anything for my best friend's new girlfriend. I have never seen Drew so happy."

"Believe me, I am over the moon, I hope we get to know each other better," I replied and thanked her for doing whatever she could to help us.

"Me too," Greg said. "Wait, we are having a cookout tomorrow afternoon.

Would the two of you like to come?"

"Aww, thank you, but we're going to Woodstock tomorrow," I replied and turned to face Drew.

"Yes, but I can change it to Sunday. I would love to spend some time with them, I have been neglecting my neighborly duties and my godson."

"Okay, it's a plan, what should we bring?" Drew asked and I knew he was delighted they asked us to join them.

"Just yourselves, we want to spend more time with Anna and get to know her better," Stacy replied.

"We'll both see you at one-thirty," Drew said. After a glass of wine and a warm get-to-know chat, we got up to let them have the rest of the night to themselves.

I hugged Stacy, Greg, and Kevin before we headed over to the house to get ready for dinner. It was so nice outside, we set everything up on the back deck.

"Sit down sweetheart and relax. Drew put his hand on one of the reclining chairs adding, "I will get everything ready for us."

"Are you sure, you are always the entertainer?" I giggled like a child. "Speaking of entertaining. How about you give me a show tonight?"

Drew's face turned all red. "In person?"

"Oh, it's ok for me to embarrass myself, but not you. You are not getting away with this one mister. I want my turn."

I am so erotically attractive to him. As he prepared our meal, I imagined him dancing around the house first in his underwear, then naked, making me cream in my jeans.

I blew him a kiss. "Coming soon. The Drew Show."

"Oh, my goodness. We have a name for it now." He was red and trying very hard to not be.

## Chapter 16

Drew lit the torches, poured us each a glass of wine, and turned the radio on. I smiled at him when my favorite song came on and turned it up just enough to hear while we sipped our wine in contentment.

Dinner was good, the chicken parmesan didn't disappoint us. Dusk was upon us, so Drew tossed a couple of logs into the portable fire pit directly in front of us. We sat around the fire for the longest time talking.

I headed back, wine in one hand, mouthing the words to "Keep on Loving You" by REO Speedwagon. "Drew, want to play a game?"

He snapped his neck to the left. "Strip poker?"

"No, silly, a serious one. I wrote down questions for each other to answer. It's a good way to get to know one another. It will be fun."

"Sounds fun. Shoot."

"Ok, first question. Do you believe in soulmates?"

"If you were to ask me this question over a month ago, I would have said no right away. I had given up on it." He pointed his finger at me and inhaled before adding, "Until you. Anna."

"Okay, my turn. Yes, I do believe in soul mates. Honestly, I believe with all my heart you and I have a special and spiritual connection." I looked at him. He was nodding his head at me. "How many close friends is ideal?"

"Well, over forty, of course. Isn't that the number of Facebook friends we have in common?"

"You're funny. For real."

"Close friends are hard to come by. I have of course my family and just a few very close ones that I would call for anything and know they would be there for me." "That's great," I said. "Good friends are hard to find. I have a lot of acquaintances, co-workers, gym friends, and high school friends, but honestly, I only have a few close ones. I adore all my friends and I am very grateful for all of them for different reasons. My circle is very diverse. But not all are close ones. Okay, next question, how do you like to spend your free time?"

"Before my mom passed, I really did not have much free time. I have always been very spontaneous though. I would say, 'Hey let's go to Rhode Island for the day and have lunch. I tried to include my sisters as much as I could. I like life on the go." "You are an amazing person. I spent my free time reading." I winked at him.

"Now that I found you, I live in a romance novel."

He shook his head. "My mom sent you to me."

He leaned over and kissed me. "I am never letting go of you, my precious gift." "And I am not letting you go anywhere, my handsome."

My heart smiled and we continued with the next question, "What is your biggest regret in life?"

"Hmm, I suppose not having any children. Fortunately, I have my nieces, nephews and I have my godson. They are all great kids, and I was lucky to spend lots of time with them since they were little. Almost like I had my own."

"I'll have a baby with you." "Hell, no! I'm good."

"We could always adopt." "No!"

I laughed. "Relax. Fine, no Drew Jr. or Princess Anna in our future. If you could only bring three things with you on a deserted island, what would you pick?"

"Hmm, let me think about that one for a minute. I would bring you, a backpack filled with my favorite snacks and drinks. My Asian blanket from Taiwan." He looked at me. "What? It's the warmest blanket I own. What about you, what would you bring?"

"Let's see, lots of books to read, a flame starter." I looked at him. His eyes were on me. I giggled. "Of course, I would bring you."

He laughed aloud. "You've been watching Naked and Afraid." "I love that show!"

"So do I."

"You do? Would you go naked knowing all of America will see your gorgeous body?"

"I would have to say no to that one, sorry."

"Just for the record, I would definitely be on the show. I think it's cool to be naked. Once, I went to a 'clothing optional' beach in Florida. It was my first time, but it was a very free feeling. People were walking up and down the beaches holding hands stark naked like it was normal. By the way, great people-watching experience."

"Not something I would do," he quickly replied.

"I'm sorry to tell you, but you didn't have any clothes on your list of three things to bring to the deserted island."

"Real funny, smart ass."

*Mental note. Take Drew to Howe Caverns when they have their naked day.* "What's your favorite dinner, mine is eggplant-parmesan."

"I love sushi, my favorite place to go is New York City. Have you ever been to China Town?"

"'No, maybe we'll go for your birthday. Wait. I don't even

know when your birthday is."

"April sixteenth."

I quickly took out my phone and added it to my calendar. "What's your idea of the perfect woman?"

"A real lady, someone who is genuine, honest, beautiful inside and out. Wants to be serious about a relationship. I love women who like to dress up pretty when they go out. A sexy dress, high-heels, and hosiery is my soft spot, or should I say hard spot. It makes me horny as hell to see legs. I guess I am a leg man. What are you looking for in a man?"

"First, I want to make sure he really loves me, not lusts after me. A genuine man who is honest and knows what he wants for his future. Someone who can see *me* in his future. I don't want to waste time on someone who is not worthy of my love. I love with all my heart and soul."

"Anna, you have my heart, and you have my soul. Believe me, we are true soulmates."

*Oh, that flips, jumps, hops, bounces, and everything else I couldn't name that my heart does whenever he says something like that. I want you right now, Drew, please make passionate love to me right here and right now!* I was turned on, I could feel myself resisting to pull him into a long, lingering kiss.

Even with the torches and the fire pit, it started to get cold outside. *Making love in the cold outside always sounded dreamy to me. Like they show in romcoms.* Drew suggested we watch a show. "Let me guess what you want to watch, Mad Men right?" "No, I thought maybe we could watch the movie, The Incredible Hulk for a change."

"Oh really, do you have a crush on the Hulk?"

"Maybe, no I just have an infatuation with him right now because I might get to meet him in person soon."

"Does he excite you?"

*Huh, Does Drew seem to have a little jealous streak now?* "Absolutely not," I replied. "Alright. I have it on DVD."

As soon as the movie was over, I excused myself to go get ready for bed. I put on my nighty, washed my face, brush my teeth, perfumed myself, combed my hair, and stroke a sexy pose, 'I look good.'

I stood in the doorway. Nothing, he didn't sense me there. So I had to announce my presence. I cleared my throat and let him turn before I moved.

"Wow." His jaw dropped. "The movie does that to you?" He was looking at me with such desire as I walked down the hallway in my pink-lace nighty. "We should watch more Hulk movies."

I gave him a little hip action and poured two glasses of white wine. "Cheers!

To us."

"Anna, this wine is delicious, just like you," he said and then leaned over and smothered my face with kisses.

"I can't believe I have someone to share my life with now." I looked at him, ran my fingers through his thick, black hair, and kissed him passionately.

"You are making me so excited right now," he said as he swallowed a lump in his throat, "I can't take it any longer." He grabbed my hands and pulled me down the hall into his bedroom. Threw me on the bed and started taking my nighty off.

"Oh Drew, I can't get enough of you. I want you all the time." "You make me so happy, making love to you is special." "Really? I was so afraid that I wouldn't be able to please you."

"I know you have had many years of experience over me. I want to tell you something Anna. Very personal."

"Drew, you can tell me anything. What are you trying to say, sweetheart?"

"I have had very little experience with intimacy, not a lot of practice. I dated a lot of women, but I was very shy, and I didn't feel the same way about them as I do with you."

"You were a gentleman," I said.

"I feel like everything is right with us. Another reason why I think you are my soulmate."

"Oh Drew, that is so sweet." Again, my heart burst with love for him.

He lit the candles, took off his clothes and could he have gotten more handsome since the last time I saw him naked? My heart started beating with desire. "Please come to bed," I said and held out my hand to him.

He slowly lifted the sheet before climbing into bed. He kissed me once, maybe twice and then he kept going deeper under the covers. He performed oral sex on me, and he was magnificent!

*That was fucking amazing!* I wanted to give him the same pleasure, so I crawled down and orally gave him such a great thrill. Every time he moaned; I knew he was enjoying himself.

"Anna, oh my god, how can you do that? You are spoiling me."

I grabbed his face and passionately kissed him. Then I screamed, "Drew, I need you inside me. Please."

He entered me slowly and gently.

"I'm not going to break, give it to me harder," I cried. "Oh yeah, that's what I'm talking about."

Our bodies were growing more in sync, we were getting to know what turns each other on. Sex with Drew was great. We finished our love making and cuddled.

"This is called a pillow." I kissed his nipple. "You were amazing tonight." "Are you making fun of my inexperience Anna?"

"Hell, no. You, my love, are the best lover I have ever had. I am here to tell you that you passed with flying colors. You can practice on me any time."

"Passed? He said jokingly. "Hey, did I get an A?"

"I want you to promise me from this night forward, that you

will not doubt your performance. It's not about that, we will get better each time."

"I would like to try some role-playing. I know you would get into that." "I would," I replied and wondered what my innocent man had in mind. "Let's plan our first role-playing date."

"Okay?" I replied with a bit of wonder.

"Anna, I want you to dress up like an airline stewardess and I will be a pilot." I giggled. "Then what?"

"Stay tuned for more information on the itinerary from the cockpit." "Now, I'm curious."

He turned out the light and kissed me goodnight. "We have to get up early tomorrow for the neighbor's barbecue and I want to take a walk in the morning with you after our coffee."

"Sounds good, Mr. Aviator." *This is my first night in Drew's bed, and it feels so real and right.*

I leaned over, kissed him goodnight, and whispered in his ear, "I love you."

He immediately fell asleep. I lay there for a while watching. He was exactly what I imagined – a man I dreamed about. I snuck out and went to the bathroom, put on my sweatpants and tee shirt. The pink nightie did its job. Looking at the clock, I realized it was one in the morning. I had a hard time getting to sleep, my mind was racing, thinking about the meeting with his sisters on Wednesday and him meeting my children.

Will the kids like him? Will his sisters and families like me? It really means a lot to me for them to all get to meet each other. Everything seems to be worrisome to me lately. *Stop being an over thinker, and don't put up that umbrella yet!* I realized I brought my book with me; I grabbed it out of my bag and started reading it hoping I wouldn't wake Drew. He seemed to be out like a light, he was snoring like crazy. At first, I thought I was back at my apartment and Hank was upstairs.

This place really feels like I belong here, I am comfortable and hopelessly in love. How else would you know that you are at the right place with the right one – you feel at home, sheltered, loved, cared for, and yourself.

*Thank you, Drew.* I whispered to myself. *I can't love you enough and can't tell you how much you mean to me.* I leaned in slowly and carefully and kissed him very gently on his forehead. He didn't move a muscle, and I retreated and moved under the covers. Switched the lamp off, and gave my eyes rest, hoping to have the best slumber of my life.

## Chapter 17

I woke up to the sound of birds chirping outside the window of our bedroom. It was like they were singing love songs. I rarely noticed the singing of birds at my apartment. Their songs were putting the entire surroundings in synchrony and harmony. I couldn't guess what birds were singing, but all the different voices came together in one beautiful melody. I stayed in bed for a while, listening to their song. The warbles were followed by the trilling, and a few chirps to add a distinct chord. I felt as if the birds could feel my heart was filled with love.

"Anna, good morning, my love. I hope you slept well."

"Oh yes, at first I had a hard time falling asleep, I had a lot on my mind." "What's wrong, you, okay?"

"I'm fine. I am just a little anxious about the picnic at Lake Taconic." "Don't be putting up the umbrella Anna."

"You're right, one party at a time. We must get through the picnic with the neighbors today. Tonight, we can confirm all the loose ends for the get-together. I just can't believe our families are going to meet each other on Wednesday. Anyone would be a little fearful."

*Sarah Kaye*

"Chill out, I got this all covered, remember me, Mr. Planner, and the Ambassador of fun?"

"Oh yes, speaking of fun, it was a playful time having our little sex party last night."

"Get over here you little pink nighty girl." He grabbed me around my waist and squeezed me tight.

"Hey, let's get in the shower, we have to take our walk this morning, remember?"

"Yes."

My mind was remembering the last time we took a shower together. That was a shower to remember, and the number two shower was just as memorable. Still, we made it in time to enjoy our walk together.

"Anna, come on, get your sneakers on, we have a lot of steps to get in this morning."

We walked hand in hand down the sidewalk as we began our journey. "See over there Anna?"

"Yeah."

"That was the house my grandparents lived in. I have so many memories there. One time, I and my cousin spent the night out in the woods behind their house. We woke up one morning and saw a treasure map lying next to our tent. Apparently, my grandfather snuck up late at night, planted the map, and hid an actual treasure. We thought it was real. I remember it like yesterday. My grandpa took a bunch of old fake jewelry from my grandma and put it in a box hidden in the woods. I can still remember the feeling of us finding the chest. We were so excited to tell everyone about our adventure. Both of us ran to the house so fast, we couldn't even get the words out of our mouths. We were so excited. Then we learned that gramps set us up. He was in the corner laughing his ass off. I wonder if my cousin Johnny remembers that day."

"You sound like you had such a great childhood, you're lucky."

"Yes, I am." He squeezed my hand so tight and said, "Anna, I want you to be part of my family someday."

"I would love that, and by this time next week we will be telling stories about the memories we made with our newfound families."

"I hope so." "I know so."

As we walked, I could see all the flowers growing alongside the road. There were wild ones, lilies, and Queen Ann's lace. In a flowerpot next to a mailbox geranium smelled simply delightful. I listened intently as Drew explained all the stories he remembered on that road.

"I used to sleigh ride down that huge hill," he said and pointed to the right.

"Wow. That looks like it would have been fun."

"See over there? That's where I crashed my bicycle and had to get three stitches right here," he said and pointed to his forehead.

"Oh, let me kiss that?" I jumped up and straddled my legs around him and kissed his forehead. "My poor baby."

He returned my kiss and said, "Let's start heading back, we have to get ready."

*What am I going to wear?* It's the Fourth of July weekend and I think I had a tee shirt that was red and white, maybe the jean cut-off shorts will be good. "Drew, what are you wearing?"

"Shorts and one of my shirts," he replied and looked at me. "You are always dressed perfectly for every occasion. Sexy! Just be comfortable, we are going to have a nice time, they have the best yard for parties."

An hour later, we were dressed and ready to go. Drew had on a blue button-down collared shirt, with white dress shorts and blue sneakers. He smelled just as good as he looked, and his hair was perfectly combed. I am almost embarrassed to be with him because all I had on was a warm tee shirt, cut-off shorts and flip-flops. "You look so nice and I–"

"Anna, you look great, stop obsessing over your clothing, it's about having fun."

"Okay, let's go."

"I'll race you over Mr.GQ."

It was a gorgeous day for a party, the sun was brightly shining. Drew reached into the front pocket of his shirt and pulled out a pair of goofy red, white, and blue sunglasses. They all glittered up, then he pulled out a silly hat to match. I never really saw this side of him. He was like the life of the party. Everyone was greeting him and saying, "Now the party can start!"

"Hey, everyone this is my girlfriend, Anna. I wanted you all to meet her." "Hello everyone, nice to meet you," I said and waved my hand.

People were busy socializing. One group was sitting next to the pool drinking beer, another group was sitting at the picnic table playing a game of cards. They even had a DJ there; a few people were dancing. Drew ran up to the music area and apparently requested a song for us.

"Anna, come dance with me?"

I shook my head. "Oh no, I can't."

He grabbed my hand and took me to the dance area. We danced to "Waiting for a Girl Like You" by Foreigner. We started swaying back and forth. At first, it was quite awkward, but then I just rolled with the music and realized that this was real, it wasn't a dream. It was happening, we were in love. Then everyone became quiet, and I noticed they were staring at us. Like we were on stage in some romantic musical.

"Uncle Drew!" Kevin yelled from across the lawn. "Now I see why we haven't been spending much time together, lately."

We finished the dance, and everyone clapped. I was totally embarrassed for myself. Drew was smiling from ear to ear. He wanted his neighbors and godson to see how happy he was with me.

"Let's have a beer, Anna, I told them you like your Bud Orange."

"Okay, I think I need one, or two, maybe three."

"Oh, stop. We just danced to a song, no big deal."

We ate and finished the day with tons of different kinds of desserts. I had a delicious mini eclair and a piece of homemade carrot cake – my favorite.

"Thank you, everyone, for the fun time today, we enjoyed ourselves and I am happy Anna got to meet some of our friends."

"Don't be a stranger Anna, we have to get together and talk about researching Drew's birth certificate."

"Yes, Stacy," I said and took out my cell phone. I appreciate you helping us, I'll be in touch. Let me give you my cell number."

We were headed over to Drew's when he announced he was stuffed and wanted to relax outside for a bit longer. "Let's sit and plan our adventure in Woodstock tomorrow, Anna."

"Okay!" I replied and sat next to him. *God, I love this new found life of mine, I will never take it for granted.*

## Chapter 18

"Anna, now that we are home, let's talk about our July picnic. Have you decided on the menu?"

"Yes, I just have to pick it up from the caterer."

"What?" he said, making it sound as if I had done something wrong. "I could have whipped up a great menu in no time. Why didn't you ask me to do it?"

*Geez. I didn't think of that.* "Next time I will. I didn't realize you liked to do stuff like that, but I should have known, you can do anything." *One of the thousand reasons I love you so much!*

"And I'm sure you would have come up with a far better menu than the caterers."

"When we get to Woodstock, we are going to go walk around Tinker Street. It's supposed to be a cool place. According to Google anyway. Then we will play it by ear for the rest of the day. Oh, and I want to check out the Tibetan Monastery. It's going to be an exciting day for us. I'm looking forward to another first for us."

"Sounds great. Yes, another adventure." *I'm glad I brought my tie-dye shirt and bright green shorts. Let's see if he notices I forgot my bra.* "Okay, I'll call the kids and you call your sisters to confirm everyone is onboard for Wednesday." I grabbed my phone and hit Facetime with all the kids, gladly they all picked up. "Hi, guys. Is everyone ready for our fun day? I can't wait for all of you to meet Drew."

"Yes, Mom," said my oldest.

"We are all delighted to meet this man you can't stop talking about. Mom, we have never seen you so happy." My youngest one exclaimed. Somehow I had always felt happier whenever my youngest one complimented me or said something to make me happy. I guess, it's just that mom's instinct of protecting their little ones, and the youngest one perhaps remains mama's baby for a long time. "Thank you, my love," I said and smiled from the inside out.

Before I ended the call, my daughter-in-law, Kelly asked, "What should we bring?"

"Just bring yourselves. We have everything covered."

"Okay, we will see you then, can't wait," my son said and vanished from my view.

I grabbed Drew and hugged him so hard. "I can't believe it's going to happen.

It's all coming together so perfectly. Now you call your sisters." *My tummy started to get butterflies again. I hope they like me.*

"I like the idea of Facetime group calls, I think I will do the same," he said and dialed them both in on the call.

Before they picked up, I excused myself and rushed to the bathroom because I didn't want them to see me on the screen. *Why am I being like this? Just seems like I am more nervous than usual about this, normally I am Miss Social Butterfly.* I stood in the doorway, listening.

"Hello Karen, hi Tanya, how are my two favorite sisters today?"

"We're good. Still really sad about Mom. I can't seem to shake this guilty feeling I have. None of us got to say goodbye to her."

"Listen girls, Mom will always be with us. I believe that now.

I'm excited to introduce you to Anna and I have some interesting things to tell you at the party."

"Wait, do you have a new girlfriend? What happened to Savannah?"

"No, new girlfriend. I call her Anna. When you meet her, you'll see how sweet my Anna is. The name suits her. You are bringing my niece and nephews, right?"

"Yes, they will be there. You know that they are grown-up now? And it's hard to pin them down for something like this, but they are coming because they are happy for you. You have been like a father figure to them all their lives," I heard one of them say and my heart skipped a beat.

"I do love them, tons," he replied. "Okay, see you all soon. Bye, Drew."

"Anna, are you coming out of the bathroom anytime soon?" I heard him laugh. "Did you fall in?"

"No, I am coming out now."

"Stop making this such a big deal, it's going to be great, you will love my family." He said as I sat resumed my seat and sat beside him. He put his hands on my shoulders. "And they will adore you! Now, let's go to bed, we must get up early to start our Sunday fun day." He helped me remove the bedspread to the bottom of the bed and then he declared, "Tonight is a snuggle-only night."

"Oh, I can go for that, I love curling up with you."

We got in bed, but I couldn't sleep. I kept thinking about Drew's sisters. He must have known because he started rubbing my back and massaging my head. Suddenly, I felt more relaxed. I closed my eyes. The pillow smelled just like Drew. *Thank you for sending him to me. I don't know how much more I need to thank God for Drew. Like loving Drew came naturally to me, and thanking for him being in life also came naturally to me. I won't ever stop doing either of them.*

I woke up to the smell of breakfast. "Ahh." He was brewing coffee. I stretched my arms out, took in one more deep breath, and ran to the bathroom so I could get ready to meet my prince. I grabbed my robe hanging on the hook in the bathroom and headed for the aroma. He had prepared a feast. Pancakes, sausage, and scrambled eggs. There was a table set up for two sitting on the deck, it was like we were eating breakfast at a country club. "Drew, you are just so wonderful, you are perfect in every way. I love and appreciate you so much."

"I love you too, my darling."

"Sit down and eat, we have a full day today."

"Really, fresh squeezed orange juice too? You are amazing."

We finished our breakfast, showered together, and got ready to go. I purposely waited for him to get dressed before I put my clothes on. I was standing in the doorway; he had his back to me when he asked me what vehicle I wanted to take.

"Are we taking the Jeep or the car today, Anna?"

"Let's take the little sports car. I love riding in that. Plus, it's going to be a great ride over. We will see everything with no top."

He turned around, smiling from ear to ear. "Let's get going Ms. Tie-Dye." *I wonder if he already had noticed the missing bra. I hope he did.*

Away we went, Drew set the GPS for Woodstock, New York. It was about forty-eight miles away. He went to turn the radio on but stopped. Instead, he started singing a new song. I liked it. I Googled some of the words and once again my heart started racing. "All my life I have been searching for a girl to love me like you." He was singing a song from nineteen-sixty-two. "Anna (Go to Him)," then he put on my eighties station, and I started singing. I enjoyed this turn-wise singing, we could both enjoy our favorites on the drive.

We arrived at our destination, and I could see a lot of cool places. Shops I wanted to explore, and restaurants I wanted to try.

My eyes were wandering all over the place. "Drew, we are going to have a nineteen-sixty kind of day." I jumped out of the car.

"I have never seen you so impatient, let's take our time."

"Okay, but can we stop first at that massive candle shop over there?"

"Of course, we can." He took me by the hand, and we ran across the street to Drip Candle Mountain. Inside, it was filled with so many cool candles: different styles, colors, and funky-shaped ones too.

They had a huge candle in the middle of the store, it took up half the room. There was a sign that read, "Please Do Not Light."

Drew asked, "Would you like me to buy you a candle?"

"No thank you Drew; I just love taking it all in all the different aromas." Hand in hand we walked outside and looked around. "Where to next?" "Let's go in that one. It looks funky." I pointed to an Apothecary.

"Is that a hippy pharmacy?" He asked.

"Come on, we have to check it out," I said, and Drew opened the door for me. It was filled with lots of homeopathic remedies. I was fascinated with all the different things in the store. And there it was – the CBD aisle. I smiled back at Drew. "My kind of store." As tempted I was, I resisted the urge to buy anything from there. We decided on trying something again later on and stepped out of the store before the store owner either insisted we get something or doubted our intentions. Pretty sure, he must have encountered several hippies lurking around his CBD aisle trying to pick something up.

We continued down the street, in and out of different places. We both adored looking at all the nooks and crannies the small town had to offer. We discovered a neat place called Woodstock Love Knot. Of course, we had to take a picture of us sitting in front of the place. A couple went by and offered to take our picture in turn for taking theirs. People were so friendly there, and I was impressed by the picture they took of us, it was just perfect.

We walked down the street a little further to the center of town and heard music playing. It was a drum circle; people of all kinds were sitting around playing djembe drums and dancing. It was so interesting to watch.

Drew glanced over at me and said, "Let's try it."

"You are kidding, right?" I said looking around. "They never grew out of it." "Come on, you only live once, it would be a first," Drew said.

I looked around and saw so much tie-dye. Everyone was wearing colorful tee shirts. The smell of marijuana was profound. People were dancing, drumming and really getting into it so much, I found myself nodding to the beat of the drums. A woman with rainbow-colored hair was urging the crowd to join.

"Come on you two, join our circle," she said and handed us a set of shakers and bells.

Drew and I looked at each other, shrugged our shoulders, and took them from her. "Why not?" Drew said and handed me the bells.

Once our embarrassment left us, we started to really enjoy ourselves. The people were so friendly and inviting. I had to admit it was quite entertaining. I even started to feel my body moving to the beat.

"Look at you Anna, my little hippy girl," he said shaking his shakers louder.

"Yeah, this is so much fun, can we buy some of these?" I held up my bells and pointed to his shaker.

"Let's go over to the shop across the street, it looks like they might have them."

*These can be useful,'* I thought about Drew and me dancing with shakers and bells in our hands, and of course, these could add a little fun to the parties.

"Okay, where are we going to lunch, I am famished from all the excitement of the circle."

Drew laughed and pointed across the street. "Let's go over there."

I looked out and saw an adorable little shop called, "Yum Yum Noodle Bar" and said, "Yes, let's go." We walked in and it was decorated in a groovy sixties style. Tables were placed in front of what appeared to be hand-painted shadows of people. It was very colorful and cheerful. As soon as we walked in I was full of happiness and peace.

"I hope the food is as good as this place makes me feel." "We will see."

The waitress came over, gave us our menus, and right away I noticed there was a variety of things to choose from. They offered a lot of vegan and vegetarian dishes. A few different kinds of food preferences like Thai and Korean tacos.

"I'll have the Korean Tacos," Drew said. "And you Miss?"

"I will have the Miso-Sake Cured Salmon with Chinese broccoli and brown rice."

"Good choice, anything to drink?"

"Yes, we will have two glasses of Plum Wine." He looked at me and I nodded approvingly.

"Sure. You two love birds made some great choices." Drew pursed his lip. "Is it that obvious, Anna?"

"I didn't even realize that we are showing a lot of affection towards each other, it seems so natural to me."

"Yes, it does," he agrees and kissed my hand.

We enjoyed our lunch and headed on our way to the Tibetan Buddhist Monastery. "I can't wait for this part of the adventure," I said as we walked outside. We found our car and jumped in.

"Here we go, off to Mead Mountain Rd." He reached over and took my hand in his. I just love the convertible; it makes driving up these mountains so much more beautiful. I feel so relaxed and free.

As we pulled up the road to the Monastery, there were colorful triangle flags held by a rope all the way up to the parking lot. It already seemed so serene to me. As soon as I could see the beautiful Zen gardens, I announced, "This is going to be wonderful." We entered and immediately we felt like we were in a dream. Everything in there was so colorful and gold.

We immediately felt peace wash over us as we looked at all the incredible architecture. It was spiritual for both of us. I picked up a flyer offering a fully private retreat to truly escape and find peace through Tibetan Buddhists teachings.

"Drew, this is something that I would love to do, can we look into this?"

He took the pamphlet and stuck it in my purse. "Yes, we can check it out someday, another adventure for us," he said as we followed a tour guide outside.

After listening to the guide, we were both intrigued by it all. The views were breathtaking.

"Want to head back now?"

"Yes, hey, remind me to call Andrea and Aunt Dolly. They called while we were eating lunch. You know that I fixed up my friend Andrea with my cousin, right?"

"Yes, I remember you told me you were playing matchmaker."

"Oh yeah, I am the real deal! It worked, they are a perfect match, so far." "Let's go out to dinner with them one night."

"Okay, but you better set it up, let me know and I'll tell them. I enjoyed all the dates that you planned and I want them to have a memorable experience with us."

"Okay, Ma'am," he said jokingly.

"Wait, I have to use the restroom before we go." "Alright, I'll wait."

I walked in and immediately my eyes went to the floor, there lay a dime. It was a sign from Drew's mother. Being a Buddhist, she would be happy we visited a place like this together. *Should I tell*

Drew? Would he be upset, knowing what the Medium told us? I decided to keep this one to myself.

I looked at the car and saw Drew sitting on the hood, looking at the panoramic views. I could tell he was thinking about something. I grabbed him and kissed him. "Thank you so much for this memorable day."

"You are welcome, I enjoyed it too."

I stood in between his legs, grabbed my phone, and called Andrea back. "Hey, I am calling you back, so how was it?"

"Oh Savannah, he is such a nice man. A real gentleman and, he's not married!" "Yes, he is wonderful, I knew you would get along with him." I mouthed the words, "I told you so!" to Drew and he smiled. "We want to double date some night next week with you guys, set a date and text me when it is." "Okay, sounds fun."

"See, they are a match, I do have the knack for it, maybe, and I'll start my own dating business someday." Now to return Aunt Dolly's call. I put the cell phone on the speaker phone. "Hi, Aunt Dolly, Happy Sunday. I am returning your call. I hope everything is okay." We usually have our weekly call on Monday, so I was nervous something was wrong."

"Everything is fine, sweetheart. I wanted to invite you and that hunk of yours to dinner Friday night. What's Drew's favorite meal?"

"Chicken pot pie," I replied.

"Oh, that's easy. Can I count on you guys to be here around five thirty?" Drew nodded and gave me a thumbs-up.

"Yes, we can't wait to see you again. Drew just adores you; he thinks you are the coolest aunt he ever met."

"Oh, he is a doll."

"Ok, see you then Aunt Dotty, I love you."

"Love you too, Angel."

The call ended and all I thought about was the session with Felicia. She told me to spend more time with Aunt Dolly. That scared me.

I know no one lives forever, but so far, she is doing a good job. She has the secret to a great life lived.

Even Drew had a look of concern when he told me, "It's good we are going to spend time with her. On our next visit, I am going to cook for *her*."

"Oh, she would love that. Let's ask her what her favorite meal is when we go Friday night."

"Okay, great idea."

We made it home and I quickly gathered all my things. Drew sat me down and told me to leave my things, he has cleared out a drawer for my stuff for when I stay here.

"That is perfect, I am kind of feeling like a gypsy."

"You're a funny girl, but you're not a gypsy, you are a hippy chick." "Funny, thank you for the lovely weekend filled with lots of firsts." "You're welcome, Anna." His goodbye was a long passionate kiss.

*And I was alone, again. Alone just physically, I always felt Drew around me now. I knew he was with me, in fact, I sensed his smell everywhere around me. It was as if I was enveloped by his halo. Maybe that was the reason I was content more than ever. No matter how much we deny it but people matter in our lives. And the right ones, matter a lot. I was glad I was the right one for Drew – more than finding the right one for myself, being the right one to someone was a special feeling.*

## Chapter 19

I was pulling into my parking lot and saw all these tractor-trailers along the side of our parking area. *Now what's happening?* I quickly called my source, Hank. "Hank, what's going on now?"

"They brought in more furnishings for the apartment, they had to make it look like the eighties style."

"Is he here?" "Who?"

"You know who I am talking about, Hank. Come on, I know you see everything around here."

"Yes, Savannah, Mark is here. I saw his driver drop him off with a duffle bag.

I am assuming he will be staying tonight." "Oh, really?"

I quickly moved my car over to the area where rented apartments were, then I started my stakeout. I didn't leave my car until I saw him go in or out. I turned on my radio and just sat there. This is ridiculous. I have a lot to do before seven in the morning. I called Andrea while I waited. I grabbed my phone and dialed her number.

"Hello, guess what I am doing right now?" "Planning for another adventure with Drew?"

"Uh, no. I am sitting in front of the set for the HBO movie. I am going to sit here until I see Mark Ruffalo. I am officially obsessed with this movie-making activity around here. It's a blessing I have been working during the day and busy on the weekends with Drew, otherwise, I think I might have had a problem here."

"Savannah, you're so funny. You have a prince charming already, stop fantasizing about this."

"Well, you're right, and you might have your own prince developing too. How are things going? Drew and I want you two to go out on a double date with us. Maybe we all can meet at Old Drovers Inn. It is a great old bed and breakfast in Dover Plains. It can be romantic there. How about it?"

"I'll check with Randy and get back to you. I can't believe I can actually go out in public with the man and enjoy dinner."

"Yes, Andrea. This is how it's supposed to be. I am so happy for the two of you. Can't wait to see you both together. Also, I wanted to ask you to give me the information on the divorce lawyer you mentioned that was reasonable."

"What! This must be really getting serious."

"Oh, it is. I am hopelessly in love with Drew. I don't think he is fond of me still being technically married. No one has ever made me want to reach out and venture onto this avenue."

"I am so happy for you Savannah."

"I have got to go!" I saw two men coming out of an apartment, heading toward a black Mercedes SUV.

"Was it him?"

"False alarm. I better get my derriere in the house and get ready for work tomorrow."

"Yeah, you should."

"I'll catch you later. Bye."

I moved my car to my original parking spot and started to reach for my bag, when I realized I didn't have anything in the back seat. Drew had asked me to keep some stuff at his house. My heart skipped a beat as I realized my things were in a drawer, in Drew's bedroom. This is such a big move for me.

Back in the apartment I made my lunches and packed an extra treat for Mr. Fred. I would always bring him leftovers or some sort of yummy food for him on Mondays. I think he almost looked forward to it. *I hope he likes carrot cake; I brought some home from the barbecue on Saturday.*

All set for my work week, I only had to work two days this week. Wednesday was a holiday, and I took the rest of the week off. I needed time to get everything ready for what I hoped was my upcoming appointment with a lawyer.

'*Taking a week off was a first, too. I guess with Drew, there will be a lot of firsts.*'

It was around eleven, I was so tired from dancing at the drum circle and walking the streets of Woodstock. In just a weekend, I had acclimated to Drew's smell and presence when sleeping, and now sleeping alone seemed like a struggle. I yelled at myself to go to sleep, consoling my yearning heart that I would be sleeping in his embrace soon enough.

Morning came fast and I hurried to get myself going. I found myself speeding to work to make it on time. In my rear-view mirror, I saw flashing lights. *Oh shit, am I getting pulled over?* The Sheriff went right by me, I was glad it wasn't me. I don't need a speeding ticket right now. I pulled into the parking lot and saw many cop cars, an ambulance, and fire trucks all lined up. *What's going on here?*

I couldn't imagine, maybe a fire or a gunman? *That's not how I expect my Mondays to start at work.* Everyone was running out of the front doors. I watched every move that was going on. Finally, I saw them bringing someone out on a stretcher. Someone must've fallen or fainted. I got out of my car and ran inside, stopped at the security desk, and asked, "What's going on?"

He just pointed towards my office door. I ran down the hall and entered my office. Everyone was there looking upset and scared. "What happened?"

"Oh Savannah, it was Mr. Fred. The paramedics told us he suffered from cardiac arrest."

"Oh, no!" I started to cry. They all looked at me, equally shocked. "What hospital did they take him to?"

"Savannah, he passed away, they worked on him for about a half-hour. We know how close you were to him; we are so sorry."

My boss approached me from behind. "Savannah, take the rest of the day off, and Andrea go with her please."

"Ok, we will see you tomorrow. I will make sure Savannah gets home okay. I will stay with her the rest of the day."

We both got in my car, and Andrea drove. I was shaking from being so heartbroken. I know he was in his late nineties, but I just figured he would live forever, he was in such good shape for his age. I guess when your time comes, it comes. We made it to my place and an unusual silence settled. I tossed my bag on the couch and the lunchbox with carrot cake in it fell out. I held the lunchbox close and sobbed. "I bought him this today. I was so sure that he would love it."

"He would have loved it, Savannah." Andrea put her arms around me and held me tight.

"I just can't believe it. I saw a cop car this morning and thought I was getting pulled over for speeding. I would've never guessed he was going for Mr. Fred. He lived a good long life. I am just going to miss the crap out of him. He was my buddy. I loved him like a father."

"Savannah, I know how much he meant to you. What would you like to do today? Boss gave us the day off."

"I don't know. I don't think I can think right, right now."

"Let's get out all the pictures we have of him and make a collage. You and he were always taking photos of all the parties we used to have and all the holidays we spent in the office, everyone's birthdays."

"Yeah, I have tons of those photos."

"We were his family. I think he knew it too."

"Thank you so much for being here for me, you're a real friend."

"Of course, that's what friends are for Savannah, and for playing matchmaker." "You make me laugh, thanks, I needed that."

"Let's call Drew and tell him what happened, I am sure he would want to know."

"Okay, take my phone, it's under Drew, my love." "Wow, you really are in love with this guy."

"I am Andrea, with all my heart and soul."

Andrea looked at me and whispered, "It's his voicemail."

"Go ahead and leave him a message about what happened today."

"Hi, Drew. This is Andrea, Savannah's friend from work. We had a terrible thing happen this morning. Don't worry Savannah is okay, but our dear friend and coworker, Mr. Fred passed away at work. I am sure Savannah will fill you in with all the details later. She wanted me to call and let you know. She is pretty upset; she was very close to him. Call her when you can, thanks."

"I appreciate you so much for reaching out to Drew, I hope this doesn't trigger any feelings of his mother's death for him."

"Never even gave that a thought, I hope it doesn't either."

"Let's get busy with this collage. Or should we do a slideshow with some of his favorite music playing?"

"That's a great idea."

"Let's get this together and google some music from the twenties or thirties for the background together we can make something special and memorable for him, he deserves the best of everything. You know he had no family; we were the only people in his life. That's why he was so dedicated to work and us."

"It's kind of sad thinking he had no family, he was never married, had no children and he was the only child."

"That sounds so lonely, it's a wonder why he loved all of us so much." My heart was aching. I never thought he would leave us so suddenly.

Andrea grabbed a box of tissues and picked a few out for me.

"I can't believe how upset I am, he really meant a lot to me. I just don't want to upset Drew, he seems to be in a good place right now. His sisters on the other hand are having trouble."

"What do you mean trouble?"

"Apparently, they are having some guilty feelings about not saying goodbye in her final hours."

"It really wasn't their fault; it was in the heart of the pandemic and people were dying alone everywhere. It's sad but true."

"This world went through hell and back during the COVID crisis, we deserve a break."

"Drew's break was finding me, I think his mom sent me to him. He told her he was going to give up finding someone."

"Oh Savannah, I just got chills from that story. I think you are right. You never told me what the medium said."

"Someday I will tell you all about it. I just feel like it's personal, something Drew will have to share with you."

"You have me so intrigued."

"Oh no, who's going to clean out Mr. Fred's apartment, who's going to plan his funeral? He has no one." I started to shake with fright, thinking no one was going to be responsible.

"Let's call the office and see if they heard anymore." "Okay."

"Hey, any news? We are here setting up a slideshow with all our pictures of him. We are going to pick out some music for the background."

"He loved Frank Sinatra." "That's right."

"Did you hear anything from the paramedics? Yes, they said he was gone before he hit the floor. It was quick, he didn't suffer."

"I am so glad; he must have been so scared."

"Andrea, I checked his in case of emergency form and he had a cousin that he named. She and her husband will take care of all the arrangements."

"That's good, we all have to go."

"Yes, we will shut down the office and attend, wherever it will be. You girls, go take it easy."

My apartment seemed so sad; it even was a gloomy day out. I think it might even rain today. Andrea and I finished up our special tribute and sent it to the office. I couldn't shake the feeling of not being there at the office early, maybe I could have saved him.

"You know he was scared to die, he told me so."

"I am so sorry Savannah; he will be watching over all of us from heaven." "Oh, I believe that for sure," I replied as I looked out the window and saw the lightning and heard the thunder. "Yeah, this sums up the day."

"Let's wait a little bit for the storm to end and then go out to lunch, I have nothing in my refrigerator, I am always at Drew's now."

"Sounds great, how about Madison's?" "Yeah, their pizza is the best around here."

Half an hour went by, and I opened the door and said, "Oh good, it stopped raining."

We both headed towards the car, we looked up and saw the most beautiful, vibrant arch I have ever seen in my life.

"A rainbow, Mr. Fred sent us that," Andrea said and pointed to the sky.

I couldn't believe how vivid the colors were, I was so mesmerized by it. I counted the colors of the ROYGBIV, their hues were vivid. I put my hand to my lips and blew a kiss to the sky.

"Goodbye, Mr. Fred."

We drove to Madison's; it was right down the road from my apartment. It felt good to get out of the house. The breeze was so beautiful as we walked from the parking lot of the pizzeria.

"Sit anywhere you like," the waitress said.

We sat in the corner by the window, it was private, and I really didn't want to see anyone.

"What would you girls like today?" she asked as she set two glasses of water on the table.

"I will have a glass of house red wine and a slice of pepperoni." "Do you have any specials?" Andrea asked.

"Yes, the specials are on the chalkboard." She pointed to the wall behind the counter.

"Oh, the lasagna sounds scrumptious, I'll have that and a glass of house white."

Andrea tapped my hand declaring, "We need more than a glass of wine after what we went through today."

"I just wish he was still here. My heart hurts."

"Think of all the memories we put on the slide show. Everyone had a great time with him all these years."

"Yes, we sure did." I gave her a wry grin. *But he was my friend, my fairy godfather.*

"Let's talk about something else," she said. "Like where you got that gorgeous bracelet. It looks like a piece of treasure."

"Funny you say that Drew gave it to me. It was his when he was a little boy.

His mom brought it back from Taiwan when she was visiting there."

"It's fascinating, you must've been shocked when he gave it to you." "I was, he also asked me to get it appraised by a good jeweler."

"Really? Wow! Let's go after our lunch, there is a jewelry store in Millbrook." We munched down our lunches and off we went to the jewelry shop.

"It kind of did come from a treasure chest. A wooden box that Drew's mother had had for a very long time. It was filled with lots of neat things."

Andrea and I went into the store, but at first, I was reluctant to take the bracelet off. "Ms. Rowe, you have yourself a fine treasure there, it's made of a very hard gold from Taiwan. If you were to lose this in a brook and it sat for a hundred years, someone would find it in the same condition it is right now." He handed it back to me.

"Wow. That's so cool."

"Do you want to know how much it's worth?" "Yes, please."

"Ms. Rowe, this piece of jewelry is worth about six thousand dollars." "Are you serious?"

"Yes, you could get a second opinion, but I believe mine is accurate. It all depends on how much gold is going for at the time of appraisal."

"I think I will just leave your store with this knowledge of your assessment.

Thank you so much for your time."

"You're welcome. By the way, I saw you eyeing those engagement rings, maybe I will see you soon with your special someone."

*Just hearing him talk about a ring filled my heart with excitement. Will I be Mrs. Drew Hart someday?* Speaking of Drew, the phone rang. I had his speaker phone. "Drew."

"Anna, I just listened to Andrea's message. How are you, sweetheart? I am sorry for your loss, you must have been devastated."

"Thank God, for Andrea. She was right there for me." "Good, do you think we should cancel the picnic?" "No, I need my family now more than ever."

"I knew you would say that."

"I took the rest of the week off. I figured with the picnic on Wednesday and with Mr. Fred's death, I couldn't bear to be in the office without him. It would seem so weird knowing he died right there, and I will miss his so much not being there to greet me in the morning."

"Okay, I really want to be there with you. But sweetheart, I have to work tomorrow on a job I need to finish up, do you think Andrea will stay out tomorrow with you?"

I know he has to work, but I was sad he wasn't with me. I could have used a hug from him. Andrea was standing next to me when she yelled out, "Of course, I will."

"She seems like a great friend, can't wait to meet her."

"Hell yeah, I'll call in tomorrow," she said waving her hand in the air. "I'll go home grab a few things and see you first thing in the morning."

We headed back to my home, re-watched the tribute video we made for Mr. Fred and Andrea returned to her home, promising to see me first thing in the morning.

I couldn't shake off the thought of not having Mr. Fred meet Drew. He cared for me like his daughter, looking out for me if even Drew hurt me or said something to me. He would smile the widest smile whenever I talked about Drew and our adventures, he couldn't help himself but feel happy for me. He was truly like a father, caring, loving, watching, protecting, and preserving the memories.

I recalled when I first told him about Drew, he sang his favorite song's line. 'Little did we know, love was just a glance away, a warm embracing dance away,' he wasn't the best at singing but he tried with Frank Sinatra songs. *'Ever since that night, we've been together,*

Lovers at first sight, in love forever, it turned out so right,
For strangers in the night.'

I sang the song to myself, knowing that in this life I was blessed by some humanlike angels and Mr. Fred was one of them. Losing him was perhaps only losing his presence, his blessings and fatherly warmth will live on with me for the rest of my days in this world.

I cried myself to sleep and slept like a baby, only to be woken up by the sound of banging. I was still in bed when I realized someone was knocking at the door.

'Who could be here so early in the morning?' I went to the door wearing my sweatpants, tee shirt, and no bra. "Who is it?"

"It's me, Savannah."

"Andrea." I opened the door and looked like I had been run over by a train. I was so embarrassed, usually, I go to work dressed up and have my hair and makeup just so.

"Get in the shower," she said and walked right past me. "I have muffins," she turned to face me. "Did you make coffee?"

I shook my head.

She waved her hand at me. "I'll make it while you get ready. After we eat, we'll head to the lawyer's office. I called early this morning and asked if they could squeeze you in. I used to go to high school with his secretary. She was more than happy to fit you in."

I hugged her. "Thank you. I can't be getting serious with a man while I am still married, I know if the role was reversed, I won't stand for it." I clapped my hands and headed for the bathroom but stopped in the doorway. "I appreciate you, my friend. Hey, if Drew and I get married, I want you as my maid of honor."

"You are just happy that's all, it's very becoming on you, and you're glowing with satisfaction."

"Oh yeah, I am very satisfied, he's the best lover I have ever had."

"Savannah, I don't mean that way of satisfaction. Get your head out of the bedroom."

"Well, I am, just calling it like it is."

By the time I got out of the shower, Andrea had our coffee in to-go cups and she was waiting for me at the front door. "Come on, let's go!"

Fifteen minutes later, we are at the lawyer's office. We got out of her car. Before I opened the door she said, "Don't be nervous."

"I'm fine." We walked into this fancy office building in Poughkeepsie. It was decorated so pretty and cheerful. Not sure why divorce would be cheerful. Hopefully, I would have a simple divorce. We would just have to decide about our home. I was sure thirty-two years together would mean nothing to my soon-to-be husband and would tell me he wanted the house. He could have the house, but I wanted half of what it was worth.

The secretary came out into the waiting room, and said, "Ms. Lawson will see you now."

"Hello Savannah, nice to meet you. I am Janet Lawson, and I am going to get you that divorce you are looking for and going to get you all you deserve."

I sat back in my chair and let out a breath of fresh air. "Thank you so much, Ms.

Lawson. I hope he doesn't give us a hard time."

"Don't worry about anything, we will take care of it all."

"That is such a relief to hear."

"I see you did the paperwork in the waiting room; I appreciate that. I'll have him served by the end of the week. I just need you to fill out your statement of worth for me. Then it's an appraisal on the house." She raised her eyebrows. "Trust me, I will get you half. Either he buys you out or we sell the house and split the profit."

"Sounds like you have done this before."

"Have faith in me, I am an excellent lawyer and promise to get you what you are entitled to."

*My mind was racing with anxiety, I was terrified.* I stood up. "Thank you." "That was quick. Are you ready to go?" Andrea asked when she saw me.

"Yes, I am, this was harder than I thought." I waved to the receptionist and told Andrea, "I have paperwork to fill out."

"Let's go back to your place, I will help you."

"I think I am going to keep this a surprise for Drew. I want to see the look on his face when I hand him my divorce papers."

"Oh, I'm sure he will be happy about not dating a married woman."

"Don't rub it in lady, you know some things about dating married people and that's all I am going to say."

"I am glad that's over. I have a man now that doesn't require being kept a secret. I have Randy!"

As soon as we arrived at my apartment, we sat at my dining room table and got to work. "Andrea, do you want something to drink, tea, coffee, or some bottled water?"

"English breakfast tea, please," she said adding, "Let's get you a divorce, oh, and don't forget to write out the check for the retainer."

"Oh yes, that's very necessary." *Ten thousand payable to Lawson & Rose Law Office.* "It will be worth every cent. Drew will be so proud of me."

## Chapter 20

Andrea spent the rest of the day and evening with me until Drew arrived holding two bouquets of flowers. "Anna, are you okay? I was so worried about you. I hurried over as soon as I got done with work. I am so glad to see that beautiful face of yours," he said as he kissed me a million times and gave me the tightest hug.

"That's my cue to leave, I will see you two soon," Andrea said and picked up her purse.

"No, please don't go," Drew said to her and handed her sunflowers. "Stay, I want to thank you for taking care of my Anna. I am sure she had a nice time hanging out with you."

*If he only knew just how sad today was for me.* "Andrea, Drew is right. Stay. Have a glass of wine with us."

"Thank you, but I really must be going." She winked at me and shook Drew's hand goodbye. "Thank you for these, they're my favorite."

I closed the door behind her, turned around, took one look at him, and instantly felt better. "I am so happy you are here." I kissed his forehead. "The past two days were very sad. I am grateful to Andrea for taking time off to make sure I wasn't alone, but my heart is so grateful to see you. Am I crazy needing you for everything? I don't think I would have been as devastated if I packed a bag and gone to your house. I love you so much Drew." I started to cry ugly tears.

"Oh Anna, I am so sorry I did not offer my..." he paused. "Our home. You should have stayed with me. I could have held you in my arms and comforted you." After he kissed me, he said, "I am in love with you more than you know."

I inhaled deeply and instantly felt at ease again. "You're here now. I'm sorry I must look horrible." I pushed the hair back from my face.

He put his hands on my shoulders and told me I looked beautiful. "Have you eaten anything in the past two days?"

I shook my head. "I can't eat when I am upset, but if you are hungry, I have a pot of Hungarian stew one of my co-workers sent over."

"Let me do it," he said. Spun me around, patted my derriere, and told me to go take a nice bubble bath.

An hour later, I walked into the kitchen wearing my favorite Adidas sportswear and a touch of lipstick. The table was set for two. A bottle of wine and my flowers in one of my beer steins. I laughed knowing I had a couple of vases in the cabinet over the refrigerator.

"There's my girl. Wine or Bud Orange?"

"Wine please," I said and sat down in the chair he pulled back for me. I tipped my head back and he kissed me. "Thank you," I said as I inhaled his cologne.

For the first time in two days, I ate everything in front of me. Drew offered to take me out for ice cream, but I declined. I just wanted him to hold me. He took me by the hand and told me to sit down with my feet up while he cleaned the kitchen. He lit several candles, turned on the radio, and poured me another glass of wine. When he finished cleaning the kitchen, he came out to the living room and sat down on the couch. I got up and sat next to him, resting my head on his chest. My body was aching for him. I think he put a little too much cologne on. It was driving my inside crazy. I rubbed his leg, crotch and knew he missed me too.

"Let me make love to you, I need you and you need me," he said and stood up before taking my hand and leading me to the bedroom.

He turned off the lights, lit a candle and put on some romantic music. I watched as he turned down the bed, closed my eyes and he slowly took my clothes off.

"Come, Anna, lay down so I can mend your troubled heart. Are you up for making love?"

"Yes, it would be just what the Dr. ordered for me."

"Well then let's get started." He took off his clothes exposing his erection and I wanted him inside of me, but he turned me over, grabbed the massage oil, and started to rub my back, my butt, and my legs. My insides were screaming for him to make love to me, but instead, I whispered, "This is exactly what I needed, more please."

"Anna, I would do anything for you."

"And I would you, now your turn. Let me shine your ass with this oil." "Okay, boss."

I was back in the moment. Frisky, free, and I was with my man. Before we knew it, there was oil everywhere – something about the slippery, scented feeling on every inch of your body. He slid his penis in me like butter. "Oh, this feels so good, Dr.'s prescription was just perfect."

We lay in bed talking for over an hour. We talked about our plans for the picnic. He admitted that he was a little nervous to meet my family, especially my sons.

"I have a butterfly tummy just thinking about meeting your sisters and their families. I hope we have enough food. I ordered a to-go picnic for twenty-five people. Do you think it will be enough?"

"It should be, I am sure my sisters will bring stuff too, even though we told them not to, they never listen."

"Ok, that makes me feel a little bit better. I'm sure my daughters-in-law will do the same."

"Next time Anna, leave the planning to me, I love doing that kind of stuff, and I can see how anxious you are about entertaining."

I sat up. "You got that right." "Oh, I almost forgot."

"What?" I replied hoping he had good news.

"I have a big surprise for you, hand me my jeans please." He pulled an envelope out of his back pocket and handed it to me. "Open it."

I opened the plain white envelope and there were two airplane tickets to Arizona. "Next week?" I looked at him knowing I would never get the time off from work, not after these past two days. "Drew, oh my god, we are going to visit your father?"

"Yes, he can't wait to meet you."

"Wait, this is so crazy, how did you pull this off?"

"Well, I texted Andrea and asked her to get in touch with your boss, ask him if you could take that week off, of course, he said yes."

"This is the most surprising thing I have ever received in my life. I can't believe this time next week, we will be in Sedona, Arizona. I have always wanted to go there. Thank you for treating me like a queen, I love you so much."

"Of course. I love you more."

"I do! What's your father's name? Do you think he will like me? Oh no, will we sleep in the same room?"

"Anna we are not teenagers, we are two grown adults, of course we will stay in the same room. And yes, he will love you."

"What should I call him?"

"Call him John, that's his name."

"I can't believe you pulled this off, that darn Andrea, she kept a good secret." "Yes, she did," he said adding, "Let's get some rest, we have a big day tomorrow at the lake."

"I agree, we are in for a grand day. Drew, I can't keep this in anymore. You had a surprise for me, and I have one for you too."

"Really? Alright. Surprise me?"

"Andrea took me to see a lawyer this morning and I filed for a divorce; my husband will be served by the end of the week."

"I am so proud of you for going through with this, I have to admit that I was a little concerned that you were still legally married."

"Well, I won't be by this time next month. The lawyer said everything should go smoothly. In fact, I won't even have to see him because of COVID, everything is done virtually. How great is that?"

"That's perfect, that could elevate some of the stress of a divorce. I pray it goes smoothly for you. I will be right here by your side every step of the way."

"Yes, fingers crossed. And thank you for everything." I gave him the biggest squeeze ever.

My life was finally coming together perfectly. Everything I ever wanted and needed was in my line of sight. The bad memories are being replaced with beautiful ones. I no longer have bitter feelings about my past. My life has turned around in so many ways.

"Goodnight, see you in the morning," he said and kissed my cheek tenderly.

He held me in his arms until I slept.

## Chapter 21

My eyes opened when the alarm on my phone went off. I lifted my head to see his handsome face, restful, and at peace. *'I will wake him up. In a while.'* We had to hurry up for the big day, still, I wanted a couple of moments to myself. *'Am I being irresponsible?'* My ever-so-worried mind nudged me to get up, but I resisted. *'I have all the right and time to do this. I love this man.'* I traced his face with my finger, careful enough to not wake him up. I wanted to remember every inch of him, every tiny wrinkle, every mole, every line, and every freckle, just everything about him. *A few years ago, I wouldn't even think of falling in love with another man after my husband. And here I am, with my dream guy. With my soulmate.'* I smiled at the thought and lightly tapped his chin.

"Wake up Drew, today is the day our families meet. Please tell me everything is going to go smoothly."

He opened his eyes and shook his head. "Calm down, it's going to be a great day. I packed some fun things to do. My Jeep is already loaded."

"Sounds good, but we have to get up, shower, dress, pick up the food and head over to Lake Taconic by noon. I told everyone to be there by one."

He stretched his arms out and pushed the covers down to the foot of the bed. "What exactly did you order for food?"

I reached over to get my cell phone from the nightstand. I read the order form. "I got assorted pinwheel sandwiches, fried chicken, a pasta salad, macaroni, and potato salads. Oh, and watermelon. It's a great package, right? It also comes with all the paper supplies plus a red and white picnic table covering."

"That sounds delicious, but ..."

"Yes, I know you could have done it all yourself." "You bet I could have. Next time ..."

"You'll do the catering, I know," I finished the sentence and leaned in to kiss his stubble. "I promise. Next time we have get-together, you can prepare everything, and I will assist you. I also have a box with some bottled water and some bottles of lemonade. I'm sure the kids will bring beer and wine."

"I think we might be all set for today. Wait until you see what I bought for the kids and for us big kids, too."

"Surprise me, it seems to be the theme for us these past couple of days."

He got out of bed and said, "Get in the shower and see what surprise you get in there."

I grinned knowing he was up to something. Again. "Meet you in five." I jumped in the shower. Drew shouted, "Google play strip tease music."

"Oh boy, surprise number three coming towards the shower." I stepped inside the shower and waited for his 'surprise.'

"Open the shower door Anna, I'm coming in." He started dancing and removing his clothes as he came towards me.

"You're a sexy stripper, get in here now." I laughed at Google's song choice. "Respect" by Aretha Franklin.

"Thanks for making me smile." I kissed his lips while he started soaping my back.

"That's what I am here for." As he bent me over in the shower.

We finished our shower and got ready for the day. I decided to wear jean shorts and a tank top with Spiderman on it. Drew loves that Marvel character. "Anna, I think you need to bring your bathing suit."

"I do? Why?"

"It's part of the fun I have planned." "Alright, I will throw it in my bag."

Drew wore his bathing suit for shorts and a button-down collared shirt. "Geez, you even have to dress up for a picnic?"

"Yes, I love to look presentable, although a little while ago, I wasn't so dressed up."

"Ha, ha. Magic Drew."

"Oh, you are way more 'magical' than I'll ever be."

Off we went. He was right, the Jeep was loaded. All we had to do was pick up the food. "I hope they give us some ice for the salads. I don't need to get sick today. It's going to be a hot one and I need to keep the salads very cold."

"Stop overthinking, everything will be fine." He touched the side of my face. "If they don't give you any ice, we'll stop at the gas station on the way, and I will buy some."

Drew left the air on in the Jeep, while we ran into the store. "Hi, I am here to pick up the picnic package for Savannah Rowe."

The man behind the deli counter looked at me and said, "Yes, I took your order over the phone. This is a perfect day for a picnic. Let me get your boxes." He handed two boxes stacked together to Drew and a large brown paper bag to me. "I hope you have a wonderful time."

"Thank you, we will," Drew said and I echoed his sentiments.

Then he picked up an even bigger box and said, "Let me bring this out to the car for you."

"That's very kind of you." I rolled up a ten-dollar bill and stuck it in the pocket of his apron.

Drew opened the back door and of course, he had the perfect spot to put all the food on. Aluminum foil with curled-up edges in case something spilled. He even had a cooler in the back. We were almost to the lake when Drew looked at me and put his hand on mine. "It's going to be a good day, you'll see." Then he kissed the back of my hand.

As soon as we pulled into the parking lot, I noticed my son's car parked next to the walking path entrance. "James and his family are here already. I wonder where Michael and Summer are?"

"Give them time, it's not even one yet."

We got out of the Jeep, and I introduced Drew to everyone. James gave a wink and a thumbs-up, he liked Drew and I couldn't be happier about it.

"Follow us over there," Drew said and pointed to the picnic area.

He pulled the Jeep up to the picnic area where we were going to be setting up for the day. It was a nice shady area. "Perfect," I said. It was a beautiful day; the skies were so blue and not a single cloud in the sky. As soon as we started to unpack the Jeep, in came my other son Michael and his wife.

"I wonder where my sisters are, maybe they got lost. I hope I gave them the right directions."

"I heard you on your video call the other day, you definitely told them where and what time to be here," I said looking around for anyone driving slowly. Then we both looked up and their cars were at the front check-in booth. I took a deep breath as my butterfly friends woke up. They parked next to Drew's Jeep and got out of their cars. Right away, I noticed their hands were filled with all kinds of goodies for the picnic. *Yep, they're related.*

"I knew they would bring stuff," Drew said as we walked over to them. "Savannah, this is my family, this is Karen, my older sister, and her two kids. Oh my God, you are both so ground up now. Brian and Molly are my nephew and niece."

"Nice to meet you," I said adding, "I have heard so much about all of you." "Uncle Drew, we both have wonderful news for you today, both of us got engaged last month."

Drew grabbed them both, hugged them, and told them congratulations. "I didn't even know that you both had serious relationships going on. Please bring them around so we can meet them soon. Our family is growing."

"We will," Molly replied and stepped back.

"Savannah, this is my younger sister, Tanya, and her son, Zeek."

"Hello, nice to meet you both." I looked at Tanya and said, "I believe you work with my son Michael."

"Yes, I do. Sorry, I laughed at Drew when he told me he was dating Michael's mom. I thought you were an old lady."

"Well, do I look like one?"

"No, you are very pretty and look very young." "Thank you, Tanya."

I noticed my sons were looking at me. "Let's all go over to the table so I can introduce you to my family."

"Savannah, don't forget to video call Samuel, he's going to be waiting to meet everyone too," Drew reminded me and then brought his family over to introduce them to my kids and grandchildren.

Five minutes later, all the kids were playing with a kickball Drew handed them along with some other lawn games.

I caught my breath before it left my chest. "Michael, Summer, James, and Lynn, this is Drew."

"Hi, glad to meet you," Michael said as he extended his hand to Drew. Drew shook his hand and then James'. "It's a pleasure to meet all of you."

James told him, "Our mom has been crazy ever since her first date with you." I grinned at that. *Yeah, crazy in love.*

"Savannah, your grandchildren are simply adorable," one of his sisters said.

I looked over to where they were playing kickball and said, "Kelly and Andy love playing kickball. Lynn is the best twelve-year-old I know. They are my life."

Drew looked back at me and said, "Those kids look just like you, Anna." "Thank you, I'll take that as a compliment."

"We need to get the food out and start eating," Drew said as he raised his eyebrows.

The women all asked if they could help get things set up, but Drew told them to mingle. "I will take care of everything."

"This is why I just adore this man. He takes care of everything." His sisters both smiled at him.

Twenty minutes later, Drew called out to us, "Everything is ready. Come eat." The tables were set as though we were at a planned special event. I noticed how everything was set with a thought as if to make it easier for everyone to reach everything on the table. I put my hand on the small of his back and kissed his cheek. "You are simply the best!"

## Chapter 22

"Mom, everything looks delicious," James said adding, "Did you and Drew make all this?"

"No, I have to confess, the deli down the road from my apartment made it. I wish we could take credit." I rubbed my knee up against Drew's. "Next time, we all get together and I hope it's soon, I promise you'll all get to taste the many wonders of Drew's cooking."

James nodded before saying, "It's so nice to see you smiling so much. You're a new person, the same mom, but a happier one."

"Yeah, and laughing," Michael said and then held his Coors Light can up. "To Mom and Drew."

Everyone held their drinks up, even the kids. It made me feel good inside knowing I had their approval.

My sons knew I wasn't in a fulfilling marriage and am glad they are seeing me in a different setting, a genuine one. I hope they learn from me and Drew. Because this is what a loving and satisfying relationship is supposed to be like. They were raised in a household that didn't show much affection, sad to say. But those memories are fading away. This is the second half of my life, my happy life.

Everyone finished eating, even the kids loved the food. I think everyone enjoyed the company too. It was nice to have everyone here all at once. I was glad that we got to have Samuel meet everyone on the video call. It all felt so right.

Then we heard Drew yell from the parking lot. "Everyone ready for the real fun?"

The kids raced over as fast as their little legs could go. "Wow, what are all these water toys?" Andy asked.

Drew took the portable air compressor out of the back and started blowing up all these cool water toys. The kids' eyes were as big as saucers. "Are we going to play with these?"

"Yes," Drew said, as he handed each child something. "We are all going to have some water fun today."

The weather was perfect for it. I grabbed all the bottles of sunscreen from the back seat and told the kids, "Line up, its sunscreen time."

My daughter-in-law Summer echoed my sentiments. "We don't want any sunburns today."

When Drew started to blow up the inflatable island big enough to hold eight people, my two sons and his nephew ran to help him with it.

"We are going to lay back and relax, you kids can use the openings to swim through."

All of us, except Michael and Summer piled on the island. They took a cooler with beer and wine in it and sat on a blanket under the shade tree.

We put it in the water and floated it while the kids wrestled with it. Then we kicked them off and paddled across the lake and back. It was so much fun. It even had a place to hold our drinks.

"Oh yeah, a place for my beer," Kelly said.

"It couldn't get any more perfect," I remarked as I placed my drink in the holder and straightened my back a little. I wanted to remember this day for years to come. 'Never going to put my umbrella up, again,' I thought to myself. 'My overthinking never got me anywhere except for the deep, dark corners of my mind, the place where I don't ever want to be.'

"Hang on Kelly, I have a couple more fun things for us to do today," Drew said and dived into the water.

The kids kept saying how much fun they had.

"We want Drew to come to all the picnics from now on," Lynn said. Apparently, Drew made a big hit with everyone.

"Next up, Spaceship Squirter. I brought two, one for each of you guys," Drew said before blowing them up.

"This is so cool, are we really going to have a squirt gunfight?"

Lynn looked at Andy and said, "I bet you I am going to win."

Drew explained to the kids how it worked before handing them out. "This inflatable has a built-in squirt gun with a constant supply of water, you will never run out of water. Go have fun with them, kids"

I believe Drew was their new forever friend. '*I hope he is, I want him to be liked by my grandchildren. That would mean the world to me.*' He made the biggest hit with them. While the kids were busy playing in the water, the adults sat near the lake watching them and enjoyed some adult conversations.

I told Drew's sisters, niece, and nephews how it was so great to get to meet them. Of course, they agreed with me.

"Savannah, would you like to go shopping at the mall with us tomorrow? I heard you are going on a trip to see Dad next week. You are going to need some light clothes, it's so hot in Arizona."

"Sure, I am off from work for a while and I do need to buy some new things, I would love to go. It will be a girls' day out."

"Okay then, it's a date."

Drew turned to me with a smile on his face, blew me a kiss, and gave me a wink. Almost like he was trying to say, "I told you everything was going to be fine." And I inwardly said to myself, "I know." I blew him a kiss and mouthed I love you to him.

It seemed like my sons, their wives, and Drew's sisters' kids were all getting along, they were all about the same ages. That was nice to see too.

Everyone seemed to be having fun.

The kids didn't want the day to end, but it was getting late and most of us had to work the next day.

"I appreciate all of you coming today and I hope to see more family get- together," Drew said.

After everyone packed up and headed home, Drew grabbed my hand and led me toward the most magnificent sunset. "This is such a beautiful ending to an even better day. You were a big hit with my family. I just love you so much."

"I love you too, Anna." He kissed me as the sun went down over the mountain.

It was something out of a love story.

"Come on, let's get going, we have some more cleaning up to do," I said thinking about my day with his sisters. I was excited to have a trip to the mall with them. We'll have more time to talk. When we got in the Jeep, I asked Drew for their phone numbers so I could confirm the time and meeting place.

"Done."

I looked over at him. "Hey, I just realized I am going out with your sisters tomorrow, we have a dinner date at Aunt Dolly's on Friday and then we leave for Arizona on Sunday."

"You have a lot going on these days." "I love it!"

"Do you know I love the most?" I said.

"That we are all coming together as one big happy family." "You bet we are."

We got done with cleaning, loaded the stuff we intended to take in the jeep, and drove toward home. The glorious sunset has subsided and the night with all its glimmering stars covered the entire sky. My night and days had never been better, I loved, and truly cherished every season and phase of my days.

It's true, with the right person in life, you appreciate the entirety of life and have much more appreciation for even the little things.

We were both exhausted when we arrived home. Drew insisted on unpacking the Jeep so I went inside, made myself a cup of tea, and made my arrangements to meet with Drew's sisters at the mall.

"Drew, I am so happy that I am going to get to know your sisters better tomorrow. I am really looking forward to it. We're meeting up at ten. I want them to know how much I adore you."

"They adore me too, Anna."

"Well of course they would, if you treat them like you treat me, then they have themselves a gem for a brother. You might be just one of a kind."

"Thanks for making me feel so special, it's just my personality, what you see is what you get. I'm just myself, I don't know anything else."

"That's what makes you so unique. You're my diamond in the rock. Your sisters are lucky to have you, close families are hard to come by nowadays."

"Let's go to bed. If you're meeting them by ten, you will have to leave here by eight thirty."

"Yes."

We were both so excited about how our family day, neither one of us could go to sleep right away. I laughed listening to his stories and remembering the events of the day.

"Did you see Lynn's eyes when I told her she was going to have a squirt fight with her brother? Or when they asked me if I could come to all the picnics forever?"

"Yes, they love you. I, on the other hand, am always the one worrying about them drowning or getting sunburn. I am not a fun person like you. Did you see the way James and Michael were watching us together?"

"I did see that, I think they are so happy for you, for us. They don't know my story yet, the one where I almost gave up on finding the right woman."

"Well, did you find her, Drew?"

"I found the most beautiful, genuine, trust-worthy woman I could ever dream of finding."

*'Thank you, Mom.'* I said as I looked up.

He kissed my forehead. "Good night, Anna."

"Good night," I replied and set the alarm for seven and shut off the light.

The sun took a lot out of me yesterday. I could hardly open my eyes the next morning. Drew slid over to me and said in his gentle voice, "Good morning, my love." "Good morning, it's going to be a good one too. I am having so many great days and nights with you."

"Well, get used to it, dear."

*My life is just too good to be true, I never want to wake up from this beautiful dream.* I stretched my arms out in front of me.

"Anna," Drew yelled from the bathroom. "You better get moving, the shopping mall is calling you."

"I hear you, getting up now." I jumped in the shower and got ready to meet Tanya and Karen. Being so excited to go, I rushed around the house searching for my keys. I had so much going on the past couple of days. I forgot where I left my keys.

"Found them. See you later, Drew."

I was supposed to meet the girls in the Macy's parking lot, that's easy. As I reached the mall, I followed the signs to Macy's. I pulled in and they both were waiting near their car, they waved me over to park next to them.

"Hi, Savannah. We are so happy you agreed to come with us

today. You are going to love Arizona and our dad," Karen said.

Tanya agreed and then added, "You are going to melt this time of year there." "Well that's one of the reasons I am here with the two of you, let's go find some cute outfits for the trip."

Tanya laughed. "And I have good taste Savannah."

"Great, I need some advice on what they wear out west. All I can picture is very colorful Aztec-designed clothing. But, I love that style."

"When we go to lunch today, remind me to tell you all the good places we visit when we see Dad every year. Drew didn't visit because he took care of Mom," Karen explained.

"Girls, Drew's life has changed since he met me, could you tell?"

"Yes, and that's why we want to give you this." They handed me an envelope.

I opened the card, it read, "Savannah, thank you for coming into our lives, not just Drew's but ours too. We love you! Love, Tanya and Karen." My eyes teared up just reading it, my heart was full of exceptions. They loved me, they want to include me in their lives. Who sent me this man, this great family? I know who, as I thought of all the dimes and the meaning behind them. The medium told us that Drew's mom was sending us signs. Maybe this is one of them. My life was so content and complete. Now to meet Drew's father. *'I hope he likes me too.'*

"Hey, let's go shopping," Karen said.

We entered the store. Of course, it was overwhelming for me. I wasn't even sure what I wanted or even needed. I have never experienced the heat of Arizona in the summer.

Tanya told me, "You are going to need a lot of jackets."

"Jackets!"

"Yes, it might be swelteringly hot outside, but inside, it's like a freezer in every restaurant, store, and even at Dad's house. It's like walking into a freezer. But, we know Drew will get you anything you need when you get there, if you don't pack it."

"I'm so glad you enlightened me on that. Thanks."

"Look at this jacket, it's got all the colors of Arizona, the turquoise, oranges, greens. You will look like a real Sand Cutter. A genuine Arizonian."

"I love this, it's perfect. Now, I would like to look at a nice linen shirt for Drew. I know he has so many clothes, but I want to treat him with something new for the trip."

The girls looked at each other. "She's a keeper. His other girlfriends were takers, not givers. They used him and he didn't even know it."

"No worries about that with me, I promise." "Good, our brother deserves the best, and no less."

*Boy, these sisters are very protective of their brother. But in a genuine way. Nothing wrong with worrying about your sibling ending up with the wrong person. I know my children looked out for each other in that way.'*

"I am starving, let's eat. Shopping does that to me. How about Applebee's?" I said.

"Sounds yummy, they always have the best salad bars," Karen said and pointed toward the restaurant.

"Table for three, please," Karen told the waiter who escorted us to the freshly cleaned table.

*'Drew would be so happy to see us girls bonding like this.'* As we were seated, my phone rang, it was Drew.

"How's it going? I hope you guys are having a nice day so far. I wanted to let you know, I just got some good news. Stacy called and said she got all the paperwork in order for us for our passports. She was able to pull some strings in the town hall and expedite everything. All we need to do is get our pictures taken. She said CVS or the post office will do them."

"Great news! Maybe tomorrow we can stop at the store and get them done. I will text her and thank her for doing this great favor for us."

"Wonderful, see you later. Don't spend all your money in one place," he said jokingly.

Of course, we all ordered the delicious-looking salad bar. It looked so appetizing. And it was all-you-can-eat, which was my kind of meal. I love to eat, one of my favorite things to do. I was lucky that I exercised to keep my girlish figure.

*'Why am I saying that I have gained ten pounds since I met Drew? I guess happiness looks good on me.'* That's what I keep saying to myself.

The waitress brought over our water and asked us if we wanted a cocktail. "No, thank you. Water is fine for now."

I excused myself from the table and went up to the counter. "Please take my credit card and put our bill on it please?"

"Sure."

We all finished our lunch and were deciding on a dessert. "What looks good to you, girls?"

"We love carrot cake, our mom used to make it all the time," said Tanya. "Let's all have some in honor of your mom," I replied and waved to our waitress.

"That's a great idea, I only wish she could be here for this girls' day out, she would have really loved you, Savannah," Karen said with a tear in her eye.

I explained to them mine and Drew's story about how we met, and how we think their mom had something to do with it. They listened to me with such concentration on their faces.

"What do you mean, Savannah?"

"We met the day after my birthday, the day after your mom's passing. I had an overwhelming feeling to reach out to your brother after I sent him a friend request on Facebook. I never reach out to people, I really don't. We both feel your mom sent me to him. Drew had told me that he told his mother he was giving up on finding someone. Your mom told him he was going to find a woman, he just had to be patient. When he least expects it, then she will come. Literally, that's how it happened. We met for ice cream and haven't been apart since. We always feel a sense of her presence."

"Spiritual?" Karen replied.

"Yes, we even went to see a medium a couple of weeks ago and your mom came through."

"What do you mean?"

"The Medium Felecia described your mom to us and she shared her messages with us."

"This is crazy, I can't believe that Drew would go for something like this, what are you some kind of witch?" Karen asked.

"No, Karen. I am not, but I believe in the afterlife and I also think they can send us messages through spiritual individuals."

"I still can't believe our brother allowed this to happen."

"Don't be upset, calm down everyone in the restaurant is looking at us. I am sorry I mentioned it, it was a very memorable experience for both of us. My mom came through too. Your mother also spoke through Felicia stating that she didn't want your sisters to feel guilty about anything."

"Really?"

Both girls were listening to every word I spoke to them. After I told them that part, they seemed like they believed the story I was telling them.

"What else did she say?"

"You both need to talk to Drew about this, I probably should have left this conversation for him to have with you two. I'm sorry, let's not talk about this anymore today. Let's just talk about something else."

"Okay, yes, we'll ask Drew about it. Thank you for being so

open with us and trusting us with this." Karen concluded the conversation on that topic.

"It's perfectly okay," I calmly mentioned, inwardly hoping that I didn't ruin the good relationship I had with them so far.

"So, tell me all the cool places to see in Arizona? Tell me a little about your Dad.

John, right?"

"Yes, his name is John Hart. He is a really cool man. White hair with a long white beard kind of reminds you of Santa. He is the sweetest man, would do anything for anybody."

"Well, I guess Drew gets that from him. I can't wait to meet him. He will be picking us up at the Sky Harbor International Airport on Sunday. It's only a few days away. I can't believe your brother surprised me with tickets."

"He must really care for you, he has never taken anyone to meet Dad ever! Any girlfriends anyway. This is why we know you're the one. His other girlfriends were nothing like you. If mom sent you to him, she picked the perfect match. We just adore you, Savannah."

"Thank you for saying that, it means so much to me to hear you girls say that." "Savannah take out your notepad on your phone, type this down. You have to go to The Chapel of the Holy Cross, Cathedral Rock, and Montezuma Castle National Monument, and have a picnic at Oak Creek's Red Rock Crossing. These are only a few places, just wait until you get there, then look up on Google places you must see while in Arizona. Or just ask Dad. He has been living there for over twenty years."

"That sounds wonderful. I am getting so excited about the trip. I have been taking lots of time off of work since I met Drew. I never took any time because I never had anywhere or anyone to go places with. Now I do."

"Oh yes and you have found the perfect man to take you to

places," Tanya said, patting my hand lightly.

We all enjoyed our carrot cake while Tanya and Karen talked a little more about their mother and how they all baked different things, mostly on weekends.

"Drew always loved cooking. Have you tried anything that he cooked?" "No, sadly I haven't. But he promised he will cook something for me, soon."

"Oh, you have to try it. It's world-class. I would say if he was a chef, he would have earned himself a couple of Michelin stars easily." Karen said as she enjoyed one bite after another of the carrot cake.

"Oh wow! That good!" I almost exclaimed.

"I don't know about you two, about I am enjoying this carrot cake. I can't think of anything else. This is so good. After Mom's, this is the best cake I've had." Tanya had the last bite of her carrot cake and sat in her chair with her eyes closed. "You know you had good food and eaten to your appetite when you feel sleepy."

"But we can't sleep, right now. Let's finish up our shopping." "Wait, we have to pay the bill first."

"No, it's all taken care of girls." "Wow, thank you so much sista!"

"You're welcome! Anytime, I enjoyed every minute of it. Let's get that linen shirt for Drew I saw in American Eagle."

Off to a few more stores and then I can call it quits. Shopping wasn't fun without Drew with me. Matter of fact, I felt a sense of loneliness without him. I realized I was with his sisters, but it just didn't feel right. I missed him so much. Seemed like I am getting very attached to him.

"This is the one." As I ran into the store and grabbed the shirt off the rack. "This olive green shirt matches his eyes, he looks so handsome with this color on. I can't wait to spend a whole week with him in Arizona. This life is getting real and I love it." I finished up my purchase and we headed back to the parking lot. We all stood there for a while saying goodbye.

"It was so much fun hanging with you Savannah. We both enjoyed getting to know you better. If mom picked you out for Drew, then we concur. We love you!"

"Talk soon."

"And we are definitely trying that cake again," Tanya said.

"You're in love with that cake, aren't you?" Karen chuckled a little.

"We will try it again the day I come back from Arizona." I felt the same way, it was perfection.

We hugged each other and went on our way. I do believe my life is as perfect as I dreamed it could be. *'I hope Drew will not be upset with me that I spoke to his sisters about the Medium.'*

*'It's okay. They are okay with it,'* I kept convincing myself.

## Chapter 23

I drove back to my apartment. Not only was I going to be away from Drew all day, we did not have plans to see each other that night because he had to work the next day. I decided to spend my day packing for my trip. I have the cutest luggage set. It has a black and white polka dot print on it. "I get to use it. Am I really going on a jet plane with Drew?" I tossed the smaller suitcase on the bed and started filling it with my under garments. I must remember on our way to my aunt's house tomorrow to tell Drew about my conversation with his sisters. He needed to tell them what Felicia told us. *'It's not my place and I can't believe it came out during lunch. It just seemed like the right time. I probably should have kept my mouth shut. Not my place and I hope Drew isn't agitated with me. If he is quiet on the ride after I tell him then I will know. He tends to get quiet when he is deep in thought. Not me, I love to express my feelings and thoughts. Sometimes, I think Drew wants to shush me.'*

I sent Drew a quick text telling him goodnight and hoping we could talk tomorrow about my day. I asked him to meet me at my apartment by four. Aunt Dolly was expecting us for dinner at five-thirty.

The thought of Drew being upset with me didn't leave my mind all night, however, I still managed to catch a few winks and got up early for the day.

Four o'clock on the nose, Drew pulled in and I ran to his car. "I missed you so much," I said and then added, "I am so glad we are right on schedule for dinner, thanks for getting to my place on time."

"You're welcome, I know how much this dinner with your aunt means to you, and I remember what the Medium told us."

"Yeah, that had been on my mind a lot. I don't know what I will do when she passes. She is the next best thing next to my own mom."

Driving down Route 684, I realized any visit could be my last and I wanted to make sure my aunt knew how much she meant to me. I was extremely glad she was able to meet Drew and at least know how much I was in love with him and how much he adored me. And I was more than thankful for that.

We pulled into the driveway. It seemed strange after I mentioned any visit could be the last, it only made me enjoy her company to the fullest more now. We knocked on her door, and I swear I could hear her practically skipping to answer it. "Hello my loves, come in."

"Oh my, something smells so good, did you make chicken pot pie?" I asked and hung our coats up in the hall closet.

"Yes, I made it for this hunk of yours," she said and pointed to Drew. Drew started to giggle and turn red in the face.

"Come sit down, do you want a glass of red wine?" We both said, "Sure."

"How was the traffic coming down?"

"It was not bad, everyone was going north for some reason," Drew said. "Well that's good, I enjoy driving up your way, and it's very relaxing for me." Aunt Dolly already had the table set and she even pulled out her good dishes the ones that were my grandmother's. Those were old. We sat in the living room talking for a few minutes before she said it was time to eat.

"Dolly, this food is fantastic, you made it right? Your niece here likes to get catered food when she has guests over."

"Really? That is funny." Aunt Dolly winked at me before asking, "Would you two like dessert?"

"Maybe later," I said.

"Drew, could you follow me in the parlor for a minute, Savannah will clear the table."

"Ok."

I was still in the dining room when I heard her say, "What are your intentions for my niece?"

There was about a minute-long silence before Drew answered her. I carried our dishes to the kitchen, set them down quickly, and stood at the door holding it open just enough.

"Well Dolly, I am falling madly in love with Savannah and I plan on keeping her for the rest of my life."

"Do you see marriage in your future?"

"I do, but Dolly, do you realize that Savannah is still legally married? She has hired a lawyer to start the proceedings and I believe it's going smoothly. Her friend Andrea is helping her with the paperwork since she had gone through a divorce recently. Of course, I am there for her every step of the way. It needs to be done. Then I can honestly say that I see marriage in our cards. I could see us having a beautiful life. We do have another half of life to live."

"Okay, I feel confident then in what I am about to give you right now. Drew, hold out your hand, this was my grandmother's engagement ring. It's vintage. I want you to give it to Savannah if you two get engaged."

I swallowed the lump in my throat. Tears were streaming down my face.

"Oh my Aunt Dolly, this is the most beautiful ring, you can surely tell it's a very old piece. The emerald cut diamond is exquisite and the band is so unique."

"It sure is one of a kind, just like my niece, she is just like a daughter to me, we have so many memories together and I know she will take it hard when I pass. I think this will remind her of the family when she wears it. Old and new families. She told me she met your sisters and she is about to go meet your dad in Arizona. She is very excited about it."

"Yes, she is super excited for the trip, we have to start packing tomorrow." "Keep this ring in a safe place and give it to her if and when you propose." "I will."

'Oh my god, I can't believe I am hearing this, is he really thinking of getting married? Is he just saying it to make my aunt happy? I wonder what the ring looks like? I have never seen it before. When I was eavesdropping I heard an emerald cut, it's got to be gorgeous!'

I went back to the dining room and I continued cleaning off the table, trying to hold back my emotions, I didn't want them to know I heard every word. I turned to face them when I heard her ask.

"Who wants dessert? I made a carrot cake."

We both looked at each other with our eyes bulging out of our heads, it was our favorite cake. Drew stood up and told her, "We both love carrot cake."

"Did I tell you about the carrot cake I had with your sisters?" I whispered to Drew.

"Uh, I don't recall."

"Oh. I'll tell you about it."

"Right, if you two are done with your little Chinese Whisper game, Savannah, go make a pot of coffee for us, then we can sit and bullshit a bit before you get on your way. You know I hate it when you drive in the dark."

My aunt still made her coffee in an old percolator. It made

the whole house smell like a cafe.

Drew sat back down at the table and said, "That smells so delicious."

I set the table using her old vintage tea cups and saucers. I knew they were my grandmothers. They looked like they were iridescent and looked so pretty. I also brought out the matching cake plates.

"Thank you, Savannah, it looks so pretty, and the coffee should be done now," Aunt Dolly said and sat at the head of the table.

*That was my cue to go get the coffee and serve it with the cake.*

"So Savannah, how is the divorce going?"

"I am glad you asked, I forgot to tell Drew so I'll tell you both now. My lawyer called me today and told me my husband's lawyer called and offered us a buyout for the house, two hundred thousand, and we will leave each other's retirements alone. I accepted the offer and we should be divorced by the end of the month. The longest part is to wait our turn for the judge to sign the document and be recorded."

"That is great news, after all, you were married over thirty years and you deserve half of the house. I am glad it's going so smoothly. Sometimes things can get very ugly and stressful. Thank God things went well," she said.

Drew looked at me and smiled ear to ear. He basically told me once he didn't want to be dating or falling in love with a married woman. I know if the role was reversed, I wouldn't commit to a married man either.

"Okay, we finished our dessert, the bullshit session is over. I have a show to watch," Aunt Dolly announced and we went on our way.

The car ride home was fun, we cracked up laughing at some of the things my aunt was telling us. I think dementia was starting to settle in because she kept repeating herself. It makes sense, after all, she is in her late nineties. *'I don't know what I would have done if she wasn't here. I can't thank my aunt enough.'*

"So Drew, what was the big secret?"

"Oh, just your aunt making sure I had good intentions for you."

"I am so sorry she put you through that, she must be losing it."

"No, it was kind of cute, it shows how much she cares about you, I know your mom passed away over twenty years ago and she took over as your mother figure. She is just protecting her loved one."

"I guess, if you put it that way."

"Why didn't you tell me the news about the divorce?"

"Honestly, I forgot. You were pumping gas when the paralegal called and I was so excited to visit my aunt. Then you got back in the car and started telling me a funny story. I forgot to mention it. It wasn't done on purpose. I want to share everything about my life with you. I will always tell you the truth and never leave you out of anything that happens in my life. I hope you feel the same way."

"Yes Anna, I know it wasn't intentional and I will make sure to communicate with you on everything in my life too."

"I am glad you said that because honesty and loyalty is a deal breaker with me Drew. I was lied to my whole marriage and I want to start my new life with open communication. It's a very important part of a relationship. I know you haven't had many, but I am telling you this now."

"Duly noted. And I will ensure it happens from my end. Don't fret." "I believe you." I held his hand and gently kissed it.

"Okay, about our trip, are you excited about it? Have you Googled Sedona yet? It's an amazing place. You are going to love it. My father is so excited to meet you. He is telling all his friends that his son and daughter-in-law-to-be are coming into town." "That's cute." I tapped his leg. "I like the way that sounds. Hey, tomorrow is Mr.

Fred's memorial service. Do you want to attend with me? I know that you might have some work to finish before our trip. I can go alone; all my coworkers will be there. It's okay if you can't make it, I totally understand."

"No way are you going to that service without me. You don't understand Anna, I am here for you. I am not your soon-to-be ex-husband who left you alone to go deep sea fishing the day after your own father died. We are a couple and that means we go together."

"Thanks, Drew, you are my rock. I love you so much, thanks for coming into my life."

*'I find him so attractive whenever he sounds protective about me. Just the right type of protectiveness; the type that makes me feel warm and loved all over.'*

"Thank you for coming into mine."

We both looked at each other and lifted our heads to the sky and said in unison, "Thank you for bringing us together."

"By the way, what time is the service?"

"It starts at ten and it's on Hooker Avenue in Poughkeepsie."

We pulled into the apartment complex parking lot and Drew got out to open my door. "Come on, let me walk you inside."

"Thank you Drew for going to dinner and making memories with my aunt." I kissed his cheek adding, "She adores you."

He grinned from ear to ear. "I adore her, too. And you're always welcome." After he kissed me back, he unlocked the door to my apartment. "Good night, I will pick you up at quarter to ten."

I squeezed his hand. I wanted to say stay, hold me, but I knew he would want to go home and change his clothes. I got ready for bed, dreading the idea of tomorrow. It would be a long, sad day.

I wished Mr. Fred was there at my wedding, soon-to-happen wedding. He would have been there like my father, taking care of everything and even feeling teary at seeing me as the happiest bride.

## Chapter 24

'Mr. Fred will be so missed.' I opened my phone and looked at all the albums and reminisced about all the memories we all made at work. *He did have a good life, he had all of us.* I set the alarm for eight.

For some reason I awoke very early, the birds were chirping outside my window and the sun was shining brightly. I realized why they say that birds sing. There was nothing more relaxing than listening to all kinds of bird songs. It was very peaceful. *'Maybe this is Mr. Fred letting me know he is at peace.'*

I looked through my closet, thinking about what I should wear. I realized that there was a favorite dress that Mr. Fred was fond of. It was a turquoise color dress with some fancy embroidery on it. I grabbed it in his honor. I looked at the clock and realized I needed to get going, Drew would be here soon and I didn't want him to wait for me. I jumped in the shower and thought about how lucky I was to have Drew in my life. Knowing he doesn't want me to go through this alone means the world to me.

I sat on the porch dreading having to say a final goodbye to my best pal at work. It will never be the same without him there. Drew pulled in at nine-forty-five. "Hi sweetheart, you ready?"

"Yes, I am. I was just replaying all the fun times and the interesting talks I had with Mr. Fred."

"You hold onto those good memories it is what gets us through our losses. It's the only thing that gets me through missing my mom. Oh, by the way, I had a voice message from Tanya asking me to call her and explain the medium encounter with her. I guess they are very curious. You left them hanging. I will call them later after the service. We need to pack today for our trip."

"I'm so excited. I know, I will spend all afternoon and evening getting ready. What time do you want me at your place to head to Bradley Airport? I think noon should be good."

"Yeah, noon will be fine," he said as he stopped at a red light.

"I am nervous about being on a plane for so long. I have never flown for more than three hours."

"Did you bring a book like I suggested?"

"Yes, between sitting at the airport and flying those five hours, I should be able to finish the whole book."

He chuckled. "I am going to watch a couple of movies, The Adam Project and Top Gun Maverick."

"Well, it sounds like we both have a good plan. I can't wait to meet your Dad." "You will soon enough."

"When I told the kids I was flying to Arizona to meet your father, they started teasing me saying Mom it sounds like it is getting serious. My granddaughter said he's bringing you home to meet his parents. Woot woot!"

"Well, it's true. I want him to see how happy we are and how much my life has changed since I met you."

"Yeah, life has changed. I know happiness now." He looked at me with all the fondness, and I could have cried for being the one he was fond of.

I took a deep breath as Drew pulled into the parking lot. "Thank you so much for coming with me today," I said, holding his hand.

We walked in the funeral home hand and hand. This is not something I am used to, and it feels so right.

I introduced all my coworkers to Drew, and of course, they all said the same thing. "We have heard so much about you these past few months."

Drew replied, "I hope all is good."

Everyone told him how happy I had been since meeting him. That made him smile.

We sat and listened to the beautiful eulogy made by our boss. He definitely lived a full life. *Rest in peace Mr. Fred.* Everyone was going out to lunch, but we declined because we had lots of things to do.

Andrea came over to me, gave me a big hug and kiss on cheek. "Have a great time away and when you get back we will have to go out on a double date. Things are really great with Randy. He is amazing. Thank you for connecting us. Really, you are an angel."

"Oh, I am so thrilled to hear that Andrea. I will call you as soon as we come back."

I paid my last regards to Mr. Fred and called it a day.

## Chapter 25

I spent all day Saturday packing and unpacking, listening to the weather forecast for the next seven days. *'Oh my God, it's going to be a hot week!'* Of all weeks, the weather was supposed to be one-hundred and ten five out of the seven days we were going to be there. But, it didn't matter. I was going to be with Drew and meet his father. This was something you couldn't put a degree on. I finally packed up the lightest clothes I could find. I remembered what Drew's sisters told me about the air conditioning being on very high everywhere you went. So, I packed a few cardigan sweaters, as crazy as that sounds.

I headed over to Drew's with all my things ready to go. I was so excited for this trip. I had my own itinerary in my head for things I wanted to see in Sedona. I didn't realize how spiritual some of the places were. It sounds like my kind of town. My butterflies were back but in a good way.

Drew was waiting on the front porch for me when I arrived. He had a familiar smile on his face. The one which makes his dimple stand out even more.

"Are you ready, Anna?"

"Oh yeah, butterflies and all."

"Don't be nervous, it will be a wonderful time." He took my luggage out of my car and put it on his own.

As we drove to the airport, Drew was reminiscing about all the fun trips to Arizona he took throughout the years since his father moved there. He told me it took him a very long time to forgive his dad for divorcing his mother. "I basically gave up my life to care for my mom. Sometimes I wonder what my life would have been like if my father didn't leave. Would I be married now? Would I have children?"

"I bet that is always something that is in the back of your mind. You can't change anything that happened, but everything happens for a reason. You know, if your father stayed with your mother and he was the one taking care of her, we might not have met and we wouldn't be on our way to a fantastic vacation."

Drew looked over at me, grabbed my hand and kissed it. "You are right, it was worth it all. I waited a long time for you, Anna."

"And I for you, Drew." *'Almost too good to be true.'*

Drew handed his key to the valet and we jumped on the shuttle bus to the Delta departure area. Our luggage was tagged and sent to the plane. We sat at Dunkin Donuts and enjoyed a cup of coffee and a Danish before walking around the airport for an hour. The airlines just aren't the same anymore. No more snacks and drinks, you have to pay for everything on the plane. "

It's really happening," I said to him as we boarded the plane.

"Airports are the best people-watching places," Drew said. As he stared at all the stewardess walking by.

"Geez Drew, take a picture, it will last longer. What's up with the staring problem?"

I almost felt embarrassed and disrespected by the way he was looking. I think his head would turn a three-sixty every time one went by. This was the first time he made me feel this jealous. *Doesn't* he know I am right here, or that I can see him undressing them with his mind? I didn't like the feeling at all. Then the light went off, I remembered him talking about the fantasy that he revealed to me one night. He wanted me to dress up as a flight attendant. Oh, Drew. I whispered in his ear, "Do you want to join the mile-high club today?"

"What? Why are you saying that?" His face turned three different shades of red.

"Remember what you told me about a fantasy you had? And how I suggested we dress up as a pilot and stewardess? I actually was thinking when you told me that for more of a Halloween party costume idea. But, I am game if you want to try."

"Anna, you watch too many movies, you are so silly. Besides, we would never fit in the bathroom together."

"Okay, I guess maybe I do watch too much television. But, I know how much you like Halloween and you mentioned you go to costume parties, so I will accompany you to the first party as a flight attendant. What happens afterward is our private trick or treat."

"That's a plan. I will hold you to it, Ms. Fly with Me."

We heard on the loudspeaker, "Flight 525 to Phoenix boarding at zones one through three."

"That's us. Thank you for this trip." I kissed his cheek. I had my neck pillow already around my neck, book in hand, I was ready to fly. We sat in our assigned seats, of course I wanted the window seat. I love to look out at the sky, it's so magical. One time, I flew in a thunder and lightning storm. It was amazing. You could see the strikes of lightning, one after another like it was my own personal fireworks show. This will be a five-hour flight, so I have to stick to my itinerary. Site seeing, finishing my book, and taking a nice nap. Then I figure we will be landing by then and Drew's father will be there to pick us up. It's a two-hour drive to his place in Sedona. My eyes will be peeled out the window. If the places I saw on the internet were as beautiful in real life, then I would be in awe of everything. My face might be even peeled to the window the whole ride back. There goes my sheltered life again, Drew had brought so much excitement and adventures to my life since I met him. I appreciate him so much. I looked at him and blew him a kiss.

"What was that for?"

"Just for being you, and for taking me on another first. I love you, Drew." "Ditto Anna. I can see you are so delighted to be going to meet my father."

After looking out the window for ten minutes I opened my book and traveled to Rhode Island reading about a beautiful love story. The next thing I heard was the Captain on the loudspeaker saying, "We are getting ready to descent into Phoenix International Airport."

We both looked at each other and clapped with excitement. "Drew come look out this window, it is so beautiful!"

Our landing into Phoenix was so smooth I turned to Drew and said, "What a beautiful landing."

"Yes, Anna, it's a wonderful start to a great week. Let's go get our baggage and look for Dad," he replied and laughed. "Just keep your eyes peeled for a cool-looking dude that looks like Santa Claus."

"That's not very nice." "Oh, you wait."

*I can't imagine Drew's father looking like St. Nick. Drew is so clean-cut and very Asian to have a dad who looks like jolly old St. Nick. Well, I will soon see for myself.* As we turned the corner, I saw a man, who Drew described to a tee, standing there with a sign, 'The Hart's.'

'Okay, he looks charming.'

"Dad, you are really funny!" Drew hugged his father before introducing me to him.

His father gave me a long hug and whispered in my ear, "Thank you for coming and I am so happy to finally meet you. You have changed my son. He is so happy and fulfilled with his life now."

I imagined him to be a loving father, but he exceeded my expectations. I didn't expect him to hug me and say what he said to me. *'They all genuinely like me.'*

"Hello! Dad, I am here too, you know."

"Oh yes, how was your flight, son? And, I am so glad to see the two of you. We are going to have a blast this week."

We waited patiently for our suitcases to come around the carousel. I was dying to get outside and check out the views. We had a two-hour ride back to Sedona. "Here comes my polka dots! Drew yours is right behind it. Let's get out of here."

"You're not too enthusiastic are you, Anna? Oh Dad, I call Savannah Anna for short. You can, too."

"Alright, let's get going, Anna. Arizona is waiting for you."

We finally found the car, after three times scouting parking lot. We loaded the luggage in the back of the truck. Drew's father asked him to drive. With his father being seventy-eight, I had hoped he was not experiencing dementia yet."

"Kids, we are driving home all the way on SR 179. That's got the best views. Anna, watch out the window, you are about to see the most magical place. Very spiritual here, too. When you see the red rocks the Chapel of the Holy Cross will be next. Wouldn't it be nice to get married at that Chapel?"

"Oh Dad, you are getting way ahead of yourself here. We are happy just the way we are right now. Besides, you know Anna isn't officially divorced yet either."

"Well, I think you guys make the cutest couple. You look so in love and so meant for each other. I am so happy for you both.

Maybe, there will be a wedding someday. I'm not getting any younger. I can start looking forward to your wedding."

"Of course, Dad," Drew said and smiled at me.

"I don't think I have ever seen anything more beautiful than I am seeing right now." I banged my head on the window as I looked back. "It's breathtaking."

"Stick with me Mrs. Hart and you will see it all."

Anyone could tell they are related. They might not look alike but I could tell they have a lot of the same personality, which is a great thing. At least I know how Drew will act when he gets his father's age. *I might want to revisit that statement at the end of the week after spending all this time with both of them.*

Drew turns around to the back seat and asks me, "Are you hungry?"

Of course, I was, it was a very long flight, and peanuts and pretzels can only go so far in this belly. "Let's stop somewhere halfway to the house."

"That sounds great," Drew said.

Drew's Dad suggested we stop in Prescott to eat. "I know a place that has fantastic food. It's called Prescott Junction. They have the best burgers."

"Yes," Drew answered. "By the way, we are not fussy at all."

"I see that you guys are eating out all over the place. You know I watch all your Facebook posts. I am always getting ready to open up Facebook and there you guys are eating out somewhere or on your adventures. Honestly, I am glad you have found someone, Drew."

"Mr. Hart, thank you for having us, we appreciate you picking us up and letting us stay at your place."

"First, call me John or Dad, Mr. Hart was my father." "Sounds good, John."

*'John does sound more personal but it felt like he accepts me as a part of his family.'*

We got off the exit towards the restaurant. It was amazing seeing all the cactus everywhere. "Where's the grass?" I asked.

"Did you forget Anna, It's a desert?" "Oh yeah."

"Let's go eat, you guys need a good meal."

The menu looked so good. I was going to have the wild-west-wagon cheeseburger, which comes with an onion on top, barbecue sauce, and fries.

One look at the menu and Drew's eyes got as big as saucers. If that is even possible for an Asian man. "I want the all you can eat shrimp, an endless platter of golden mini shrimp, fries and their soup, salad, and the fruit and frozen yogurt bar." John laughingly said, "You must be real hungry, son." And ordered the Rio Grande chicken topped with a roasted poblano pepper and pepper jack cheese with lettuce, tomato, and chipotle ranch sauce for himself.

*I hope he has some tums in his medicine cabinet, he is going to need them later.*

The waitress took our orders and told us she would be back with some water. The place was very nice, but it was freezing. I remembered what the girls told me about this. Boy were they right. I should've realized they knew what they were talking about, they have visited many times. I wanted to run out to the vehicle so I could grab my sweater, but realized, it would sound crazy considering it was over one hundred degrees out. We finished our dinner and back on the highway we went. John said we had about one hour until we arrived at his house. It was starting to get dark and I couldn't really see much so we used the rest of the way to chat.

"Anna, have you heard about the Pink Jeep tours around here?"

"Yes, I did see them online, I am hoping that Drew rents one for us for a day and we can explore."

"What about the vortex, did you do your homework on that?" John asked and pursed his bottom lip.

"Oh yes, that's what I am most curious about, the pockets of energy believed to aid in prayers, healing, and meditation."

"We have the best art galleries and boutiques here, too," John said and then paused before adding, "My ex-girlfriend loved all the cute shops."

"Ex?" Drew replied. "What happened?"

"She owned one of those witch shops, she claimed to be one of those people who can talk to the dead. There are a lot of people like that around here. She even had a website where she told fortunes for money. She even had a PayPal account set up. A real scam artist."

I saw Drew look at me in the rear-view mirror. I leaned forward and whispered in his ear, "Oh no, maybe we shouldn't tell him about our experience with Felicia?"

## Chapter 26

Drew stopped at a traffic light, cleared his throat, and looked at me. I smiled back at him. Then he put his index finger to his lips. I guess that would be a hard no on telling his Dad about our medium experience.

A minute later his father pointed to a group of large red rocks. "Anna, did you take a picture of that?" Before I could put my cell phone down and answer him he said, "You kids must be exhausted, I have the bedroom and bathroom all set for you. You should be very comfortable. You have the whole wing to yourself. Just like a honeymoon suite. Hint, hint." He said, winking first at Drew and then at me.

"Dad, let' s just get this straight, Anna and I are just getting to know each other and yes there might be a wedding in the future, but for now we are purely happy with each other just the way it is. No more nudges about marriage. Got it?"

"Yes, I got it," his father said, sounding more deflated than I felt.

I was confused. He told my aunt we were getting close. Now, he's telling his own father, "No more nudges." What the hell? Frigging butterflies in my stomach and they're not happy. I had a strange feeling something, or someone was happening. I looked at Drew in the mirror. Asshole was smiling. Is he leading me on? Does he really have plans to make a future with me? Why is he all of a sudden adamant about changing the subject? Is he one of those guys who are afraid of commitment? *Don't put up the umbrella before it rains, Savannah.* I looked out my window and told myself to enjoy the beautiful state of Arizona. Then I forced myself to relax and try to experience some amazing things while I was with Drew.

*'It will all turn out to be okay, as far as today is going well, our future will be for the best of us. Remember, you are his miracle and he is your dream guy.'*

We arrived at his father's house. It was a typical home in Arizona. The walls were made of stucco, the colors were mostly bold orange, and turquoise.

Even though I was convinced somehow that all was well, I still could not stop thinking about what he said in the car. The last thing I wanted to do was sit around and listen to them talk about nonsense.

"Drew, I'm going to bed, the time change is going to take its toll on me tomorrow."

"You're right," he said and followed me toward the bedroom. "Goodnight pops, we will get up early tomorrow and make you a great breakfast."

"Goodnight kids. See you in the morning," Drew's dad headed to his bedroom with his cute little dogs following behind him.

Drew immediately climbed into the bed, I headed for the shower. Then I had to join him because the bed was calling my name.

The bedroom was so cute, all decorated Aztec style, and beautiful wall hangings surrounded the room with the cutest comforter set for the bed. I felt very Western. The house definitely had a woman's touch with all the decor. The question was, what woman? The witch? *I chuckled to myself as I lay in the bed.* I looked over at Drew who was sound asleep.

*God, he was so beautiful. I am so in love with this man. I hope I don't get hurt. He won't hurt me. He is different. But doesn't every woman with a man thinks her man is different? There is nothing different about my feeling that Drew was different. And that is a scary thought, as I know several women out there who aren't happy in their relationships. But I am happy, genuinely happy and you can't pretend genuineness.* I rubbed my eyes a little, palmed my face, and tried to calm myself. *I am not a pessimist. I am not going to put up the umbrella. We are good, it's all good.* I took deep breaths and felt myself calming down.

As I started to fall asleep, I remembered that I was supposed to send a text to the kids and let them know I landed safe and sound. I could not go to sleep, so I texted the boys.

Drew woke up before me, I don't recall when exactly I fell asleep. I could hear Drew in the kitchen, perhaps scrambling around trying to find pans to cook breakfast for us. I also smelled the aroma of freshly brewed coffee. I don't think I ever craved a cup of coffee as bad as I did this morning. Maybe, it was the Arizona air. I was so happy to see the windows were open. I was able to get some fresh air before the blazing heat set in for the day. I could hear all the birds, they were singing different songs. Must be a different species of bird in the West.

Whatever songs the birds were singing, they made me feel so happy. I grabbed my robe and headed to the kitchen. "Do you need some help with breakfast?"

"No sweetheart, I got this."

I think he knows by now that I am not very domesticated. I love that he wants to cook and take care of me. I spent many years taking care of everyone else, it feels nice to be treated like a princess.

*How did I get so lucky? I hope I get luckier. I hope I get married to him.*

"Good morning, kiddo's. Anna, how did you sleep?" "Great, thank you," and sipped my coffee.

John walked over to Drew and put his hand on the small of Drew's back. "I love waking up to the smell of bacon and eggs. I forgot how much you like to cook, Drew."

"Dad, Anna loves to cook too." Drew looks at his dad and starts to laugh. "Really funny Drew, why are you making fun of me? Go ahead, tell your father about my entertaining practices, I don't care."

"Dad, she likes to get things catered, I told her that I could have whipped all those dishes up with no big deal."

"Yes Drew, I understand now how lazy I may look to others now. I just don't like the stress of cooking and having people not appreciate me. Honestly, I like when you do it for me."

"I'll wear the chef hat for you any day."

"Ha-ha," I said as I noticed Drew had the table outside on the deck all set and ready for our breakfast.

His dad said he appreciated waking up to a wonderful breakfast. "I am so happy to be able to share this week with you two. You know you don't have to include me in all your excursions, I understand you might want to be alone sometimes. You know I am an old man now and can't do some things I used to be able to do. Son, getting old stinks."

"Dad, you look wonderful, I hope I am in as good of shape when I am your age."

"Thanks, that makes me feel good. Maybe, I should ignore what my ex-girlfriend revealed in that fake reading she gave me."

Drew set the platter with the eggs and bacon on the table and it hit hard enough to make me jump and then asked, "What did she tell you?"

John shook his head adding, "It was stupid and it's not going to come true. That is why I got rid of the crazy nut."

I whispered to Drew, "We need to find out what she told him."

He nodded in agreement.

"No more bringing up my ex, just like no more hints about marriage." "Deal," Drew said and filled my plate with more bacon than usual.

John finished eating his breakfast, he looked at Drew and asked, "How are your sisters doing since your mom's death? And how are my grandchildren taking it?"

"They're ok. I think there is a little guilt going on. We didn't get to say goodbye in person. We had to look through the glass to say our final goodbyes."

John winked at me and replied, "They will be okay, it's still very fresh in their minds."

"Dad, did you know that Anna and I met the day after Mom passed?" Drew said as he sat back in his chair and smiled at me.

"Yes, you told me the story on the phone. I remember getting chills as you explained the story. I think your mom sent Anna to you. She knew how much you wanted someone in your life and you were getting to the point of giving up."

Drew and I both looked at each other and couldn't believe that he thought that, too. Even he thought we were sent to each other.

"Why do you think that, Dad?"

"Well, look at the timeline, your mom left this earth one day and the next day you meet the woman you have been waiting for your whole life. Son, it's a no-brainer." "I never looked at it being cut and dry like that. Thanks for sharing your point of view."

Drew's father picked up the glass pitcher of freshly squeezed orange juice and asked me if I wanted a refill. I noticed it was almost empty and said, "No thanks."

Drew quickly replied, 'I'm good too, Dad."

When John poured the rest of the juice into his own glass, Drew and I looked at each other with pure validation. There was a dime stuck to the bottom of the pitcher. "That's weird, where did that come from? It must have been on the table, sometimes I empty my change from my pockets on this table. It must have stuck to the table when I cleaned it off last time." John looked at Drew and then at me. "Why do you guys look like you saw a ghost?"

I stuck my hand out and asked, "Can I have that dime, John?"

"Not sure why you want it, but of course you can have it. You do know that we have the same money here in Arizona as you have in Connecticut, right?"

Drew laughed at his father's antics.

"Yes, I am blonde but not that ditzy. It's something that Drew and I have been finding all over since we met. It has a spiritual meaning to both of us." Even though he has had a bad experience in the past, I felt compelled to explain myself. "Alexa says it means a loved one's soul is trying to let you know they are watching over you." "Oh no, you guys don't practice that witchery, do you? I will have to take you and drop you off at my ex's house."

"We will tell you more about it when we have more time. I have to get showered and ready for this wonderful first day in Sedona."

"You two go get ready, I will do the dishes. Thank you for the delicious breakfast."

"You're welcome, Pops."

After breakfast, I was sitting on my ass watching Drew help his father put the dishes away when I heard his father say, "I am so proud of you, and I can clearly see how happy you are with Anna. Maybe your mom did have something to do with sending you your perfect match."

"Pops, remember our deal?"

"Yes," he replied and closed the cabinet door. "All I am saying is I'm excited for you and I can't help but want to tell the world about your newfound happiness. Being in your middle fifties could've been hard to find someone without a lot of baggage. Anna is good for you. I can see it. Nowadays most single girls have lots of issues going on in their lives. Something you don't need."

Drew put his hand on his father's back and said, "I agree."

"Son, I think I will stay home today while you and Anna go exploring Sedona. I've seen it all. Honestly, my knees are not in good shape. I am having a lot of trouble with them."

"I think you should see a doctor, is this something that your ex mentioned in your reading?"

His father threw the dish towel on the counter. "Hello! The deal. Remember?" "Oh yeah, just get it looked at as soon as possible, please. Okay, so Anna and I will leave within the hour and be back around seven. How about we go out to eat when we get back?"

"No, I will have a nice dinner ready for you when you come back. Just send me a text when you are headed home. I'll surprise you, it's been a while since I cooked for someone."

"Pops, don't go crazy, we are not fussy."

*Is it rare for children to share such a bond with their parents?* I was watching television, switching channels, and finding something to watch until father and son chatted. I stopped briefly at a channel that was playing a Frank Sinatra song. *I was glad that my children share that bond with me and I found someone who has a similar bond with their parents.* I started singing along to the song while keeping an ear out for their conversation to end.

"Well, I like to arrange and cook good food for everyone and especially my son and his dear girlfriend."

"That's really sweet of you, Pops." "Now you two get going."

When I heard his father say get going I shut the television off and grabbed my cellphone. I intended on taking a lot of pictures while I was there.

"Thanks for letting us use your car while we are here." "Don't worry about me, I have the truck if I need anything."

"Anna let's get going, and don't forget your water bottle and sunscreen."

We arrived at the parking lot of the Pink Jeep Tours just as they were opening the gate. I was so excited to get to see Sedona in a Jeep, nevertheless a pink one! One of my favorite colors. I can't wait to take some photos and post them on Facebook. No one would believe me unless they saw pictures of this amazing place.

The tour guide met us as we got out of the car.

"Hi, I am Carson, your tour guide, here is the flyer to explain the different tours we offer."

We looked at each tour and our eyes got bigger each time we turned the page.

Each tour listed in the pamphlet was better and longer than the one before.

"Oh my god, how are we going to decide what we want to see?" I asked. "It's so overwhelming."

Carson explained every excursion to us and we finally decided. We were going to take the Sedona 360 East Tour. It included a visit to the Chapel of the Holy Cross, Cathedral Rock, Tlaquepaque, and Airport Mesa.

Drew put his arm around me and said, "Remember we are going to be here for five days. Long enough to see everything on our list."

"I know, but it's so overwhelming and breathtaking. I can feel how spiritual it is here. Now, I understand all the hype."

Carson got in his Jeep and we snuggled up in the back seat. When Drew kissed my cheek he said he was excited to see Sedona through my eyes. "I know Sedona or any place whatsoever will look a thousand times more beautiful through your eyes." "I am flattered. Thank you so much for this compliment. I will make sure I don't miss out on any of the views."

I looked at the panoramic views and told Drew, "God made this world so beautiful, I can only imagine what heaven will look like."

"Sounds like the spirits getting to you already," Carson said and then reached into the box on the seat next to him and handed us each a pink baseball cap with the "Pink Jeep Tours" logo on them.

"You're going to need these out there in the desert today; it's going to be a hot one." Drew said as he took one of the hats and placed it on my head, "Now you won't have Jeep hair."

"No, but I look so dorky in it, but not as dorky as you do."

"Pink is my color, Anna!"

"Sure, whatever makes you happy."

Carson handed us these neat pink earbuds. "I will be narrating everything to you as we go. The rough terrain can make things hard to hear. So where are you two from?"

We both answered, "Connecticut."

"Oh." He paused before glancing in the rearview mirror. "Are you two on your honeymoon?"

"No!" Drew answered, which seemed to be very loud coming through the earbuds. "We are just dating for now."

*'God, Drew. Don't bite the guy's head off.'* I looked at him and shook my head wondering if he was getting paranoid about the subject of us getting married. *'And why do you need to be so loud and insist on this?'*

"Huh," Carson replied. "You act like honeymooners who are so in love." Drew looked at me and said, "We're in love." Then he blew me an air kiss.

I pretended to catch it and put it on my heart, but my insides were screaming, "Are you still in love?"

The wind was in my hair so I tucked it under my hat. Never mind, it was getting really hot out and my nose felt like it was on fire. The dry heat was killing me.

Carson asked if we wanted cold water. "You need to stay hydrated on days like this. Did you know that Elvis made a movie here? Hollywood loved to film their movies in Sedona."

My eyes lit up and I said, "I can see why, it's picture-perfect in every way. I will have to tell my friend Mark Ruffalo all about this place."

Drew almost snapped his neck looking at me. "Sure Anna, he's your best friend now. You haven't even met him yet."

"I've seen him, Drew." I smiled at him. "And he wraps up the movie at my apartment complex, I plan on introducing myself to him."

Carson spoke up, "Are you serious? The Hulk is making a movie near you?" "Yes, it should be coming out on HBO at the end of the year."

"Cool. I'll be watching for it. Hey, make sure you both have your seat belts on." "Yes, sir," Drew said.

We started to get into some bumpy terrain. We seemed to be at a higher elevation, my ears were popping.

Both of us were in awe of the breathless views, the towering cliffs, and all the red rock formations. Something you cannot describe to anyone so I started taking pictures.

"Would you guys like to stop to take some photos?"

"Yes, please. No one would ever believe I saw this view even if I tried to explain it," I said as I moved the microphone closer to my mouth.

Carson parked the Jeep and told us where to stand. "Both of you stand over here, it is an iconic spot to take photos."

We both put on our best smiles and posed together proudly.

"You guys sure do look good together, you are even dressed alike."

I didn't realize it but Drew and I both had on khaki shorts and a white tee shirt. Then the pink hat made the cake. We must have looked like geeks. I guess tomorrow I will have to check our wardrobe before we leave.

Carson took some gorgeous photos of us, but how can any photo come out bad with this backdrop? Breathtaking.

"Come on love birds, let's get going, we have a half hour left of the tour."

We got back in the Jeep. Drew put his arm around me and kissed my cheek. "I am so glad to be here with you Anna. I love the innocence on your face, it's like you were blind and you have your sight for the first time."

"Your compliments are getting better," I chuckled as I said it. "Oh, Drew, it's just so beautiful, I saw the pictures on the internet, but in real life it's magical. I feel like I am in another world."

"You, are in my world." "I am, Drew, I am."

We visited the Chapel of the Holy Cross and Cathedral Rock. Drew not being a Christian wasn't interested. I made sure I took pictures. It was something indescribable. Maybe, Drew's Dad will come back with me and visit the holy places. Before I knew it, we were back at the entrance. There were about 20 pink Jeeps lined up waiting for the next tour. We were glad we came early and had to experience the place to ourselves without the noise of the crowd around us. I turned around and snapped one more photo, this time I would post these photos with captions written just for these places. We got out and thanked Carson.

"It was a pleasure having you as our tour guide," Drew said as the two shook each other's hands.

"You're most welcome. Come back soon and visit us again. This place is magical every time you visit it." Carson said with a rather cheerful tone.

"We will," I replied and we headed our way.

"Come on Anna, let's grab a quick lunch and do some window shopping."

## Chapter 27

We made it back to John's just in time for his dinner he had prepared for us. He had an assortment of shish kabobs. "Delicious John, thank you for your hospitality, how about dessert?"

No one answered me, so I looked in the freezer and grabbed the chocolate chip and the coconut ice cream to serve for dessert. I popped my head into the dining room and asked, "I'm serving ice cream. How many scoops?"

They both answered, "Two, please." I love ice cream, so I filled our bowls with big scoops.

"I am stuffed. That ice cream was yummy," John said.

We were still in the living room, relaxing with big fat bellies. John stood up and said, "Let's go to Jerome tomorrow."

I immediately grabbed my phone and googled it. "Ahh, it's a ghost town?" "Yes, it's a very neat old Arizona mining town," John said and grabbed all of our empty bowls.

"Sounds cool, Pops."

"Yes, I love ghosts, gold, and silver," I said and clapped my hands.

John looked at me and smiled. "I knew you would. Let's plan

the next three days. Jerome, then Blazin M. Ranch and then we will visit Flagstaff. We might even see some snow."

"Snow," both of us shouted!

"Yes, kids. Then I want to host a dinner here at the house for all of my friends to meet you two."

"That all sounds great." Drew looked at me and I nodded in agreement. "I would love to meet your friends. How about your old girlfriend? I would like to meet her too if you are on speaking terms."

I thought his father would get upset with Drew for even mentioning her. When his father went into the kitchen, Drew whispered in my ear, "I am curious about her."

John came back and said, "It's funny you say that because she called me today, she heard through the grapevine that I had visitors and she asked to meet the two of you. I told her I would ask you if you were interested and get back to her. So, I guess the answer would be yes."

"Yeah, it would be cool to meet her," Drew replied.

Then his father told us her name. "Vera is unique. As you will see soon enough.

I will call her and invite her to dinner."

I was still sitting in the living room when I turned the television on. I wanted to catch up on my soap, The Bold and The Beautiful when Drew interrupted me.

"I can't believe we are going to meet that crazy ex-girlfriend." "I can't wait. Maybe she will give us a reading."

"Anna, you are always getting into that hocus-pocus part of everything. Maybe, *you* are a witch."

"Maybe? At least I am a good one." I laughed aloud. "Perhaps, I cast a love spell on you at Fudgy's Ice Cream."

"Are you serious? Now I know why I fell madly in love with you from the start." He kissed me on the back of my head and added, "My long-lost Sanderson sisters."

"Someday I will tell you the spell I used, but for now show me how much you love me and make love to me tonight."

"What? In my Dad's house." He raised his eyebrows. "Fine, you don't have to twist my arm."

"So, when are we going to bed?" As I winked at Drew and tiptoed to the bedroom, using my index finger for him to follow.

"Goodnight, Pops. See you in the morning."

As soon as we entered the bedroom, Drew closed and locked the door. Then he put down shades and turned off the lights.

"Paranoid, much?"

"No, I just feel weird making love to you in my father's house. Anna, you know I'm old fashion."

When he turned around I was standing there naked as a jaybird. "Get over here Mr. Old Fashion." Then I pushed him on the bed and climbed on top of him and whispered in his ear, "Thank you for the wonderful day. I am so happy being here with you."

"I am so glad you feel that way, now show me how happy you are Miss Hocus Pocus."

I slowly undressed him as if it was our first intimate night together. I needed to be close to him. I had to show him how much he meant to me. First, I went down on him, but he pulled me up to meet his lips. Our love-making was great, even though I could tell he was trying to be quiet and inconspicuous. Once again, we connected with each other in the darkness. It was kind, gentle, and yet kinky.

"I enjoyed that so much," he whispered in my ear.

Drew ran to the bathroom to wash up and he even brought me back a warm washcloth. "Wow, Anna that was fun." As he handed me the cloth. "We have to make love in the pitch dark more often. It felt like we were trying to hide from the world. Even in the dark, our passion for each other is strong."

"I feel the same way: sexy, wanted, and like I belong to you."

When I handed him the washcloth, he told me, "Bring your sexy to the shower, we have another big day planned for tomorrow and it starts at seven a.m." In the shower, we both realized how burnt we were. Our shoulders were flaming.

"Tomorrow we need to lather up with sunscreen," Drew said as he handed me two towels.

"Absolutely," I replied.

When I plugged my phone in I noticed I had a text from Drew's neighbor, Stacy. I read her text aloud, "Everything is good at the house. No burglaries or bear sightings so far and your passports are at the town hall. Hope you are having a good time. See you soon. Stacy."

"No bear sightings, that's a relief," he said and we both laughed. We finished our shower with brief lovemaking and returned to bed.

## Chapter 28

We were driving back from Jerome to John's house when we decided to go to the market to get the food for the dinner party. "What do we need, John?" I asked hoping for something new to try. "Do you have a menu in mind?"

Drew pulled over, put the car in drive, and turned around to look at me. "Anna, you are not even thinking about organizing this soiree? Ha-ha," he added and I stuck my tongue out at him.

"You are so humorous, Drew. I was married for many years and I cooked for three boys."

"Hey, you two," John said. "It's not my first dinner party."

"We know Dad. I just think it is funny my sweet Anna is even considering another event." Drew looked at me adding, "I like taking care of you. You deserve to be pampered for the rest of your life. Dad and I will do the shopping, preparing, and cooking."

"Drew, you earned the title 'saint' as far as I am concerned. You took care of your mother for many years. That couldn't have been easy and now you want to take care of me."

"I love you, Anna." He put the car in drive before adding, "And I have no regrets when it comes to my mom."

I saw his father nod and I wondered if he knew just how much Drew sacrificed his own heart for the sake of taking care of his mother. We rode in silence for the next few minutes. We pulled into the Safeway and I pushed the cart inside. After John handed us the list he turned and headed toward the cold cases. Drew and I headed down the first aisle.

I glanced down and said, "Looks like the menu is going to be chimichurri and chimichanga. We grabbed the chicken, refried beans, salsa, sour cream, Colby jack cheese, green onions, and a dozen avocados. "Wait, how many people are coming?" I asked wondering if we had enough food.

"Pops never told me, I better text him before we check out. How many of your friends are coming to the dinner party?"

"Ten people including you two."

"Anna, enough for ten. Can you run back and grab another package of chicken and a pack of wraps while I locate my father and tell him we are ready to leave? Wait, are you sure you are up to meeting everyone?"

I snapped my fingers and ran down the meat aisle. I suddenly felt like I was on that grocery shopping show, where you are only allowed a few minutes to get everything. "Oh no! I forgot the dessert. Shit, maybe I am a little rusty in the grocery store." Hurrying around the store, "Excuse me, excuse me, can I get through?" I finally got the extra ingredients and a box of chocolate cupcakes. Easy. Finding my way back up to the front of the store, I saw Drew and his father looking at me like I had three heads.

"I won, supermarket sweep."

"What?" his father said and shook his head. I laughed. "It was my favorite game show."

"Yeah, yeah. What's with the store made cupcakes?" Drew asked with a look of 'Oh, Anna!' on his face.

"There's a bakery on the way," his father added and I handed the box to the cashier.

"Sorry, I'm with the chef of the year."

John put the beer on the checkout counter next and then proceeded to pay for everything. "I insist," he said pushing Drew's hand away.

She laughed. "Let me guess. Chicken Chimichanga." "You're cute and clever," Drew said to her.

I snapped my neck to look at him. His father's eyes got wide. *Did he just flirt with the little blonde cashier?* "Let's get out of here," I said as I crossed my arms over my chest, covering my frozen nipples. I'm freezing my ass off. Why does it have to be fifty degrees inside?

Drew pushed the cart to the car. I sat in the backseat fuming.

"We still have to stop at the liquor store because according to your menu, the drink of the evening is going to be a Prickly Pear Margarita," Drew said as he put the car in drive.

"Make a right out of the parking lot and it is on your left about two blocks down the road."

I stayed in the car while Drew and his father went inside. We were bringing in the groceries inside when I slipped on one of those cacti in John's yard. "Dam, why can't you have grass like everyone else?"

"We are in the desert Anna," John explained to me as if I didn't know where the hell I was.

Drew set the last bag on the counter and yelled to his dad, "You have two messages on your home phone."

"Hit the button to listen to them," he hollered back. Drew picked up the pen and hit the button.

"John, it's Vera, I had a spirit visit me last night. I would like to come by and tell your son what it was all about."

"No way," John screamed. "It's happening! That damn nightmare is about to come true. I just can't deal with that nut."

I could tell that John was getting very upset. He started getting all red in the face and sweat beads were forming on his forehead. It was clear he was under some stress regarding this woman.

"John, how about we call her back and invite her to come by tonight? Instead of coming to the dinner party, we will have our own personal meeting. Make her feel like she is a special guest. Tell her we are so interested, we asked to meet with her privately. That way you won't be so stressed when your other friends are here."

"Anna has a point," Drew said agreeing with me. "What do you think?"

"Give me that phone, I'll call her." John dialed her number, and put the phone on speaker. She picked up after the first ring.

"John, I am so happy you returned my call, I need to talk to Drew right away."

"Yeah about that. We have to cancel tomorrow evening, but if you want to come by tonight for pizza and salad, Drew and Anna would like to meet you."

I whispered to Drew, "Cancel? If she is a real medium spiritualist, she will know he is not telling the truth."

Drew rolled his eyes, shook his head as if I didn't know what I was talking about.

Vera immediately accepted the invitation. "Yes, but I need to meditate before I come over, I have to let the spirits come through."

"We'll see you at six sharp," John said and gave us a smirk. "See all of you then."

He grabbed the menu for Pisa Lisa. "I'll order. I have to make sure we get a veggie pizza. Vera is a vegetarian."

"Pops, that doesn't surprise me at all," Drew said laughingly. "Me neither," I said.

"Yeah, yeah. What do you kids want on your pizza?" John picked the phone back up and dialed their number. "It's John, can I get two large pies, one all vegetables and the other pepperoni and sausage, two orders of garlic knots, and a large garden salad."

"What time do you want it delivered, Mr. Hart?" "At a quarter to six, please."

"No problem, see you soon."

Apparently, he must get takeout from this pizzeria place often.

Half an hour later the doorbell rings, and we all look at each other wondering.

## Chapter 29

John went to open the door, "It better not be the pizza all ready."

We were all surprised. It was Vera and man she was a winner for sure. Her hair was bright red, long, and snarly, almost like she was moving toward the dreadlock look. Her face was covered with makeup, not the usual concealer and eyeshadow, mascara, or blush. It was a little on the eccentric side. Her eyes were made up with thick black eyeliner, with wings that almost reached her ears. The eyeshadow was a sparkly purple that belonged to a twelve-year-old that didn't know any better. Her cheeks were as bright red as her hair. I had all I could do to not laugh. She looked like a clown. I couldn't help but notice she had a tattoo of a cross on her chest. She dressed kind of like a prostitute to meet John's family. Her clothing was a tie-dyed shirt that was cut down the breast area and jeans with holes in the knees, of course, her cowgirl boots bedazzled with purple rhinestones, matched her cowgirl hat. She smelled of patchouli. She held up a stalk of smoldering white sage. She almost knocked me over when she boldly pushed by us waving the burning bundle. "I need to cleanse the house and remove all the energy," she said. The three of

How the hell does she know what I said to his sisters? I could feel my face getting flushed. Drew reached over and rubbed my hand.

John stood up and said, "Enough! Vera that is enough. You have caused my son and his girlfriend pain. Get out of my house, now!" He walked abruptly toward the front door.

"But, I have more to tell them."

He picked up the rest of her pizza and handed it to her. "Here, consider it a donation. Goodbye!"

She left and not by choice. He pushed her out the door. John was so upset that she caused such a ruckus that he almost started to cry. He came back to the table and drank his beer, emptying his glass entirely. "She's gone, now let's eat our dinner in peace."

*How did she know about the dimes?* I was so struck by her reading that I didn't fully realize how angry and embarrassed John felt. And all the noise that just happened and died as soon she left.

Drew leaned over and hugged me as tight as he could. "Don't listen to her. You keep on loving me and dreaming about us all you want."

"Yes, but?"

"But what? The dimes. Anna, every time we find them you post about them on your Facebook page."

"You're right. She really had me for a minute. I was like how does she know all these personal things?"

"Calm down and eat your dinner."

"Yeah, I suppose you're right. Thank you for reassuring me. You do love me, right?"

"Of course, with all my heart and soul, Anna."

We ate dinner and there were no conversations as such after it, we just thanked John for our stay and retold our experiences at Sedona. But I couldn't let go of what Vera said. *Does she know more about us? Has she been studying us? How did she know what I said to Drew's sisters? What more she wanted to tell us?* For one moment I wanted that clown-looking witch to tell us the complete reading, I was fuming yet somewhat scared.

*'Is there an unseen trouble on our way to marriage? Is our relationship not going to last?*

The umbrella was up and high in the scathing hot desert. This was not the end I expected from my visit to Arizona.

## Chapter 30

As I go through all the photos I took from dinner, I asked "Are you boys finished with the cleanup? Let's all sit down and relax; we had a very emotional day with your crazy Vera. I honestly hope you don't see her anymore. She is a bundle of crazy!"

"Oh no Anna, you can be sure of that. Especially after tonight. I will be blocking all contact with her. Hand me my phone, son."

"Here Pops, I don't blame you on that one."

"Blocked from Facebook, blocked from my life. She's not treating my family like that and getting away with it."

The next few days were great. Drew helped me with getting rid of the nagging prediction Vera made. I found my interest and focus again on visiting Arizona. We visited Flagstaff for the day and the other day we went to this real-life Western show that served a chuck wagon supper while watching the western style stage show. It was fantastic. We thought we were really in a Western movie with gunshots, actors dressed as cowboys, and all. John teased us because he was only there about fifty times since he lived in Arizona. He kept on telling us what was going to happen next. He was so happy he got to experience it with us. Drew was fascinated with the costumes.

I caught him eyeing all the pretty cowgirls. And he caught me catching him eyeing the cowgirls.

Our last night was here and John and Drew were cooking for the dinner party. "Pops, what did you do with the jalapeno peppers? I need them to make homemade guacamole."

"Drew you are going all fancy on me; I just buy the jar stuff." "Oh, you and Anna both."

I ran over and slapped him in the butt, "Stop making fun of me all the time. I can't help it I am not a chef like you. But I am not complaining, you're a great cook."

John shouts over to me "Anna, could you please set the table for eight?" "Where are the paper products?"

"Anna we are using my Mexican-style dinnerware tonight. They are in the cabinet." John points to the dining room china cabinet."

I grabbed all the plates, bowls, cups, and saucers for eight. "What about serving bowls? I see those here too."

"Yes, grab those too, it's going to look very festive here tonight. Let's even play dance music tonight. I love asking my Google to play whatever I want. That was the best gift you gave me. I have been enjoying it so much. It's almost company for me."

"I am so glad, Pops."

The doorbell rang, John opened the door and there everyone was, all his friends and neighbors. He introduced us to everyone. He has a lot of nice friends. Everyone was so happy to meet Drew and me. He must talk about us a lot because they knew everything about us.

John brought everyone into the living room and introduced us. "Everyone, this is my son Drew and his girlfriend Anna. This is their last night here; they leave for Connecticut early tomorrow morning. Kids, this is Pete and his wife Carrie, they live next door. Over here is my friend Lance, he has been my friend since the first day I moved here, he lives in Cottonwood, and this is my friend Mary and her three grandsons, Carl, Donald, and Nicholas. Mary has her grandsons live with her to assist her with daily living. She's so lucky to have her family care for her."

"So nice to meet everyone, I am so glad my Dad has so many friends around here. I hate that he lives here all alone, but now I feel better that he has all of you."

"Thank you all for keeping him out of trouble." Lance spoke up, "John where's V tonight?"

"Do not bring her name up in this house, especially tonight, she was already over here. Shook up the whole house."

"Okay, understood," as Lance took his finger and circled his ears. "She's a real crazy one. I hope you all are fine. And I am sorry John you had to go through it." Lance patted John's shoulder as a gesture of consolation.

'Well, after what she did and said John does need a consolation.' I truly felt embarrassed for him and a second-hand embarrassment for Vera, what a fool she made out of herself.

"Everyone take a seat, let's get this party started. Google play party music, and everyone, grab my famous Prickly Pear Margarita."

The music was just what we needed; it changed the aura of the room. Everyone enjoyed the music and the very delicious meal made by the Hart men. Mary's sons cleaned up the table and loaded the dishwasher. You could tell they were really good boys. She is lucky to have a family like that to take care of her. You could tell she was very feeble and needed help. It always warmed my heart whenever I saw a family coming together and being there whenever you need them the most. Tonight, warmed up my heart.

We all said our goodbyes while we walked everyone out to their cars. Drew walked Lance home.

Drew was going to give Lance his number and ask him to call

us if he thought there was something we needed to know. I think Drew felt a little guilty knowing we were leaving in the morning and his father would be alone again.

"Anna, I gave Lance my number as you suggested. He said he would check in on him more often and let us know if anything was going on we needed to know about."

"'That's' perfect. We have eyes and ears on him now."

"Let's go to bed Anna, we have a very long plane ride to Bradley tomorrow. I am almost thinking of getting a car service to take us to the airport instead of Pops driving. It's been a long tiring week for him. It's a long ride back in the car alone."

"Whatever you think Drew. Would your Dad be upset if we did that?"

"It doesn't matter, I don't want him to have that long drive back. You know I probably could ask Lance. He did ask who was taking us to the airport and he looked a little concerned when I said my Dad."

"Pops, we are going to ask Lance to take us tomorrow, is that ok with you?"

"You know, I was going to see if you could ask one of Mary's grandsons to take you. I just don't feel strong enough to do it."

I could tell Drew was upset when his father admitted he was having some troubles with his health. He is used to seeing his father much stronger.

John came into the room and said, "I already called Mary and she was going to send Carl to pick you two up at six in the morning. Make sure you are ready, sometimes the traffic to the airport is heavy. You don't want to miss your plane."

"Alright then we have to go to bed, are you getting up with us, Pops?" "Of course, see you in the morning. I will have coffee ready for you two." "Goodnight."

Six a.m. came fast, and we were all ready and waiting on the porch for Carl to come. Before we left, we had coffee that John specially brewed for us, and for sure it tasted unusually delicious this morning. I insisted he let me know the secret ingredient, but he refused saying he would save the same coffee for our next visit, and hopefully as a couple. I knew I blushed a little at that remark, however, our tight schedule didn't allow us to sit and banter some more. Soon enough, Carl pulled into the driveway with a black BMW 740 Sedan. It was beautiful and looked very comfy. I guess Grandma had some money.

"Good morning, Carl, thanks for taking us, we really appreciate you doing this for us. Get in the back Anna."

"I would do anything for John. He is an awesome man. He is my grandma's good friend. Hey, you guys have a safe trip. Nice to meet you, hope to see you back soon."

Before we knew it, we were at the airport and waiting to board Delta flight 416 to Bradley International Airport.

## Chapter 31

At nine a.m., we boarded the airplane. Found our seats and of course, we fought over the window seat. I won. Twenty minutes later, the captain said loud and clear, "Buckle your seatbelts, we are about to take off."

As soon as we were in flight, Drew and I both fell asleep. I woke up and realized that we had slept the entire five hours. I looked at Drew and said, "The Arizona heat kicked our asses." I nudged him, "Honey, wake up. We are home."

Drew took my hand in his. "I love the way that sounds."
"What?" I smiled at him.
"*We* are home."
"Yes, and we are back to colder weather. I can hardly handle when we change our clocks back every year, let alone being in a different time zone."

"I'll make sure you go to bed early tonight." I thought he was going to reach up and grab our carry-on, but instead, he lifted me up out of my seat and stuck his tongue in my ear, and then whispered, "We have a lot of catching up to do."

"Catch up? What kind of game is that? Can we play in the dark?"

I winked. "Huh?"

"There is something about plane rides and watermelon gummies that turn me on."

"And I thought it was all me." He lifted our baggage down and walked down the aisle.

I followed him wondering if he was upset by my joke.

As soon as we got in the car, he turned on the radio. He must have turned on the radio to change the subject or to shut me up.

"Drew, you know me so well. I need my tunes to sing on our rides. I started singing, "Daddy" by Tyler Wood. I looked at him and said, "I miss him already."

"Who? Carl?" He slapped my leg. "Yeah, I miss him too. It was a good time, we made lots of memories and I am glad he got to meet you."

"Meeting your father meant the world to me. Thank you for an amazing trip. I will never forget the magical memories we shared there."

I sang all the way home and before I knew it we were in the driveway. Of course, Drew had to honk the horn letting the entire neighborhood know we were home. I laughed when Greg and Stacy came running out of their house.

"How was your trip?" They both asked.

Stacy hugged Drew first and then me. "You know I have your passports." "Yes, I told Drew when you texted me. He was so happy you did that for us.

Thank you so much. I can't believe you made it happen!" "You guys get settled in and we will see you soon."

"Yes, we have to get together for another barbecue and I will tell you all about our amazing trip."

"That sounds good, I will text you during the week."

Drew asked me, "Where do you want your suitcases? He looked at me as if I had a choice. "In the house or in your back seat?"

It was Sunday night and I had to work the next day. I replied, "In the back seat."

"I don't want you driving home if you are tired. Let's have a cup of coffee, then you can head home."

I tilted my head and replied, "Can we watch an episode of Mad Men?"

After he put my luggage in my car, I followed him inside. While he made the coffee, I turned off airplane mode on my phone and the dings started coming in. All three of my sons left the same text: *"Mom, are you home yet?"* Andrea also left me a message, *"Hope you had a great time and can't wait to see you at work tomorrow."* I smiled from the inside out and read his father's message aloud, "I hope you made it home safely. Miss you guys already. It was nice to meet you." I text each of them back home, "Home, safe and sound."

Drew kissed the back of my head and said, "I microwaved some popcorn for you." He set the two cups of coffee and bowl on the coffee table.

Our coffee was in clear cups and I noticed he even had frothed milk on top. It looked so tasty. "Aww just what I needed." It reminded me of our trip to a Barista Coffee Shop. I took a big sip.

Drew leaned over, wiped my milk mustache, and kissed me. When he sat down next to me he appeared sad. "I am going to be so lonely tonight without you. I wish you would stay, you could always get up early and drive to work from here." He looked at me and I melted. "Please?"

I felt his eyes on me, but it was just too much. "It's a long drive and I have a lot to do at home before I go in to work. I have not been there in so long. I am sure my desk is piling up with more than I can handle."

He exhaled.

As soon as Mad Men went off, he kissed me goodbye before I even stood up. "Make sure you keep your window down and turned the radio way up."

I sang all the way home. As soon as I pulled into the parking lot, I saw lights, cameras, and people everywhere. Yay! Great, I still have a chance to meet the Hulk. I grabbed my luggage and headed to my door, and when I did I saw Hank looking out his window. I waved for him to see me. He opened his window and shouted, "Welcome home Savannah. We missed you around here. Do you need any help with your things?"

"No, I am good," I hollered back and then asked, "Is he here?"

"No, I haven't seen him. Hey, I will be down tomorrow with your envelope from the landlord."

"Okay, thanks, Hank. See you then."

Of course, my neighbors Bela and Orshi heard all the commotion going on outside and they both popped their heads out their door and softly said, "Glad to see you home safe, dear."

"Thanks, I had a wonderful time, Drew's Dad is such a cool guy." "Savannah, that's a big step you know, meeting his father."

"I know, it's getting serious. I think?"

"We can have a cup of iced tea on the porch tomorrow after you come home from work, and you can tell us all about your trip."

"I would love that."

I dropped all of my belongings onto the floor and made myself a cup of soothing Sleepy Time tea. It took me a while to unwind, I put some of my clothes away and looked through my mail. I was glad I decided to come home. I picked out my clothes for work, and I grabbed a can of soup for lunch since I had nothing in the house to make. I rinsed my cup out and climbed into bed, sent Drew a quick text, "I'm home." When he didn't reply I figured he was hurt by my going home.

*'I still love you, Drew Hart, with all my heart.'* I whispered to his photo I had in my phone. I looked through the photos, smiling

at each one of them. *'We actually look good together.'* I thought and felt myself feeling sleepy. *'Guess, the tea has kicked in.'* I put my phone on the side, after checking the alarms and closed my eyes.

When I got to work, everyone was there ahead of me, except for my friend. His desk was empty. It was my first time at work without my dear friend, Mr. Fred. It was such a sad feeling.

Andrea came over to my desk with a small bouquet of tulips from Adams Fairacre Farms. She said, "We all thought you might need a little bit of cheering up today."

"Yeah, I know it seems so strange, him not being here."

Andrea hugged me. "I'm glad you're back. You look fabulous. I'm so jealous of your tan."

"I'd like to say it feels good to be back, but honestly, I am exhausted." I looked at her and as if she knew what I was about to say, we both said in unison, "Lunchtime."

Then I looked at my inbox and of course, it was overflowing with paperwork. It was time to get back to reality. And the reality was tiring, before lunchtime I was exhausted, it felt like I had run a marathon. But with my brain and not my legs.

My tummy was growling so loudly. I did not have to look up at the clock to know it was noon.

I saw Andrea stand up and waved me over. "Come on, let's take our lunchtime walk." She held up a brown paper bag. "I made your favorite sandwich and I even grabbed you your own bag of chips." She flashed me a smile. "I knew you would not have time to go grocery shopping."

"You're right, my cupboards are bare. Thank you so much for thinking of me."

We both grabbed our sunglasses and headed out the door. We ate our lunch at the picnic table outside our office building.

"Andrea, this turkey and cheese sandwich is delicious, I love the pretzel roll, and oh that Dijon mustard is yummy. You are very creative, this is a gourmet lunch if you asked me. Have you cooked for Randy yet? You are such a good cook."

"You do realize I only made you a sandwich right? I really didn't take much time making it. Do you even cook anymore?"

"Not really." I replied and then added, "We eat out a lot and Drew enjoys making dinner for me when I am at his place. He is a fantastic cook. He told me we were going to make homemade sushi this week. That's going to be fun. He showed me the seaweed paper and the bamboo rolling mats. His mom must've taught him. I think I am going to buy some sake for that night."

"You two have been having such a fun life since you met each other. I normally would have been jealous, but, I have Randy. We are enjoying each other and we're getting very close. We are really connected in every way."

"*Every* way?"

"No, not like that Savannah. We are taking it slow in that department. We were almost at that point, he asked me to stay over one night when we got home late from a date and I did, but we just cuddled. It was so nice."

"Oh, I forgot something. Wait here." I ran to my car and got the bag of goodies I brought back from Arizona for the office gals. "This is for you, I got it from the Trading Post." It was a sterling silver toe ring with a beautiful turquoise dragonfly on the top.

"It's beautiful, I love turquoise. You are so thoughtful."

"Arizona is a very spiritual place, dragonflies are a symbol of peace and harmony. Everywhere we looked we saw them. Even in the airport, the floors had them in the tile all through it."

"Wow, that's cool, thank you so much."

"You're welcome," I said as she gave me the biggest hug. "Now let's go for our walk."

"So, how was Drew's dad? Did you like him? Did he like you?"

"Yes and yes. We had a wonderful time and made a lot of memories. Drew was very proud to show his father his newfound love."

"Awe that's so nice, I can't wait to see all the pictures you took. The ones on Facebook are so beautiful, maybe someday I can visit there."

"Maybe, this week you can come over and we can get a pizza and I will show you everything. I actually took about one thousand pictures. I'll put them on a slideshow for you. Watching them on the seventy-five-inch television makes it feel like you are right there. I will let you know what night is good."

"Perfect. I'll bring the beer. Bud Light Orange, right?" "Good memory, girlfriend."

"Back to work we go, lunchtime is not long enough. But, I have plenty to do."

Three o'clock came fast, I knew my neighbors would be waiting for me. They are so anxious to hear about my trip. As soon as I came around the corner of the building, I could hear Orshi talking Hungarian to Bela. She must be bossing him around, usually when they don't speak to each other in English. She was arguing with him. "Savannah, you're home from work." She dropped her argument and turned to walk toward me.

"Yes, let me change into my comfy clothes and I'll be right over." I love wearing my tee shirts and baggy shorts after work. Especially since all I have been doing is eating lately. Things are starting to get tight on me. "I'm all yours now." The table looked so cute. It was all decorated with a cardinal theme. "Where did you get this tablecloth? It's beautiful. Look, you have matching plates and cups too. This is lovely, thank you for having me over." I took a sip. "This tea is so good."

"It's sun tea," she said. "It's been brewing all day, did you notice there was no sugar in it? Bela wanted me to add some sweetness to it."

"It was just perfect. Your porch gets all the sun during the day. Someday I will retire and enjoy my porch. It's so peaceful, you have it decorated so beautifully with all the hanging plants. Look at those petunias, how many colors do those flowers come in?"

"Aren't they lovely? Our daughter brought that over last week when she visited. She must have stopped by Adams before she came. They have some gorgeous hanging baskets. Now tell us all about your trip."

"It was like nothing else in the world I have ever seen. The natural beauty was spectacular, it was very spiritual and the company was wonderful."

"So you like Drew's Dad?"

"Yes, he was a great host and he loved having us around. I really enjoyed getting to know him. I loved seeing the bond between Drew and his dad. It was like they picked up where they left off. I think after his dad divorced his mom, there was some tension at first for a while, which is expected. They must have worked it out. Oh, and we got to meet his crazy ex-girlfriend. Let's save that for another iced tea time story."

"You have me curious now, I won't let you forget to tell me that one."

"I won't. I have to get going, Drew is supposed to call me soon. It seems so odd that we are not together, it's only been one night since we returned from our trip."

Alexa was ringing. I quickly fixed my hair. I was so excited to see Drew's name pop up. My heart was actually racing.

"Hello, Mr. Hart."

"Well hello, Ms. Anna. How was your first day back to work?"

"It was good, Andrea brought me a bag lunch and we ate outside before our walk. Of course, my desk was filled with paperwork and my computer had tons of emails to read. But, it was nice to see everyone. Oh, they bought me a bouquet of tulips for my desk. They wanted to cheer me up since it was the first day back without my pal being there."

"That is so nice of them. Andrea is a good friend to you, how's her love life going?"

"Good, she seems happy with Randy. I think they're a perfect match."

"Maybe they could come over for dinner, here at my place. I would love to cook for them."

"Sounds perfect. I will set it up for next week sometime."

"Speaking of next week, I have good news and bad news. Good news is I want you to come to Block Island with me, a customer has a house there that needs some electrical work on it and he offered me to stay the whole weekend. Bad news is I won't be able to see you until Friday because I have a big job I must finish before leaving."

"Oh. My. God. I have always wanted to go there. Count me in. What time are we leaving?" I was doing a happy dance. Literally, jumping up and down.

"Oh, good you're excited. Friday night, we'll take the late ferry from Point Judith."

"Drew, life is good with you by my side. Bye, honey." I grabbed my phone and immediately Googled things to do in Block Island.

My eyes lit up brighter than the phone after asking Google, "What is there to do on Block Island?" 'Known for its bicycling, hiking, sailing, fishing, and beaches. Glass Float Project, Mohegan Bluffs, and the self-guided bike tours.' I felt like calling Drew and asking him to put our bikes on the back of his work van. My mind was running in many directions. I wanted to make the most of our time there, too. There were so many exciting things we could do together. How much could we get in a weekend? Drew will be working most of the day, but our evenings will be free for all this excitement. And nights too, I laughed at the naughty thought.

*'Ahh, life is so good with Drew.'* I swiped the photos of the place

and couldn't wait for us to be there.

## Chapter 32

Drew was very busy all week working and I hadn't seen him since Sunday night. He is such a hard-working man. I missed him so much, it was the first time we were apart for that long without seeing each other. Each day I kept changing the itinerary learning more about the island and what it had to offer. I can't wait until we leave this afternoon. I left the office at three o'clock and it was finally Friday. Before I got to my car, my cell phone rang.

"Anna, I've been busy and I apologize for not communicating with you the details of our trip. Could you be here at four-forty-five? Pack up your bathing suit and some sundresses and active wear and bring your hiking boots. We are going to go orb hunting."

"What is that?"

"It's actually called The Glass Float Project. I will tell you all about it on the car ride to the ferry."

I immediately joined their Facebook page and got all the inside information about this interesting hunt. I threw together my weekend bag and headed over to Drew's. I was so excited and intrigued by this island adventure we were about to embark on.

"Glad you made it so quickly Anna, you must be delighted to

take this trip. I haven't had time to even think about fun on the island, it's going to be all work for me. Well, not all work, of course, some play too."

"And that is where I come in," I hugged him and kissed him on his neck.

I threw my bag in the back of the work van and sat in the front seat waiting for Drew to load some of the material he needed to work on the house with.

Drew hopped up in the driver's seat, looked at me, and said, "Well, this is a first for you. Are you ready to be my apprentice for the weekend?"

"Of course, I can't wait."

"Our ferry leaves at seven tonight, so we will be right on time. So, the Glass Float Project, what do you know about it so far?"

"Oh yes, I read about it. I hope we find one. It says here that you have to register the number of the orb and where you found it on their website. Sounds like a really fun scavenger hunt. It says the Glass Station Company hides five hundred and fifty orbs every year. Each orb is numbered and dated. They keep inventory that way."

"Maybe we will be lucky and find one. I just joined the Facebook page for Glass Float Project. It looks so fascinating. Everyone who finds one posts a pictures of themselves holding it. Look at these happy faces. I hope we find one."

"How do you like riding in the van? It's different from what you are used to, we are always either in the Jeep or the BMW."

"Doesn't matter as long as I am with you. There is something that I don't like about it."

"What's that?"

"I am so far away from you, I can't reach you to hold your hand or sneak a kiss in, these damn seat belts."

"You can sneak in as many kisses as you want once we get to the house. You are going to love this place. It's right on the ocean."

"I feel like I am in a spaceship here, it's so high up in the air and I can't believe the dashboard is lit up like a UFO."

"I know, I still haven't figured out this new van of mine. There are so many bells and whistles in this thing."

"As long as I don't have to drive it. I can just sit back and sing. Where's the radio?"

"That is the only thing I have figured out so far. Eighties station?" "Of course." I sang all the way to Point Judith.

We made it right on time for the ferry. Drew backed up the UFO, aka, the work van and we got out and took the stairs to the top of the deck. "Do you want a cocktail?"

I looked around. "They have a bar on here?" "Yes, they have some snacks too."

"I'm impressed. I'll have a bloody Mary."

"Let's go outside and watch for the dolphins."

"There are dolphins here?"

"Oh yes, there are."

"I feel like a child who is excited to watch dolphins. This is so exciting."

Drew grabbed my hand and led me outside. He put his arm around me and kissed my cheek. "I have missed this all week."

"I missed you too, but I was busy searching the internet on Block Island all week."

"We just got back from Arizona and you are all set for another adventure." "Honestly, it doesn't matter what or where we go, I just love spending time with you. The more we spend time together I realize how much you mean to me." "You are so sweet Anna, I love you." As he moved my hair that was blowing in my face.

"It's so windy out here, can we go in now?"

"We should go down to the van in a few minutes anyway. We should be pulling up to the island in about fifteen minutes."

I couldn't believe all the vehicles that were on the ferry, everything from tractors, trailers, trucks to motorcycles. The ferry apparently didn't look like it could hold all these vehicles. Or these vehicles weren't that heavy, after all. Finally, it was our turn to disembark off the ship.

"This is so beautiful and exciting. How far is it to the house?"

Drew laughed. "The island is only about six miles long and nine miles wide." "Great! We need to find an orb. I plan on hunting every inch of this place." "First, we have to work and then we can play."

"You're right, I am just loving this island magic."

We pulled into the driveway and the first thing I saw was a painted rock showing the number of the house with a blue anchor. It appeared as if most of the homes had a painted rock at the end of their driveway.

"Ready to see the house?"

"Yes, as I heard the waves playing in the background. This is amazing, I am not going to be able to sleep. I'm too excited being this close to the ocean."

"You really have been sheltered. I am so glad that I am the one to let you experience all these adventures. Now let's take a tour of the house. The owner sent me pictures of all the rooms, so I am familiar with the house. We have six bedrooms to choose from."

"Six? I want to see all of them, please. Then I will pick one, or I could pick two because we are going to be here for two nights."

"Whatever you want."

Drew took me through the whole house, each room was decorated with a different theme. I picked the mermaid room for the first night and the lobster room for the second night. The mermaid room was painted sea green, with all of the accessories being mermaid related. There was a ten-jet tub right there in the room and a king-size bed. The attached bathroom had a huge shower with two shower heads and a handheld sprayer. The room had French doors opening up to a beautiful deck facing the ocean. "I swear I could sleep right here tonight. I love the sound of the waves."

"Would you like to sleep on the sand next to the ocean? I will send you down with a pillow and a blanket."

"Stop making fun of me, I'm just so excited."

"I know, I'm sorry. It's just funny to see you react to some of these new experiences you are having."

"Can we go out to eat tonight? There are so many great restaurants here on the island."

"Really? How do you know that?" "Google, duh."

"Of course. Sure, pick a place. I will unload the tools and material off the van while you look."

I looked and found a cute little bar with a great menu and it had good reviews. "Drew, I like Club Soda."

## Chapter 33

As soon as Drew finished unloading his work van, we headed over to the restaurant. We called an Uber to come get us because Drew didn't want to drive the van around the island.

I heard Drew holler at me from the porch. "The Uber will be here in 10 minutes, are you ready?"

I yelled back, "Yes, I am. Can we take a walk on the beach afterward? I will wear my flip-flops and grab a sweatshirt."

"Yes, that sounds great after we eat. We can walk off our dessert."

"It will be so romantic, I can't wait." I picked out a sweatshirt and made my way to where Drew was standing waiting for the Uber. *Something tells me Drew isn't the kind of guy you would want to keep waiting, especially when it comes to services like Uber. I hope that Uber guy isn't roaming around and is on time. I don't want his mood spoiled.*

Our Uber driver was right on time. We got in the back seat and Drew said, "Thirty-five Connecticut Avenue please."

"Oh you are going to Club Soda, that's the coolest dive bar I have ever been to, you two will love it."

I swear we were only in the car for five minutes and we were there. Drew paid the driver and we got out. We could smell the delicious food cooking as we walked in. Drew pointed to the wall. "Look what it says."

It was a huge poster that read: "I love/heart Dive Bars, Block Island, RI."

We both looked at each other and I said, "Dive Bar, oh no. I hope it's going to be good."

The bartender came over to the table with some silverware and napkins. He asked what we wanted to drink and handed us each a menu. Then he told us they were having an 'open mike' night.

'What's open mike mean?' I whispered to Drew.

Drew looked at me and said, "Anyone can go up to the stage and sing."

"Oh, wow, maybe I will sing. You know I love those eighties."

"No, let's just eat and get out of here, we have a beach calling our names tonight."

We ordered our drinks and our meals all at once so we could hurry and get our walk-in. We both had a beer and the Club Soda Special – a cheeseburger. As we waited for our dinners, we looked around the bar. There was so much to see, beautiful artwork by a local artist that wrapped around the walls, all different kinds of games to play, and an old-fashioned jukebox. It truly was a real cool dive bar just as the Uber driver had described. You could tell the bar was filled with locals, and everyone seemed to know each other.

The bartender came over with our beers. "Your burgers and fries will be out in a few minutes. Did you want dessert?"

"Yes, we will split the bananas fosters," I replied.

"Great choice, I'll make sure it comes out right after you finish your meal," he said.

"I think he surmised that we were in a hurry," Drew said.

I nodded. Our dinner and dessert were even better because we got to enjoy the locals singing their hearts out. I wanted to stand at that mic so bad. No one sang an eighties song but the locals here had real talent at singing, specifically the young girl with an electric guitar, it felt like she was having a concert and we all were her audience grooving to her voice.

"That was very entertaining," I said as we paid our bill and told the bartender, what a great meal and we will be back again. I whispered in Drew's ear, "Now, we get to go for our whimsical stroll on the beach, you know we are sleeping in the mermaid room tonight."

"Yes, are you implying we might see one tonight?" "No, I just love being out here right next to the ocean."

Drew took my hand and we walked from the bar to an access to the ocean. It was just starting to get dark. We walked for at least an hour straight. The smell of the ocean was so relaxing, that I felt myself breathing it in and exhaling as hard as I could. I just couldn't get enough of it.

"Let's buy a house and move here."

"Are you crazy, these houses are millions of dollars." He stopped walking. "Unless you are a millionaire and you're keeping it a secret from me."

"No. I am only wishing. Look up, there's a falling star. Make a wish Drew, I know I am. It's just so perfect here. Thank you for bringing me along on this job."

"You're welcome. You know we have to work really hard tomorrow. I'd like to finish up so we can have the whole evening and Sunday morning to enjoy the island."

"I promise I will be the best apprentice you ever had." "Anna, I have never had anyone work with me before." "Well then, I guess I will be the best one."

"Yes, you will."

We walked a little and Drew and I mentally visualized our house, if it was here. "You know, it would have all glass walls," Drew said.

"That's risky, but really amazing. And oh, we can have our house only in shades of black, grey, and white."

"And you draw that inspiration from a movie?

"Of course, I have seen such houses and they look stunning, just extraordinary."

"I like those shades, though, make your house seem mysterious." "But we are definitely going to have a mermaid room."

"Heck yeah, the only colorful room in our black and white house." "It would be really nice, wouldn't it?"

"It would be." Drew smiled and we continued the rest of our walk in silence. Before we knew it we were back at the house. Drew looked at me and asked,

"Are you going to be my sexy mermaid tonight?"

"You bet I am, on our walk, I kept imagining the two of us all alone in this gorgeous ocean-view house. Oh, all the things we could do." I reached for his hand and we headed up the stairs to our Friday night suite. "I swear, if we were staying a few more days, I would sleep in every bedroom in the house. A different one each night."

"Oh, that could be very exciting, but for now let's enjoy our room tonight.

Would you like to relax in the Jacuzzi tub first?"

"Yes, I swear there is sand in every nook and cranny on my body." Drew filled up the tub and said, "Come on, let's make a splash." "Are you going to fall in love with me tonight Tom Hanks?"

"I am already in love with you, my beautiful mermaid."

The jets were on and we were in bliss. Drew grabbed me over to him and sat me on his lap. I could feel he was very excited. I sat on top of him and guided his cock inside me. Drew grabbed my face and started kissing me so passionately. It was so erotic, the sound of the jets reminded me of ocean waves. It felt like we were making love in the ocean. It was so exciting for me. Nothing like the first Jacuzzi tub together in Mystic. We were more connected, emotionally and physically. The tub jets stopped and so did my heart.

"Did we break it?"

"No, it has a timer on it." Drew laughed. "That's one of the things on the list from the owner for me to check out. He mentioned the timer wasn't working properly."

I inhaled and replied, "Should we restart it and go another cycle?"

"No, let's get out. I have better plans for our night, right over there on that king-sized bed." Drew winked at me, "Come on my sweetness, and let me make love to you."

I looked at him and realized how much I loved him, that dimple and every damn thing about him.

"Wait," Drew said, "Let me go get a bottle of wine and a couple of glasses for us. The owner told me to help myself to anything, including his wine cellar."

"Oh sure, I could enjoy a glass of fine wine tonight."

Drew came back with a bottle of Alter Ego, Margaux-2019. "This was the cheapest bottle I could find down there."

"Should we even open it? We should put it back."

"No, he said to take anything from the cellar."

"Alright, let's open it, I saw an opener on the end table over there."

Drew opened it and he poured us each a glass, it smelled rich. It was delicious.

I raised my glass and made a toast.

"Cheers to us, life is too short to drink bad wine."

"I agree, but normally we wouldn't be drinking a two-hundred-dollar bottle of wine."

"True, but let's enjoy it while we can."

We sipped the delicious wine trying to enjoy each sip, it was so smooth. Before we knew it, we drank the whole thing. "Get in this bed now, we have to get up early, we have work tomorrow."

"Yes, I know my boss. But let's do this first. As I jumped on top of him and started riding him like a horse. We made love until we both climaxed."

"Well, I think we should buy more wine for ourselves, more often. And that's without your famous gummies."

"I'm glad you enjoyed it, now let's get some sleep. I promise to be the best apprentice."

"Goodnight sweetheart." Then he kissed my forehead.

## Chapter 34

The alarm went off at six a.m. I looked at Drew and said, "It's not a dream, last night was wonderful. Everything about it, the dinner, beach walk, and the sex was like a fantasy come true."

"You're my fantasy, my dream that came true." He stroked my hair and rested my face in his palm.

"I love you, my handsome," I blew a kiss to him.

"I love you more. But today I need my apprentice. So, let's get up my mermaid, it's time to buckle on your work belt for the day. I'll meet you down in the basement. I ordered breakfast sandwiches from Door Dash, it's sitting on the table with a glass of orange juice."

"Thank you, I'll eat and report for duty as soon as I finish."

I grabbed my work clothes and work boots, got dressed, ate my breakfast, and met Drew down stairs.

"That was fast, I guess you are taking this job very seriously."

"Well, the sooner we get it done, the more we get to explore the island.

Remember orb hunting?"

"Oh yes, pray to the island gods that we find one today."

Drew was concentrating on the service panel box. "Oh yes, I see where the problem is." He pointed. "Right here. This is such an easy fix, when I replace some of these fuses, the owner's troubles might be gone."

I pulled my chin in. "As easy as that?"

"Cross your fingers and pray again to the island gods."

Just as soon as he replaced the fuses and I saw the look on his face – it was literally like a light bulb went off.

"It should be all fixed, go upstairs and check those lights in the bedrooms that were having problems, and go plug in your blow dryer in those outlets that I pointed out were not working."

I raced up the stairs, hoping the problem was fixed. I thought we could start our orb hunting real early and do all the things I had on my list to do for today. Sure enough, everything worked. I screamed down the basement stairs, "Drew it's all fixed, I think that was the issue the whole time."

"Oh really, you're sure? You are a very fast learner for your first day on the job as an apprentice. Only teasing you, yes it was the problem. Let's shower and get our hiking boots on."

I went up the stairs and jumped into the huge shower. Not sure why, but when I was singing my heart out, I felt like I was an American Idol contestant, the acoustics was amazing in there. My song for the judges was 'Happy by Pharrell Williams.' Drew came up the stairs laughing at me.

"Yes, Anna I realize you are so happy. You sound like you have a microphone in the shower with you."

"I know, it's amazing, come join me."

"Well, I will but I'm not sure about joining in on your singing. It will have to be a solo."

"But duets are so fun."

"Sorry, you don't want me as your partner for this."

As soon as the song was over, we dressed and were ready for the day.

"I saw last night that the island has cheap gas. I'd like to fill the old gas hog before we leave on Sunday."

"Let's do it now before we get so excited after we find our glass orb and forget all about it," I said.

We pulled up to the gas station, it was a little hole in the wall. I guess you can't have a big corporate gas station on a little island like this. Drew left the van running and jumped out.

"Sweetheart, grab my wallet, it's in the middle console." "Here you go, hurry Drew."

I sat there tapping my foot thinking come on, make this fast, I want to start our adventure. I could hear the gas gobbling down to the bottom. "Were we empty?"

"Almost, it's so cheap here. I am almost finished. I just have to go inside and pay. Do you want anything? I am getting a couple of bottles of water for our hunt."

"Good. It's supposed to be very hot and muggy today."

My nose was glued to my phone. I was on the Glass Project's Facebook page. I saw someone already found one this morning. "Hurry Drew, we are wasting precious hunting time. Next, I heard Drew's phone ding with a text. I figured it was the owner checking in. I lifted my head up from my phone and saw his fancy dashboard all lit up.

The text was displayed on the screen for anyone to read: "I know you are busy, but could you add ME to your list of things to do? When you were here last week you never said when you were coming back. Eve."

After I read it, my heart sank to the floor. *What the fuck was that message about? Who is Eve and why is she texting my man.* I started feeling nauseous and sweating bullets. I felt like I was going to faint. What does she mean add me to your list to do? Do what? I have never heard the name Eve out of his mouth ever, and why did she say it when you were over last week? Wait, I didn't see him all week long last week. Did he spend time with her last week? He said he has a lot of work to do before our trip to Block Island. Was his work called Eve? Who is this bitch? I immediately took his phone and deleted the message, I checked his list of Facebook friends named Eve. I saw no one. He has over one thousand friends and not one named Eve. Maybe that is her nickname. All these crazy things were going through my head. I think my heart might be broken. Is Drew the man I thought he was? Am I naive in this game of dating? Maybe he is a player and I am just a fling for him. I can't even think straight right now. Oh no, here he comes.

"Here is your water, my love, I got us a couple of Danishes too. It's a cute little store inside. The people were so friendly. Sorry, it took so long. Anna, are you okay?"

Drew looked at me and knew something was wrong. "What's the matter? You look like you saw a ghost. Block Island is known for its ghosts. They even have Ghost Tours in town. Anna, we could call and sign up for the tour for tomorrow if you would like" in it.

I looked at Drew and grabbed the closest plastic bag I could find and threw up. "Oh my god, what's wrong, why did you throw up, was it the egg sandwich from this morning?"

"No Drew, I want to go home now!"

"Well, the good thing is we are only five minutes away. I'll get you there in no time and I will drop you off and go get some Ginger Ale for you."

"NO! I want to go home to Pleasant Valley." "What? Why? Please tell me."

The whole time getting back to the beach house I continued to throw up. I never experienced this before. *I think I am dying from a broken heart.*

*Eve, who is this Eve? I am a side chick, after all, all this was too good to be true. How can I be so stupid to think this dream-like life was something that could happen in real life? I felt used. 'A thing to do,'* who talks like that? What are they doing? Drew, out of all people, I never thought he would betray me like this. I loved him. Did he not love me? All this time, he didn't love me. I felt disgusted at myself, for being used, for being so open, and for loving so dearly.

## Chapter 35

The ferry ride seemed longer than before. Maybe, because it was a quiet one. I refused to get out of the van. I went as far as to pretend I was sleeping. On any other day, I would have taken his sweet gesture as kind and loving. Drew grabbed a blanket out of the back of the van and put it over me. He had no clue what was wrong. Laying back in the reclined position I had a lot of time to think about the situation. It was killing me not to say anything. Maybe, it is a big misunderstanding? *The Drew I know would never sneak around behind my back. Would he?* I started to cry.

"Anna, wake up." He nudged my side. "I'm stopping at a store. Do you need anything for your belly?"

I looked over and shook my head. "Are you sure?"

I nodded.

"Should we stop at an Urgent Care? I am really concerned about you." Barely making eye contact, I gently said, "I just need to go home."

"We will be home in about a half-hour. Hold on, sweetheart. As soon as I get you all tucked in I will make you a cup of hot tea."

"No, I want to be in my own bed in Pleasant Valley. I want to go home."

Drew looked at me with concern and confusion. "Can you tell me why you want to go home? Are you mad at me for some reason?"

I just looked at him, with a tear in my eye and said, "I don't want to talk about it." My heart was aching, it wasn't just an emotional pain, it affected me physically, and I could feel my entire body feeling drained. I couldn't lift a finger, it was as if a wrecking ball had hit me.

"It?" Drew said.

"I'm sorry Drew, I just can't. Let me go home tonight please."

"Of course, you can do whatever you want. I just wish you would talk to me."

As soon as we pulled into his driveway, I gathered my things and put them in the back seat of my car. When he kissed and hugged me goodbye I thanked him for taking me. I wasn't sure if it would be the last time. I wasn't sure of anything at that moment. I drove back to my apartment, parked my car in a different spot so no one knew I was back yet, and headed in with my overnight bag in hand. It almost felt sneaky. I didn't want anyone to know I was home or that I was upset. Not ready to handle talking to anyone. I have to process what exactly happened Saturday after reading that text from Eve. Who the fuck was she? I was mentally exhausted. I decided to go straight to bed. I didn't even text Drew to say I made it home safely. As soon as I realized I didn't send him one, I got a notification from Drew, trying to Facetime me. I immediately declined it and sent a reply. "I made it home safely. I am going to bed. Good night."

Drew immediately responded by saying, "Please tell me what's wrong."

I just ignored the message and went to bed. Tossing and turning, my mind was setting up so many different scenarios. Then, I remembered not to overthink anything right now, I needed a few days apart from Drew to sort this out.

I woke up Sunday morning with an emotional hangover. It's exhausting to have that gut instinct and try to ignore it. I swore after my husband cheated on me I would never trust anyone again. But, Drew came into my life and I thought I had found a man worth my respect. I went out to the kitchen to make myself a cup of coffee when I heard a knock at my door. I looked through the peephole and the Fed-Ex man. I grabbed my robe and opened the door. "Can I help you?"

"Are you Savannah Rowe?" "Yes."

"This is for you." He handed me a pen and pointed to the envelope. "Please sign here."

After I signed for it I took the envelope and said, "Thank you, have a great day."

As soon as I closed the door, I noticed it was from my lawyer. *Oh yeah, a real fucking great weekend I am having.* I quickly opened it and there it was. Signed, sealed, and delivered. My divorce papers. Of all times. It had to come today. Apparently, it was overnighted by my lawyer, they knew I was anxious to get this over and done with. I didn't even know they delivered on Sundays. Well, I am officially divorced and I can't even share it with Drew.

I promised him I wouldn't keep anything from him, but until I knew what was going on with this mysterious woman, I was just going to keep it a secret from him. I needed to tell somebody. I would call Andrea and tell her the good news, after all, she was the one who gave me the lawyer recommendation. But, I didn't feel like talking to Andrea either, I just wanted to be alone. My whole world felt like it was falling apart. Everything I thought was going so great, just collapsed in one text. I looked in the mirror and saw this pitiful middle-aged single woman, with black mascara running down her face and a head of hair that was sticking straight up in the air. "Oh no, I answered the door looking like this?"

'I can't go to work tomorrow, shit I am going to call in for

*Sarah Kaye*

the whole week. Andrea will answer the phone when I call tomorrow, I'll tell her about the papers and say I caught a bug while I was away. *A bug named Eve.*

What a way to start a new single life. Maybe, I wasn't meant to be with Drew? Maybe, I should have stayed married to my ex-husband and be treated like a nobody for the rest of my life. I must have done something wrong to deserve a shitty marriage. I didn't think I would ever find a wonderful man like Drew. Wonderful? Maybe he *was* a womanizer and I just didn't see it. I didn't see any red flags anywhere. Wait, I did remember him staring at the stewardess in the airport. Or when he was flirting with the cashier. Should I have said something then? Or maybe, I should have listened to what Vera had to say. She did say, "You are not the girl for him." Was she right?

*Wait stupid, do not put up the umbrella before it rains!*

I looked at my phone and saw that I had seven missed calls and ten text messages from Drew. How am I going to deal with this? Please tell me what to do. I looked up as if she could hear me. Why did you send us all of these dimes? I ran over to the jar I was keeping them in and emptied them onto the bed. Holding each one and asking, why are you trying to send us signs? I sat on my unmade bed and just reminisced about each dime and where we found them. I stayed in bed all day and all night, watching I Love Lucy reruns. The only show that can make me laugh no matter what was happening.

I woke up to the theme song from the show and thought, *Oh no, it's Monday and I have to call in.* I immediately grabbed my cell phone. I had ten more messages and missed calls from Drew. *What am I going to do?*

"Andrea, I am not coming to work this week, I am very sick."
"Oh god, are you okay?"

"Yes, call me later when you get off work." "Of course, talk then."

'Yes, I am very sick. Sick of shitty men. Sick of shitty people. Sick *of myself. I am sick of this love, I disgust this love. I despise this love. I wish it for no one, not even my enemies.*

*I am sick from this heartbreak, which has no healing.*

I took my pillow and held it close, muffling the sound of my sobs.

## Chapter 36

At exactly four pm on Monday, the phone rang. Of course, it was Andrea. I could barely think, let alone rehash the whole story to her at this point. I was emotionally drained. I let the phone go to voicemail. Then I quickly sent her a text, "I'm sorry, I can't talk right now. I promise to call you soon."

Andrea texted back, "You better or I will be on your doorstep to find out what's going on with you."

I knew she meant every word. She's been such a great friend to me. I am grateful to have her in my life. I can't even think about my life without Drew let alone admit to anyone that my fairytale life is over.

I struggled the rest of the day, trying to eat something but my gut was in full instinct mode. I swore I would never let those feelings of doubt enter my body ever again. All those old feelings of wonder came back when I thought my ex-husband was still cheating on me. *How could I let this happen? Why are those feelings coming back? I just can't do this again, I'll never learn to trust a man again if this is true. If Drew was cheating on me with this woman named Eve.*
I decided to eat some toast with jelly and called it a night. My bed

was still in disarray, I think it might even stink. *Who cares?*

It was Tuesday morning, and the doorbell rang. I looked at my phone and I had one missed call and two text messages from Andrea. *'Oh no, this must be her at the door. Of course, it was.'*

I opened the door to Andrea with two grocery bags full of stuff, her backpack around her and her keys hanging from her mouth.

"What the hell is going on?" she mumbled, trying to get the words. "Why didn't you answer your phone or my text?" Andrea put the bags down and grabbed me, she gave me the biggest hug and kiss on the cheek I ever had. "Now please tell me what's going on with you. I am worried sick."

I could see she was staying for a while because she had her overnight backpack on. "Okay, come into my bedroom."

"What the hell is going on here?" Andrea saw how disastrous my room was and also saw my wall. "Is this some sort of crazy game you are playing?"

I actually didn't even realize what I had done, being so distraught these last few days, I had printed out at least one hundred pictures of our adventures together and taped them to the wall. It practically took up one side of my room. Now that Andrea had seen it, I realized how crazy it looked.

"Savannah, please tell me what is going on. I am worried, I am literally shaking inside, and I need to know. Please."

I started to cry. She held me in silence for a while, I tried to speak but the words didn't come out.

"Take your time, my love," she kept consoling me.

"Drew and I were having a great time on Block Island," finally I managed a few words, pulled myself from her embrace, wiped my stream of tears and continued, "We went there so he could do some work for a customer." I inhaled before adding, "I even helped him. We finished early and we were planning on doing a bunch of things on the Island. I was so happy, until he stopped for gas, went inside to pay for it and his cell phone rang."

"Yeah? So, please finish."

"A text from a woman named Eve came across his dash." "And?"

"I am so sorry," I said trying to hold back my tears. I couldn't stop crying every time I think about him going to her house.

"What did the message say? Maybe, she's a customer."

"The message said that she wanted to know when he was going to put her name on his "things to do list" and how they never went over a date to come back and do the work when they were together last week."

"Why is that so bad?"

"I never saw Drew the whole week before we went to Block Island. He said he had a lot of work to do. Oh, Andrea. I think he was with her."

"Oh, that does sound suspicious."

"See, I knew it, he's cheating on me. My gut is right, it's never wrong."

"Let's just sit down at the kitchen table and have something to drink, you look like shit. When was the last time you changed your clothes or took a shower?"

"I don't even remember."

Andrea made me a cup of tea and showed me all the stuff she brought over. The office sent a get-well card that everyone signed and she brought a bunch of Mark Ruffalo movies for us to watch.

"Savannah we are having a girl's night tonight. We got Oreos, we got ice cream, we got popcorn, and this huge sub from Panera Bread, and I know you love those."

"Sounds so nice, but I am not in the mood for all this tonight."

"I am not leaving here, you are stuck with me for the night. Let's take a walk around the apartment complex, you need some fresh air. Here, put on your slippers and this hat and take these sunglasses, I am sure you don't want to be seen like this around here."

"I don't want to go anywhere." "Get your ass up, we are going!"

"But, what if I run into my neighbors? I don't want them to see me like this, I'm embarrassed."

"No one will recognize you with the hat and glasses or the pajamas."

I walked by the mirror as I was being pushed out the door and saw a glimpse of myself. "Oh my God, I can't go out in public like this. I barely recognize myself." I reminded myself of the pitiful-looking, victimized, and cheated-on version of myself. I screamed, "No, I can't be going through this again!" Andrea grabbed my hand and we went outside.

"See how nice the weather is today? Aren't you glad we are out in this fresh air? And look at this beautiful lilac tree. It smells so nice," as she broke off a few flowers and pushed them under my nose. "Let's put these in a vase when we get back, it will make the place smell so good."

As much as I was not in the mood for flowers, the damn lilacs smelled amazing.

I gave her a wry grin.

"Stop this nonsense, you need to snap out of this right now. You need to communicate with Drew. He must know why you are doing this to him. I saw that he left over twenty text messages and ten voicemails for you."

"I don't care, my gut never lies to me."

"Don't look now, you are never going to believe who is coming towards us." "Not Drew, please tell me."

"Not Drew," she said laughingly. "Try Mark Ruffalo and he's coming straight at us."

"What, no way, of all times."

He looked at both of us and asked if we lived there, we both shook our heads.

I think we were star struck. He was so handsome in person. He asked if we wanted a picture with him. Of course, the answer was yes. At that one moment, I wasn't thinking about the rock in the bottom of my stomach or that I looked like crap, I adored his work. We took three pictures with him. One with both of us and one with just Mark, he even put his arm around us. During that one special moment, I snapped out of my mood, but then he left and my problem was still there.

"Savannah, just look at this picture. No one would ever know you are a hot mess in this photo. You're both smiling. It's a great picture of the two of you. I think you should post it on Facebook."

"Oh wow, it actually does look cool. I think I will post both of them."

"No, just the one of you and Mark. Then let's see what Drew says about that."

Within five seconds of posting the photo, Drew hit the heart button and a crying emoji.

"Savannah, come on. He's trying to tell you he loves the fact that you got to meet your hero and that he misses you. You need to call him."

"I can't," I cried.

# Chapter 37

Andrea and I sat on my black leather loveseat snuggled up, watching Shutter Island and eating popcorn. I was going through the motions trying to enjoy the movie, but inside my mind was scrambling, trying to figure out why he would do this to me. "Savannah, isn't this movie good? Can you believe we actually saw him today?" She looked at me before tapping my leg and adding, "Come on, that was so exciting, don't you think?"

I just looked at her feeling empty inside, exhaled, and replied, "Yeah, I guess."

Before we knew it we both had fallen asleep and I did not wake up until Andrea handed me my lease and said, "Come on sleepyhead, wake up".

"What's this?" I replied, yawned and took the paper from her, and explained it was my new lease. I got up from loveseat, ran to the bathroom, and met her in the kitchen with my divorce papers. "This is what you should be looking at." I handed them to her.

"Oh, my! Yay, I'm so excited for you. Come on Savannah, please call Drew. I am begging you. The longer you ghost him, the worse it will be for you."

"I want to know who Eve is. I can't stop wondering who, why, or how often has he met with her."

"Savannah, stop. Here, I made you a waffle. I found them in the freezer, not sure how old they are but you need to eat something, and I made you a cup of tea as well."

"Thank you, but I still can't eat. My gut is just in turmoil, right now." "Then call him."

I heard her sigh and then say, "What is the plan for today? What would you like to do, we can't stay cooped up like this hiding because of your damn overthinking."

"I can't think of anything I want to do, I just want my perfect life back with Drew."

"How about we ask Randy to come over today, he always knows how to cheer me up. Maybe he will come by and take us for a ride."

"I have so much on my mind, I am so sorry, I forgot to ask how you guys are doing."

"We are fantastic. I understand, but he would want to help, he is such a compassionate man and, he is your cousin. You need family right now."

"I just realized that my sons don't even know what happened yet, I am too upset to call them and tell them."

"Savannah, tell them what? You don't even really know anything because you won't call Drew back, so I don't want to hear you say you need to tell your kids anything."

I looked at the clock, it was noon. "Where the hell did the day go, I am so tired, I think I just want to take a nap. Why don't you go home?" She did not look happy. I think she wanted to see Randy.

"I will go home to grab some groceries for us for tonight, but I will be back!" "If you want to come back, I don't plan on going anywhere." After Andrea left, I went into my bedroom and looked at my room with disgust. I had jelly stains on my pillowcase. *Gross.* I shook my head. *I don't care.*

Every time, I close my eyes my mind immediately went to all the beautiful moments I spent with Drew during the past few months. My heart hurts and we are not even married. We experienced so many beautiful things that I never knew existed. We shared wonderful adventures in such a short amount of time. I thought it was real love until 'Summer's Eve' happened. *'That bitch ruined my life.'* Tears were streaming down my face and I was grateful Andrea was not with me. *"How could he do this to me? Maybe he had been using me since the first day. He must have thought I was estranged from my husband and never loved by my husband. I was just a past-time, a travel buddy or even a partner for sex."* The last bit of thought enraged me. I got up from bed and tore all those damn photos on my wall. *'Why does every photo show so much love and happiness?'* They say pictures don't lie. I took a deep shuttering breath and then jumped when my phone dinged. It was Drew. My hands started to tremble. I read his message.

"I am here. Please open your door."

I started to cry so hard. I had no idea what to do. I suddenly wished Andrea was here with me. I did not want to face him alone. I heard Andrea's voice telling me to go to him. Open the damn door, Savannah. I wiped my nose on the back of my sleeve wondering if he brought me all of my belongings. I looked through the peephole. There he was. *'The love of my life.'* I inhaled and opened the door.

"Anna, this is for you." He handed me a box and said, "Open it and then we have to talk."

*Oh no, the talk?* Now, I was really worried. What the hell was in this box? He wasn't saying anything. He was just looking at me. I grabbed a pair of scissors and started to open the box, but Drew took them from me.

"Let me do that. Sweetheart, why are you shaking? I don't

want you to cut yourself." Drew opened the box and the smell was so fragrant. He lifted the top and handed me four dozen roses. One red, one pink, purple, and a dozen yellow. They were so beautiful. No one has ever given me more than twelve. I looked at him. "What are you doing? Why are you giving me flowers?"

"It's been four long days that I haven't seen or heard from you. One dozen for every day that I missed you." He started to cry and I lost it. I handed him a tissue and my heart almost busted out of my chest. He never wiped his eyes. He reached over and touched my hand. "Please tell me what is going on with you?"

I took an even deeper breath before answering him, "Drew, who is Eve?"

"Eve? What are you talking about? There's no Eve, Anna."

"Drew, I saw a text from her while we were on Block Island. I'm sorry, but I immediately erased it because I thought it was a woman that you were having an affair with." I collapsed into a chair. "The whole idea of you seeing another woman made me sick. It broke me."

Drew knelt down in front of me, put his hands on my knees, and said, "Well, that explains it. Anna, didn't we talk about telling each other everything, including those things that we don't understand?"

"Yes, we did, but you don't understand the life I had before. Wondering if my husband was cheating on me every time a woman smiled at him. Drew, after reading her message that ugly intuition came back and my gut was wrenched. Those old feelings came flooding back to me as if it was happening all over again. I could not stand the idea of you playing around on me."

He leaned in and kissed my forehead. "Dear Anna, oh my darling. Eve is a customer and that is all she is. In fact, she and my dad were good friends." He chuckled ever so lightly before adding, "Back in the late seventies she and my father may have had a thing but considering she is seventy-nine she is a little too old for me."

I started to cry happy tears. I cried and laughed together. I slapped my hands on my forehead, reprimanding my silly head to take me to place where I didn't want to be.

"I feel so stupid. AAARGGGH!"

"It's okay, stop hitting your head," he said as he held my hands in his. "I am so sorry. Can you ever forgive me?"

"Go take a shower, you look like death warmed over." He hugged me and I knew right there he had forgiven me. He helped me to my feet and said, "I can't believe you met Mark looking like this?"

I kissed his whole face before I headed for the shower.

Drew opened the bathroom door and shouted, "Take your time, I'll straighten the apartment up."

I finished my shower, got dressed, and felt like a new person. I went into the living room with a towel on my head and one around my body.

"Ahh that felt so good. I even smell nice."

"I am sorry for the misunderstanding. I am not anything like your ex. When are you going to believe me? We have a wonderful relationship. Please tell me you feel the same way?"

"Of course I do. Drew, if these past four days say anything about me, it is that I cannot live without you."

"Seriously?" He smiled a cheshire grin. "I saw your lease on the counter and noticed your lease is up soon." He moved closer to where I was standing. "We are ready. These past few days I realized I can't live without you either." He nodded. "Let's live together."

I started bawling my eyes out. "Yes! Yes, I will live with you. I love you, Drew, and never want to live without you ever again. I promise not to hold anything from you again."

He lifted me up, swung me around and my towel dropped to the floor. We both started laughing. My heart was racing. "Guess what?" I said as I looked into his eyes. "I am officially divorced!"

"Oh, that *is* great news. In fact, let's call you landlord together."

"Seriously?"

"Yes!"

Okay, maybe I should get dressed before I call him. "Good idea. Hey, where are your vases?"

"I don't know if I even have two vases in this apartment. I am not used to receiving so many at one time."

He smiled at me and said, "I'll fill every glass in the house."

He filled every glass, and my house smelled of roses and his love.

## Chapter 38

I grabbed my purse. "I'm all ready to go out to dinner." "Where would you like to go?"

"I really just want to go to the diner up the road, it's very casual and they have great food." *My stomach finally feels empty and ready to eat a healthy meal. I fell in love again, all over, harder. Yet I know, I can't stand brokenness now, I was more fragile than a thin glass. But I knew, from here I will only be stronger, I won't be broken. Drew won't break me, or let me be broken.*

"Sounds great, I am just happy to be having dinner with my girl. What you don't realize is, I went through hell and back myself these past four days. I spent most of the evenings over at Stacy and Gary's pining over you and asking Stacy for advice. They were so concerned about me. Even my godson was trying to pull me out of my funk. We played GTA5 for hours."

"I will have to make a point to thank them for keeping you sane. Andrea was my safe haven. We should have a dinner party after I move in, we'll invite them and Andrea and Randy," I said, just as a text came through my phone. "It's Andrea." 'Savannah, where are you? I am standing at your door with Randy for five minutes knocking. I know you are here, your car is in the same place you left it."

I looked at Drew and raised my hand to my mouth. "Oh no, I forgot to let her know we made up, she must be going crazy wondering about me."

"Ask them to join us at the diner."

"That's a wonderful idea, she will be so thankful I opened the door for you. She must have told me a dozen times to call you and ask about the message."

"I appreciate her pushing you to find answers to that silly message you read.

Otherwise, who knows how this misunderstanding could have ended."

Drew pulled into the parking lot took my hand, looked into my eyes, and said, "Please promise me that this will never happen again. If anything like this arises in the future you will talk to me."

We were still in the car waiting for Andrea and Randy when I started to cry. Drew reached over, opened the glove compartment, and handed me a napkin. "Pull yourself together, we are going to have a nice dinner with friends." He kissed me on the lips adding, "I can't wait to meet Randy."

I kissed him twice on the cheek and smiled. "Here they come. He's driving his red Corvette. I love that car, he looks so cool in it," I said feeling a hundred percent better.

Randy parked right next to us and we all got out. I introduced Randy to Drew.

After they shook hands and greeted one another, Drew walked around Randy's car. "Sweet car, what year is it?"

"A 2010 Grand Sport Convertible, her name is Vegas." "Vegas, you are absolutely stunning."

"Thank you."

Andrea whispered to me, "Isn't he just amazing? I think those two will get along very well, they are both crazy about cars. Oh, and you have to tell me how this all happened. I left for a couple of hours and came back to old Savannah. Thank God. I am so happy. My heart is actually full right now, pardon me if I become a little teary." "Thank you, Andrea, for everything you do. I am grateful for a friend like you."

We grabbed a cute table for four out on the patio. "This place is different from the other diners in town. The waitress comes to take your order on roller skates."

"Really, maybe I should get a job here. I can skate like a pro," Andrea stated.

Randy replied, "Oh no. I think if you want to skate, we can go together. I am willing to learn just for you Andrea."

"That's so sweet, Randy." She looked at me and winked as if to say he is all mine and then said, "You would do that for me?" Looking at him with so much love.

"Of course, I would my sweetness."

*Yep, they are perfect together. They are that missing puzzle piece for each other. They are complete together.*

I looked at Andrea and gave her a thumbs up. It seemed they were getting along so well.

*Matchmaking will be going on my resume. I should find more matches*

"Randy, do you ever go to car shows? I love going to them. Also are you in any car clubs? There is a big following of Corvettes in my town in Connecticut. Maybe we should go to a meeting someday. I have all the schedules."

"That would be awesome, I really don't have any friends that are interested in cars. I would appreciate hanging out with you. We can have a guy's day, while the girls enjoy a shopping day or something."

"Perfect. I love the idea. Let me know when we can do that."

Our roller skating waitress came over with her tray in hand filled with water for the table and asked, "Did you get a chance to look at the menu? All you have to do is scan the barcode to read it. I'll be back in a few minutes."

"Fancy," Andrea remarked as she scanned the barcode for the menu.

Everything looked delicious. It wasn't your typical menu, with lots of breakfast items, every kind of pancake you could think of. We all decided on the Bananas Foster pancake special. My stomach needed food. I was grateful our food came out very fast. The waitress rolled over to our table with all four plates on her tray.

"Very impressive, food looks fantastic," Drew said.

We ate and had a great time. Drew and Randy hit it off and of course, Andrea and I were texting back and forth. Trying to tell her how this all happened. It was killing her, not knowing.

Then I said, "Guess, what guys? Drew has asked me to move in with him." "That is wonderful news," Andrea said. "When is all this happening? You can use my SUV and Randy has a truck, we will help."

"Great! Thank you," I said and told them, "Drew has a trailer he can tow behind his Jeep and my son's will probably help too. I think we will be able to pull this off in a single weekend. I need to phone my sons to tell them the news. I hope they are happy for me. Drew, remind me later to call them."

"I will. In fact, we'll call them together. Do you want to set it up for next weekend?"

"Yes, let's make a plan now. Andrea, are you guys free this coming weekend?" "Anything for you, my friend. Yes, we are free."

I jumped up and down, clapping my hands, "I'm moving to Connecticut." "I'm so happy for you, Cuz," Randy said and gave me a big hug.

"Thanks, I can't wait. Next weekend, I will have a new home

with Drew."

We all said our goodbyes and Drew took me back to my apartment to start packing. Andrea vowed to be there bright and early with Randy on Saturday. Things were really working out. To think just a few hours ago, I was a hot mess, ready for the nut house, all over a lack of communication. I learned my lesson.

"Call the kids," Drew said as we pulled into the parking lot.

"Yes and how am I going to tell my beautiful neighbors that I am leaving?" "They will understand, they want you to be happy, besides we can come and visit them whenever you want. I know you are going to miss your Hungarian dishes." "Oh yes. Of course, my Hungarian dishes. And what about my commute to work? It's forty-five minutes each way, that's a lot of time and gas money spent.

Should I think this decision out more before I start to pack?"

"Anna, I had this thought that I want to run by you, and now is the perfect time. Would you like to be my bookkeeper full-time? I would pay you and besides I need one."

"Really, you want me to quit my job?"

"Well, not quit, retire. You told me yourself that you have enough years and you have the age to be eligible to retire."

"Yes, that's true. Do you really want me to do this?" "Why would I ask you silly questions?"

"I am going to have a group message chat on Facetime and let all the kids know what's happening and I will let my office know tomorrow. I am making a lot of life changes these past few hours, I think I am making the right ones too."

"Yes, they are right on! I love you, girl, when are you going to believe me?" "Now, I do for sure."

Moving day came fast, everyone was at my door at seven a.m. just like they told me. It made me feel so good to know my friends and family were happy for me and agreed to help me move. All three sons were there to help, I knew they would be ecstatic for me.

## Chapter 39

It took us five trips from my apartment to Drew's house. It was very emotional for me, just a few years back I was stuck in my marriage with a toxic partner and then I finally found my independence. Never did I think that I would find true love after being in a failed marriage and in the second half of my age. I chuckled at myself, 'How did I become so brave?' I was grateful I had declared my independence in my apartment. Now, I have a wonderful man and a beautiful house to share a new exciting life with.

I hid myself in the bathroom, the sight of seeing all my belonging leaving the apartment drew me into overwhelming flashbacks.

"Anna, I have made plenty of room for your belongings, but if you need more space you let me know. Anna, where are you, sweetheart?"

I stepped out of the bathroom, stood behind him, and said, "I am right here, my love."

Drew turned around. "Oh, bring your things into our bedroom next. Randy and I put your dresser next to your surprise." He pointed toward a beautiful new vanity and I started to cry as he walked over to the closet adding, "This is your half."

I laughed silly cries. "I think we might both have a shoe problem." Drew had as much as any fashionista.

"We can find places for all our shoes. I will build something downstairs, whatever works for us. I want you to put up all your pictures of our grandchildren on the walls like you had in your apartment. You need to make this your home now."

"Our?" I breathed in before telling him, "Thank you for making me feel welcome. Have I told you how much I love you today?"

He nodded. "Yes you did." He hugged me adding, "The moment you agreed to live with me. I love you too, Anna." Then he kissed me long and hard. "How about we get a few pizzas for all these hardworking movers?"

"You are so thoughtful, kind, and sweet." I looked at him knowing I was going to be okay. "That sounds great. I am sure they are starving by now."

Hand in hand we went out to the living room. "Hey everyone, I am going to order some food from the pizzeria down the street. How about cheese, pepperoni, and a vegetarian?"

They all yelled, "Yes, please."

"We appreciate all of you helping, we couldn't have done this without you all," Drew said and I agreed. Then Drew picked up the phone and ordered the pizzas and two house salads. "Could you please deliver them to 25 Main Street? The food will be here in twenty-five minutes, how about everyone sit out on the deck and get comfortable? I will make some iced tea and lemonade for all of us."

When we walked outside I noticed the entire deck was decorated with flowers and balloons. The table was set and I heard Drew ask Google to play music for a celebration. I turned around and blew him a kiss.

He pointed his finger at me and declared, "Excuse me. Everyone, please. I would like today to be a day of celebration for my Anna. She completes me and I never want to go a day without her by my side."

Everyone held their glasses up and said, "Cheers to Anna and Drew."

Drew kissed the side of my head. "Anna, did you tell everyone that you are going to work for me now?"

"No, I didn't say anything yet." I looked at Andrea when I announced, "Drew has asked me to retire and work for him full-time as his new sexy bookkeeper."

"Mom really?" Both of my sons said in unison. "Well, he didn't really say sexy, but yes."

Everyone started clapping with excitement for Drew and me. "Starting today, I am looking forward to every minute of our new life together."

Andrea shouted, "Happily ever after."

The doorbell rang and Drew asked me to help him.

"Looks like a moving-in party?" The man said holding our pizzas.

"Yes, me!" I raised my hand and Drew smiled at me. When I saw his dimple I thanked his mother for every dime.

He handed the stack to Drew and said, "Enjoy your food." "Thank you, keep the change," I said and handed the money.

Everyone enjoyed their pizza, salad, and the music. Even though it was a long day for all of us, we were happy to be together. At eight o'clock, Drew and I walked everyone out to their vehicles and said our goodbyes. Greg and Stacy waved to us as they walked back to their house. Unlike any other time, I was alone with Drew in *our* home.

Drew lit a few candles before saying, "Now, I can open the wine I have been saving for this exact special occasion." Then he turned the soft music on, and set two glasses on the coffee table.

"May our home be a place where friends meet, family gathers and our love grows."

We both raised our glasses, and I added, "Drew that was so beautiful." I kissed his lips tenderly. "You meant every word, didn't you?"

"Of course, I did."

I had goosebumps. We kissed again and again, drank the rest of the wine, and declared to always be honest with each other.

"Anna, let's go and celebrate our first night together in our bedroom."

I followed him into the bedroom and saw a big blue box sitting on the bed. "I bought you something special for tonight."

I opened the box and saw a gorgeous red teddy with a lace tie up the front. "I love it, let me go put it on. Wait, let me take a quick shower first."

"Alright, I will jump in after you're finished, then let the night begin."

All of my bathroom toiletries were already in place, thanks to Drew. I couldn't believe how good the hot shower felt. It was as though all my stress was washing down the drain. The steam was filling up the bathroom, I was enjoying the spa feeling, I could hardly see anything in the room. I finally decided to get out, opened the shower door and there it was, the writing on the mirror. There was a huge heart with the words I love you Anna in it. Drew had used his finger and wrote me a message. My heart filled up with happiness, this man never stops amazing me. Then I realized that he had written another message on the other mirror. This one had an arrow drawn on it and said 'Look under here.' It pointed to my towel. What was this man up to now? I looked up and saw him standing in the doorway.

"So, did you like the message I wrote you?" "Of course, you are one of a kind, Mr. Hart." "Did you see the other message?"

"I was just about to look when I saw you standing there staring at me." "Well?"

"Okay, hold on." I picked up the towel and there was an envelope with my name on it. "Can I open it now?"

"Yes, please do." Drew looked like the cat who ate the canary.

I slowly opened it, knowing it was driving him crazy, and then I saw them.

There were two tickets to Taiwan. "Oh my god, we're really going?" "Yes, we leave in two days."

"Is this a dream? I cannot believe this is really happening. I have never been to another country before, nevertheless, the country your mom was born in and your parents were married."

"So, you are happy?"

"Happy? I am ecstatic, I can't wait to tell the world."

"You know I have never been over there myself, so Ms. Anna this will be a first for me too. We can experience this together. I can't wait. This is why I have been working so hard to finish jobs and working longer hours so I could save up for this trip."

"What made you decide to do this?"

"It was my mother, she came to me in a dream. Told me to bring you to her home country. I want to visit there too and maybe look up some relatives. We can do it together."

"I cannot believe this is happening. I'm going to Taiwan in two days!"

## Chapter 40

"We leave in two hours for the airport. Anna, do you have everything packed?" "Yes," I replied and told him, "I am so excited. I can't believe we are going to Taiwan. We are going to feel so close to your mom."

Drew took my hand in his, and kissed the top before saying, "I am pretty excited myself. I never imagined I would be going back to my mother's home country, nevertheless with the love of my life."

Just thinking about the nearly sixteen-hour flying time gave me butterflies in my stomach, never mind landing on foreign terrain. A place neither one of us spoke a word of Taiwanese. Drew installed an app on both of our phones, hoping to make me feel better.

I set my pocketbook down and pointed to my luggage, letting him know I was more than ready. "All the bags are packed. Let's get started on the grandest adventure of all."

Two hours later we were sitting at the boarding gate for China Airways. We sat next to each other, not letting go of each other's hands. We were never going to be apart again. Since the misunderstanding, we are so aware of each other's feelings. No one is going to pull us apart ever again. We are one.

"I already feel so surreal. And I am not even there yet." "And I miss my Mom. I feel so close to her right now."

"Your Mom is happy and proud of you, Drew. I know that for sure." I kissed lightly on the cheek and continued to rest my head on his shoulder.

We both had bought a party-size packet of chips and munched on it till it was our time to board the plane.

Then we both jumped out of our seats as we heard the intercom announce our section. "That's us Anna, we are section B, come on." We both ran toward the ramp to board the plane.

I think the flight attendant could tell we were both nervous. "Is this the first time the two of you are going to Taiwan?"

"Yes," Drew replied, "We are going to my Mom's home in Taipei."

"You picked a wonderful part of the country to visit. Enjoy your stay and your flight."

"Thank you, we will." Then Drew grabbed my face with his hands and kissed me on the lips. One of those kisses that makes you deaf in your ears. Those are the best ones. "We are going to have the time of our lives, just wait and see."

"I believe you, I do."

The plane took off so smoothly, it felt like we were sitting in our living room at home watching television together. The stewardess looked so cute in their light green dresses, with a green and red silk scarf around their neck. Of course, they were all Asian beauties. They looked similar to Drew's sisters. Thinking of that, I guess, Drew's sisters were also nothing less than Asian beauties.

"It's going to be a long one Anna, triple the time to Arizona."

"I know, as long as we are together it doesn't matter. I enjoy every minute with you."

"So I called my sisters and told them the news about us moving in together and, going away. They were very happy and gave me some names of a few relatives in Taipei."

"That would be so cool, it's almost like I would get to meet your mom through her relatives."

"Anna, I have never met any of them either, I have only seen pictures of them.

My aunts look like my mom, it will feel nice to meet them."

"Speaking of aunts, mine called me yesterday and was wondering why she hadn't heard from me in a while. I told her we were on Block Island and now we are going away again. She was so happy for us. When we get back, I want to go and visit her."

"Of course, we will have a lot to tell her all about."

"Yes, I can't wait. We can bring the notebook to show her all the pictures from Arizona and Taiwan. I can hear her now, 'You guys are like horseshit, and you're everywhere.'"

"I can totally hear her saying that too."

Fifteen hours later we landed at Taipei Taoyuan International Airport. We walked out of the plane into the airport and our mouths dropped. It was the most fascinating place. There were all these huge umbrellas hanging from the ceiling, like the ones that you get in a fancy cocktail. They were so colorful and they had hand-painted flowers on them. I looked at Drew and said, "We are in another world. Oh, Drew, it is so beautiful."

"Yes, Anna, I feel like a little kid in a candy store. I love being here with you. I love you so much."

I looked at him for a second, he was calmer, more relaxed. Happier than ever. I was so grateful to be near him, especially as we toured his mother's homeland. Hand in hand, we went to pick up our baggage and hailed a cab. The driver took our luggage, put them in the back, and asked, "Where to?"

"Golden Hot Spring Hotel, please," Drew responded.

"That's about a forty-minute ride, sir," the cab driver said in broken English. "Not bad compared to our long flight."

We arrived at the hotel, got out of the cab, and stood in front of the hotel mesmerized by its beauty. Drew paid the cab driver along with a handsome tip. I could tell it was going to be magnificent. We checked in at the concierge desk. The hotel lobby was over-the-top fancy. I couldn't wait to see our room. We took the elevator to the fourth floor. When Drew opened the door, once again, I was amazed.

"Oh my, this is something I have never seen before."

It had a king-size canopy bed with white curtains. The headboard was made of red velvet, almost to the top of the ceiling. The carpet was a black and white flower pattern. On the walls, a square black and white pattern wallpaper surrounded the whole room. The bathroom was so big, it had a large black porcelain tub with water flowing in from the springs. We felt as though we were at a luxury spa. Beautiful pottery filled with fragrant Japanese flowers filled the room with a welcoming scent. "Anna, I have something here for you." He grabbed his luggage, pulled out a small bag, and told me to open it.

It was the most beautiful silk nighty and matching robe. Lavender with Asian flowers printed all over it.

"Thank you so much, is there anything you don't think of?" I tried it on for him and immediately I felt like an Asian woman.

"It looks perfect and sexy as hell on you. You will always be my beautiful princess."

"Thank you, I love it!"

"Let's get some rest, remember we lost thirteen hours. Jet lag will make us miserable if we don't sleep. We can wake up tomorrow with a fresh start. They have a great breakfast here in the morning. Let's plan on that, then our first day will start. I have a special place I want to show you first thing tomorrow."

"I can't wait," I replied, knowing he planned the best vacations I had ever been on. "Good night, or should I say 'wan an'? That's goodnight in Taiwanese."

He smiled before kissing me goodnight. Once again, he was right. I could hardly keep my eyes open. Lying next to him, and listening to him snore felt so peaceful to me.

'*You know you are head over heels in love with someone when you feel peaceful even when they are snoring. Yes, snoring, probably one of the most annoying sounds in the world, and I feel peaceful in it.*'

## Chapter 41

At five a.m. Drew's cell phone alarm woke me up. "One annoying alarm you have, Drew."
I jumped out of bed, ran to the window and opened the room-darkening curtains, and yelled over to Drew, "Wake up! How can you not wake up by the sound of this annoying alarm?"

I couldn't explain it, but I was even more excited about this adventure than any other. Right outside our window were bright red fields of salvia. I mean they were everywhere. "Come on, Drew. Get up. I am so excited. Please get up."

Drew yawned, stretched his arms out to me, and asked, "How did my Asian beauty sleep last night?"

I kissed his forehead and told him, "It was the best sleep I had in a long while. I even dreamt about being here. I had to open my eyes to realize it was real. Oh, Drew." I put my hands over my heart. "Thank you for bringing me here."

He smiled warmly at me and threw back the covers. "My sweet, Anna." He got up, adding, "It is most certainly real." Then he looked at the clock and said, "We have to hurry and get ready because I have a driver picking us up in one hour." When he winked at me, his dimple appeared. "I have a very special day planned for us. I am only telling you one thing about it. You need to wear comfortable clothes for bicycling."

"Okay, I have a set of workout clothes in my suitcase. Where did you put the luggage last night? I barely remember, jet lag really is a thing you know."

"I agree, I too slept like a rock last night." He pointed toward the Lancaster table under the clothing rack. "We can grab breakfast in the lobby before the driver comes for us."

"This sounds so mysterious, even for you Drew."

"I just want to make the most of every day we are here, who knows if we will get a chance to come back." Before he went into the bathroom, he shouted over his shoulder, "Hey, my sister sent me the contact information for two of my aunts here in Taipei."

"That's so exciting," I said and clapped my hands. "You must feel so blessed to be able to meet them and hear stories about your mom when she was a young girl."

"I am excited about everything," he said and disappeared into the bathroom.

A minute later, I joined him in the shower. I laughed when he said no time for fooling around. I made sure to pack water, sunscreen, and hats in both of our backpacks. We both knew we had a hot day ahead of us.

As soon as we got out of the elevator, the concierge was there to greet us. "Good morning. Right this way to our complimentary breakfast buffet. Please enjoy yourselves." It was amazing that they spoke English fluently.

"Drew, look at all this fabulous food." I read the signs in front of each warming dish. "Steamed buns, rice balls, and Chinese omelets. Everything looks so appetizing."

After we sat down, a waitress appeared and asked us if we wanted Thai tea warm or cold. We both said warm. Then she asked,

"Would you like a cup of soy milk as well?"

"Sure, we will try some," Drew replied to the waitress. Apparently, in Taiwan, they drink soy milk traditionally first thing in the morning. Drew looked at me, took my hand in his, and said, "I want everything about this trip to be the most special and memorable."

I kissed his lips, and looked into his eyes. They were smiling. I gave him a wry grin in return. "I am ready to experience everything with you. Especially in your mom's homeland." We finished our breakfast in time to find our driver waiting for us at the front of the hotel in a luxurious shiny black limousine.

"A limo? Is that for us?"

"I want you to remember this day forever."

The chauffeur took our backpacks and then opened the door for me to get in. "Good morning, Drew, and Miss. Anna." The driver handed Drew an envelope telling him, "Everything you asked about is written down on the paper."

"Great," Drew told him and tucked it in his shirt pocket.

It was something out of a fairy tale. I looked at Drew and said, "I feel like I am in a fairytale."

The chauffeur turned around to us and said, "We have a three-hour trip ahead of us this morning."

"Yes, thank you," Drew replied and winked at me. "I love when you plan our adventures."

"Anna, you know I am a planner."

"Yes, and you are the best! I love you, Drew Hart."

"I love you too, with all my heart and soul," he said and kissed me long and hard.

I opened my eyes and I noticed our driver was smiling at me.

About an hour into our ride, Drew took the paper out of the envelope and when he did something fell out onto the floor. It was shiny like a key. We both looked down and there it was. A dime. We both reached for it at the same time, banging heads.

"Ouch," we both said at the same time. First Drew squeezed the dime in his own hand before grabbing mine and placing it in my palm.

"Anna, this is the ultimate sign from my mom." He had tears in his eyes. I did not cry until he got choked up telling me, "Our mother is here with us."

"Yes, she is," I replied sobbing. We hugged each other knowing she would always be with us. "She knows we are here together. Drew, I believe the dimes have guided us throughout our relationship. I can feel her presence."

Tears were rolling down his face. I reached into my jacket pocket and gave him a tissue.

"She loved you so much. And now she is watching over you." He nodded. "Over us, Anna."

I put the dime in my pocket and zipped it up. I held Drew's hand for the rest of the ride. When the driver told us we had about another thirty-minute ride before we reached our first destination, I looked out my window thinking, *wherever that may be is fine by me.*

As soon as the limo driver pulled over to the side of the road he got out, opened the door, extended his hand to me, and said, "Enjoy your day at Sun Moon Lake Miss. Anna. I'll pick you both back up at midnight."

"Midnight?" Then I looked at Drew and said, "Very romantic." "Yes, it is."

"Oh my god, I can't believe we are here. It is better than what your father described."

We were in the foothills of Taiwan's Central Mountain Range. Surrounded by forested peaks with many foot trails. Displays included centuries-old carved lintel pieces, handcrafts, and weapons.

"Yes, it sure is beautiful, we are going to start by taking a bike ride around the whole lake," Drew said as he pointed across the street.

While Drew paid for our bikes, I grabbed a flyer and read about the natural lake. Sharp Belly fish, silver candela, barbata, goldfish, and large grass carp. Then I read how big the lake was. "Drew, this flyer says the bike trail is sixteen miles. We have a long ride ahead of us."

"Wait until you see the floating flower farmers. They can be seen all over t h e lake."

We put on our helmets, and off we went. The first 8 miles were easy, I couldn't keep my eyes off of the scenery. Everywhere you looked there were huge bamboo forests, each piece was about seven inches wide. The smell of beautiful flowers was amazing.

The sights were breathtaking. Not long into our ride was the Living Basin of Sun Moon Lake. The soil was dancing with bright yellow flower blooms in the fields of the loofah flower.

"Anna, stop up ahead. We are going to park our bikes and take a cable car ride." When he said it was only a seven-minute ride. My derriere was a bit disappointed.

"I read you can see the whole lake from up there. It also said it was the best selfie spot. Make sure we take a few. I can't wait to share some of these photos on Facebook. This is so incredible, I need photos to prove this heaven on earth does exist." "We could even do a panoramic or maybe a short video while we are riding across the whole lake to include these beautiful mountains surrounding us," he said. "Great idea, you think of everything," I replied and started jumping up and down with excitement.

"Yes, Anna. I can tell you're excited. Trust me, there is more to come, my love." "More, I can't even imagine." As I looked all around waiting for our turn at the gondola lift.

"Hey," I said when Drew sat across from me. It seemed odd sitting across from each other. "I'm used to always being by your side."

"I'm more worried about us tipping this thing over right now."

I laughed aloud. "I would have saved you," I said and then read aloud, "The Sun Moon Lake Ropeway cable car offers views of the mountains and the water. Oh, don't look down now Drew, but the water is eighty-nine feet deep." I looked up from the flyer and caught my breath. A purple haze over blue-capped mountains from the lake's reflection while on the east side of the lake resembles the moon's reflection. I loved how the cable cars were all painted in bright colors.

The views were magnificent and I could see why they call this Sun Moon Lake. It was shaped like a moon on the West side and like a sun on the East side. The breeze was just so perfect. Pure bliss. "That was the best seven minutes of my life. I'm never going to forget that ride, ever," I said as we exited the cable car.

"Me either," Drew echoed. "Let's go on our next journey."

We got back on our bikes and continued for another ten miles or so. We stopped at a little outside market. Drew ordered two Chinese sausages on a stick surrounded by sticky rice and fresh vegetables.

"This is delicious, I love Asian food. I don't think I will ever be able to eat Chinese food again. There is no comparison." We finished our snack and went on our way to our next stop.

Drew agreed with me that the food was delicious. "We have about three more miles to go," he said and I felt sad. I wanted to see more.

"Anna, see that man standing up ahead?" Drew asked and then yelled, "Stop when you get close to him."

"Okay, I see him." I looked closer at the man, small frame, holding up a sign almost as big as he was. The sign said, "Drew Hart."

We both pulled up to the man and Drew handed him the envelope. "Mr. Hart, everything is ready for you." Then he looked at me and said, "Whatever wish you wrote on here will reach the heavens."

I had goosebumps. I wondered what Drew wrote on that paper.

Drew took my hand and brought me over to a huge red balloon-like canvas. It was as big as me. I could see the man who met us writing something with a thick black marker. Then all of a sudden the man lit a small fire underneath the balloon. It was a huge Chinese lantern. When it started to rise, Drew told me, "Look up, my darling."

I looked up and the fiery red lantern had words written on it. The four words I longed to hear. WILL YOU MARRY ME?

My hands flew to my mouth. I looked down from the sky, and turned to face him. Drew was down on one knee. Then he reached for my hand and said, "Savannah Rowe, will you marry me?"

I could not hold back my tears. "Yes! Yes I will marry you, my love. Oh, Drew.

My wish came true."

When Drew slipped the most beautiful vintage diamond ring on my finger, I told him I would be honored to be Mrs. Drew Hart for the rest of my life. "Wait? Is this?"

"Yes, Anna, it was your great grandmother's. Aunt Dolly gave it to me. Like my mother, she too knew we were made for each other."

We both looked up to the sky watching the lantern fly up to the heavens. I inhaled deeply as Drew whispered, "Thank you, for guiding us throughout our beautiful romance."

*Sarah Kaye*

Discover the extraordinary worlds of Sarah Kaye in her thrilling new releases of 2024. Get ready for a literary journey like no other.

Made in the USA
Middletown, DE
30 December 2023